THE TELEGRAM

BOOKS BY DEBBIE RIX

The Girl with Emerald Eyes

Daughters of the Silk Road

The Silk Weaver's Wife

The Photograph

The Secret Letter

The Italian Girls

The German Wife

The German Mother

THE TELEGRAM

DEBBIE RIX

bookouture

Published by Bookouture in 2024

An imprint of Storyfire Ltd.
Carmelite House
50 Victoria Embankment
London EC4Y 0DZ
United Kingdom

www.bookouture.com

Storyfire Ltd's authorised representative in the EEA is Hachette Ireland
8 Castlecourt Centre
Castleknock Road
Castleknock
Dublin 15 D15 YF6A
Ireland

ISBN: 978-1-83525-906-1
eBook ISBN: 978-1-83525-905-4

For my father-in-law –
whom I never knew, but whose extraordinary life
I have tried to capture and reimagine.

PROLOGUE

ENFIELD, MIDDLESEX

1915

Tilly was standing in the hall adjusting her straw hat in the mirror. She wore a bright blue, high-necked blouse that complemented her eyes, and her dark hair was twisted into a chignon. In spite of her best efforts, long strands of dark hair kept escaping the pins. She had recently started a new job and was keen to make a good impression. Sighing, she stood back to admire the finished effect. 'It'll have to do,' she muttered to herself.

There was a knock at the door.

'Can you get that?' her mother Kathleen shouted through from the kitchen. 'I'm up to my elbows in suds.'

Standing on the doorstep was a telegram boy. Tilly's heart missed a beat – telegrams rarely contained good news – but she wasn't too worried. Although her brother, affectionately known as 'Bruv', had joined the army a few months earlier, he had not yet been sent to France. In fact, he was just nine miles away, at regimental headquarters in Middlesex.

The boy handed over the telegram, and began to push his bike away down the road.

'It's a telegram, Mum,' called Tilly. 'Shall I open it?'

Kathleen came into the hall, wiping her hands on her apron. 'Yes, would you?' Her voice was tentative, nervous.

'Don't look so worried Mum. It can't be any bad news about Bruv – I had a letter from him a couple of days back. He's fine...'

But as she tore open the envelope, Tilly's face told Kathleen all she needed to know. Her mother collapsed onto the hall floor, wailing, 'No, no, no... not him, not my boy.'

Tilly sank down next to her mother as she reread the telegram. 'I can't believe it. That can't be right. They've made a mistake, Mum... surely, it's a mistake.'

Their neighbour, Ada appeared at the open door. 'You all right in there?'

Tilly got to her feet, wiping her eyes with the back of her sleeve. 'Hello, Ada,' she murmured.

'Hello, dear... I was just polishing the step when I heard the kerfuffle and wanted to check you were all right.'

Tilly handed her the telegram with shaking hands.

Ada took it, and read its contents, muttering under her breath, '*Missing, presumed dead.*' She looked up at Tilly, her eyes wide. 'Oh my God, how awful. I'm so sorry.'

Tilly was now leaning against the wall, tears streaming down her face. 'It can't be right, Ada... it can't be.'

Kathleen still lay prostrate on the tiled floor, sobbing and moaning.

'Let's get your mother off those cold tiles before she catches her death,' suggested Ada. Between them, the two women helped Kathleen upstairs and onto her bed, where she lay howling like an animal.

'Go for the doctor,' said Ada, covering Kathleen with a woollen rug. 'And where's your father?'

'He's at work. He left over an hour ago.' Tilly's father, George, was a stoker for the local electricity board.

'There's no point in trying to find him, I suppose. When's he due home?'

'Around five, usually.'

'You'd better get off. I'll stay with your mother.'

Tilly raced downstairs and grabbed her shawl from the hook in the hall. The doctor's house was a quarter of a mile away, and she ran all the way there, arriving at the impressive red-brick double-fronted house, breathless and tearful.

She yanked urgently on the bell-pull, and a maid opened the door. 'Yes, what is it?'

'I need the doctor – quickly.'

'You'd better come in,' said the maid. She showed Tilly to a smart waiting room at the front of the house. Elegant mahogany chairs lined the walls, and a plush Turkish carpet covered the parquet flooring. After a few minutes, the doctor appeared from his consulting room, drying his hands on a white towel. 'What can I do for you?'

'It's my mother... well it's my brother really.' The words were tumbling out of Tilly's mouth incoherently. 'We had a telegram, you see. They're saying he's dead, but it's my mother I'm worried about – she's collapsed.'

'I'll get my bag.'

The doctor hurried after Tilly and the pair soon arrived back at her house. Tilly showed the doctor up to Kathleen's room and then retreated downstairs where Ada was waiting in the hall.

'I'll make some tea,' said Ada, going to the kitchen.

The doctor joined Tilly in the hall ten minutes later. 'I've given your mother a sleeping draught. She should rest now for at least four hours.' He handed Tilly a small paper packet. 'There are two more doses in there. Mix one with water and give it to her later if she needs it, and the other one again tomorrow. It will just make her sleep and dull the pain. I'm so sorry, but there's not much more I can do. You have my deepest sympathy.'

Tilly showed the doctor out and then went to the kitchen to join Ada, who was spooning tea into a brown earthenware pot. Tilly sat down at the table, laid her head on her hands and sobbed.

Ada placed a cup of tea next to her on the table. 'Drink that, love. I've put lots of sugar in. I'll wait with you till your father comes home. Poor man, whatever will he say?'

George arrived just after five o'clock. He removed his boots as usual at the back door, and hung up his hat. He glanced anxiously at his daughter and then at their neighbour. 'Where's your mother?'

'Dad...' Tilly began. 'We've had some very bad news.'

As she explained what had happened, her father slumped down onto a kitchen chair. 'I can't believe it,' he murmured. 'Not my boy.'

'I know, Dad... I know.'

George looked up at Tilly, tears streaming down his weathered cheeks. 'Your poor mother. She loved that boy. This will kill her.'

Hours later, Tilly took a cup of tea up to her mother. Kathleen was lying curled up in the bed, her dark auburn hair splayed across the pillow.

'Mum... Mum, it's me, Tilly.'

Her mother didn't reply.

'I've brought you some tea... you should drink it while it's hot.'

When her mother still didn't answer, Tilly walked round the bed and knelt down facing Kathleen. Her pale skin was almost translucent, and dark mauve shadows encircled her blue eyes.

'I can't,' she murmured, rolling over to face the other way. 'I want to die.'

Tilly put the cup down on the chest of drawers and lay down next to her mother, wrapping her arms round her corseted waist. 'Oh, Mum, I do understand, I really do. I feel the same. But we must try to go on.' Even as she said the words, she was aware that she was convincing herself, as much as her mother. Her brother was the most important person in her world, and she couldn't imagine life without him.

'How can I do that, Tilly?' her mother sobbed. 'Answer me that... how?'

Tilly buried her face in Kathleen's hair, fearing her own self-control would collapse. But after a few moments she remembered what Bruv had said to her the day he joined up. 'If anything happens to me, I'm relying on you to be strong for them,' he had told her. 'As long as Mum has you, she'll be all right.'

Gathering herself, Tilly stroked her mother's hair. 'I know it will be hard, Mum,' she whispered. 'But Bruv would want us to go on. You must just try.'

Over the next few days, Tilly struggled to come to terms with what had happened. Without physical proof of her brother's death – a body, or even a death certificate – she simply couldn't believe he was gone. By contrast, her parents seemed to accept the official line. Her mother kept to her bedroom, alternately weeping and sleeping, refusing food and taking only sips of water. Inevitably, she lost weight, and seemed to be disappearing before her family's eyes.

Tilly's new employers gave her time off to care for her mother, but her father decided to go back to work.

'I can't stay here, Tilly, listening to your mother weep. It's more than I can bear. Work is the only thing that will save me.'

Two weeks went by and, one morning, after Tilly had washed up the breakfast things, there was a knock at the door. Standing on the step was the postman.

'Letter for you, love. No stamp, I'm afraid. Honestly, some people – that will be a penny ha'penny.'

Tilly went into the kitchen and took a few coins from a china pot in which her mother kept small change. She handed the money to the postman.

The letter was addressed to her parents, and Tilly knew instantly by the handwriting that it was from her brother. Her heart racing, she took it back into the kitchen, and stared at it for some time. She wanted desperately to open it, but felt she should wait for her father to return. Carefully, she placed it on the kitchen dresser, and tried to concentrate on her chores.

When George arrived home, Tilly waited patiently while he removed his boots and washed his hands at the kitchen sink. But as soon as he had sat down at the table, she handed him the envelope. 'This came for you and Mum today. I've not opened it.'

George glanced up at his daughter. 'It's his writing.'

'I know.'

'You open it. You know my eyes aren't good. Read it for me.'

Tilly carefully slit the envelope open with a knife, and removed the letter. The sight of her brother's elegant handwriting – a flowing style with a touch of copperplate that he had recently perfected – brought tears to her eyes. 'Oh Dad...'

'Read it, love... please.'

Dear Mum, Dad and Tilly,

I know you'll never understand, and maybe you'll never be able to forgive me for what I'm about to do, but believe me when I say, I can't take it any more. Army life is not what I had imagined. Something terrible has happened and the situation is intolerable. I can't say anything to anyone about it, and no one would believe me anyway. Desertion is unthinkable, so I must do the only honourable thing and end my life.

Please believe that I love you all, and try not to think too badly of me.

Your loving son and brother

PS: Mum, if you believe in the afterlife, have faith that we will be reunited one day. I promise.

Tilly laid the letter down on the kitchen table, weeping. 'I don't understand – how could he do that – end it all, I mean. It makes no sense.'

'Well, it seems pretty clear-cut to me, love,' said George.

'Does it?' asked Tilly. 'What does he mean, "something terrible has happened"?'

'I don't know. But he was always a dreamer, wasn't he? Not like the rest of us. Maybe real life in the army was too hard for him. Perhaps we've just got to accept he couldn't bear the thought of fighting.'

'No, Dad. I don't believe that. Not Bruv. No one will ever convince me that my brother is a coward. No one. There's something we don't understand – something the army aren't telling us. And I'm going to find out what it is, you'll see. We'll get to the bottom of this one day. I promise we will.'

PART ONE

28 YEARS LATER

1

NOTTING HILL, LONDON

MARCH 1943

Elizabeth

Elizabeth Carmichael ran down the stairs from her top-floor bedroom. Her feet, in their army-issue shoes, clattered on the wooden treads. She jumped the last two steps, landing with a thud on the tiled hall floor.

'Do you have to make to make so much noise?' asked her mother. Madeleine was arranging some early narcissi from the garden in a vase on the long mahogany hall table.

'Sorry, Ma,' said Elizabeth, kissing her mother's cheek. 'But I'm late. I'll be on a charge if I'm not careful.'

'What time are you home?'

'I'm not sure. I'm meeting David after work. He's got a twenty-four-hour pass.' David was Elizabeth's boyfriend. A young RAF officer, he was stationed in Suffolk.

'Why not bring him back here?' suggested her mother.

'I'll ask him. We're having supper in town, and I'm not sure when he's due back on duty – he might have to get the night train.'

Madeleine nodded. 'Well, you'd better be off.'

'I left my gas mask somewhere. You haven't seen it, have you?'

'In the sitting room, I think... on the velvet chair in the window.'

The sitting room ran the full depth of their Victorian stucco house, and was effectively one large room that could be divided into two by folding wooden doors. The far end, near the garden, was arranged with bookshelves and a mahogany dining table and chairs. A set of French windows opened onto a metal staircase leading down to the long narrow lawn, framed with herbaceous borders. The sitting room itself was at the front of the house, overlooking the road. A light airy room, it was decorated in various shades of blue – Madeleine's favourite colour.

On the grey marble mantelpiece stood a collection of family photographs, mostly pictures of Madeleine and her daughter taken at seaside resorts around the south coast – Ramsgate, Rye, Brighton. They were both dark-haired and slender, and it was often said they looked more like sisters than mother and daughter. Bookending the rest, at either end of the mantelpiece, were two pictures of a young man. Tall, with slicked-back dark hair, a full mouth and a narrow moustache skimming his upper lip, he looked like a matinee idol – Errol Flynn perhaps, or so Elizabeth always thought. In one photograph he wore uniform – First World War army issue. In the other, Elizabeth's particular favourite, he was dressed in a tweed jacket and trilby hat. In his arms he held a baby. On the back of the photograph her mother had written *Paddy and Elizabeth, Frinton 1923*. Elizabeth had no real memory of her father. He and her mother had separated when she was just one year old – soon after that photograph was taken. They had married after the first war, and divorced a few years later. Neither had ever seen Paddy again.

Her mother had kept her husband's name, and never remarried. But as far as Elizabeth could discern, there was no love lost between the couple. In fact, her mother rarely spoke of her father. When Elizabeth had asked her once why she kept the photographs, her mother explained it was so that Elizabeth could trace her roots.

'He was your father, after all,' Madeleine went on, 'and you deserve to know what he looked like. Beyond that, I have nothing to say.'

Inevitably, Elizabeth pushed for more information, but her mother replied, 'There's no point in discussing it further. All you need to know is that people are not always what they seem.'

Now, Elizabeth touched the photograph with her fingers, whispering, 'Hello, Dad...'

'Elizabeth?' her mother called through from the hall. 'You'd better get a move on – you don't want to get into trouble.'

'All right, I'm coming.' Elizabeth picked up her gas mask from the blue velvet chair and ran into the hall. 'See you later,' she called out, rushing into the street.

Elizabeth had spent her childhood and teenage years in a suburban semi-detached house on the edge of Uxbridge, where Madeleine ran a hairdressing business. When war broke out in 1939, life went on almost as normal. But in the autumn of 1940 Nazi Germany began its bombing campaign against cities and towns all over the country, known colloquially as the Blitz. Where others saw chaos, Madeleine saw an opportunity.

'A salon has come on the market in London – Notting Hill Gate,' she told her daughter one afternoon, as they sat in the Uxbridge garden drinking tea. 'The owner was killed in a bombing raid. He has no immediate family, so the property is going to auction. It will go for a song, you mark my words. No one wants to risk buying a business during a war. Apart from anything else, it's so hard to find builders to do the renovation work. But after the war women will be desperate to make the best of themselves, and hairdressers will be the first place they head to.'

'I don't think the war will ever be over,' muttered Elizabeth gloomily. It seemed to her she had spent her entire adult life 'at war' and she couldn't really see an end in sight.

'Don't be silly, darling, of course it will be over one day. I lived through the first war, remember. Everything passes... in the end.' Madeleine smiled, and poured her daughter another cup of tea.

'But Ma, it would be mad to move to central London now. What about all the bombs – surely it's too dangerous.'

'We're just as likely to be bombed in Uxbridge, darling. Trust me, there will never be a better time to break into the central London market.'

Once the salon's lease had been acquired, Madeleine bought a run-down four-storey house in Clarendon Road, a ten-minute walk from the new business. A quiet residential street, lined with cherry trees, its fine houses had once housed well-to-do families, with servants in the attics. But much like the rest of Notting Hill and Holland Park, many had now been subdivided into flats and filled with tenants. Madeleine's house was no exception. It had eight apartments squeezed into its four floors, occupied by a collection of itinerant Irish labourers. As soon as the ink was dry on the contract, she found the tenants alternative accommodation and employed them to do the building work on her house. Flimsy partition walls were torn down, the staircase and fireplaces were restored, and the rat-infested basement was turned into a large airy kitchen. In all, the job had taken over six months, but she was now the proud owner of an elegant house with a large garden, and the employer of a handful of grateful, efficient builders who were currently renovating her hairdressing salon.

Elizabeth had long been impressed by her mother's ambition. Alongside running a business, Madeleine had brought her daughter up single-handed. She had sent Elizabeth to an all-girls' school, and when the time came to consider a career, she suggested Elizabeth should train as a secretary.

'I thought you might want me to be a nurse, like you... or even a hairdresser?'

Madeleine, who had worked as a nurse in the First World War, shook her head. 'Oh no, Elizabeth. Nursing is jolly hard work, and the pay is awful. As for hairdressing – I'm building a business for our future, darling, and I want you to be management, not labour.'

At the end of 1941, when conscription came in, Elizabeth opted to join the ATS – the women's Auxiliary Territorial Service. After her initial training in Catterick – a dismal experience of damp beds in leaky Nissen huts and early-morning parades – she was gloomy about her future army career. Increasingly miserable, she rang her mother. 'Training's nearly over, and I'm terrified I'll be sent to man an anti-aircraft gun in the Outer Hebrides, or become a car mechanic.'

'Surely not,' said Madeleine. 'You're a trained secretary.'

'But Ma, the army are famous for sending people to do things that are the exact opposite of what they're good at. Everybody says so.'

'Well, let's hope someone "up there" has more sense,' replied her mother. 'Whatever happens, you'll just have to grin and bear it.'

In the end, common sense prevailed, and Elizabeth was posted to the typing pool in the War Office in central London.

She raced home in high spirits. 'Oh, Ma, can you believe it! An office job with sensible hours – nine-thirty to five-thirty! As usual, I've got *you* to thank for it. If you hadn't bought that business in London, and persuaded me to become a secretary, none of this would have happened, and God knows where I'd be now. And the really wonderful thing is there's such a shortage of billets in London, if you live within an hour's travel of your place of work you're allowed to stay at home!'

Now, as Elizabeth hurried down Clarendon Road towards the tube station, she checked her watch. If she wasn't careful, she'd be late for parade and roll-call – a morning ritual that took place at 0900 hours precisely.

The Central Line was hot and crowded. At Oxford Circus she had to run through the connecting tunnels to reach the Northern Line, and leapt onto a train headed for Embankment just as the doors closed behind her. From here it was a relatively short walk, through Whitehall Gardens, up Horse Guards Avenue and into the War Office.

In the grand entrance hall she showed her identity card, then ran up the main staircase to her top-floor office. She had recently been promoted from the ranks of the typing pool to the private office of Captain Mark Valentine, whose role was to liaise between the various armed services and the civil service. Her elevation meant promotion: she was now Lance Corporal Carmichael.

'Ah, Corporal,' he called out to her from his office. 'I need to dictate a rather urgent letter.'

'I'm sorry, Captain, but I'm due on parade,' she said, glancing at her watch. It was five minutes to nine.

'Oh, of course – when you're back, then.'

She dashed to the parade ground and slipped in behind two other ATS girls, praying her lateness had not been noticed.

. . .

As usual, her day was filled with office tasks: taking shorthand notes for internal memos, typing up reports. Messengers hurried in three times a day to collect and deliver the mail. Finally, as the office clock headed towards half past five, she began to look forward to her date with David. But just as she was covering her typewriter, Valentine called out to her. 'Corporal, could you pop in for a moment – I've just got one final letter...'

Sighing quietly to herself, she picked up her shorthand pad and went into his office.

The captain was standing at the window staring down at the street below. He began to dictate in a rambling fashion, changing his mind constantly, while Elizabeth kept an anxious eye on the clock on the wall. Finally Valentine turned to face her. 'I'll need that typed up before you go.'

'But it's already quarter to six, sir.'

'Your point being?'

'I'm sorry, it's just... I had an appointment.'

'We are at war, Corporal. I'm sure your appointment can wait.'

'Of course, sir.'

Resentfully, Elizabeth inserted the paper and carbons into her typewriter and typed up the letter at speed, before laying it finally on her boss's desk. 'If there's nothing else?'

'No, that will be all.'

Back in her office, she removed a small compact from her gas mask box and checked her appearance.

'You look absolutely lovely, Corporal.' Captain Valentine was now standing at the door that linked their offices. He had made several similar comments over the last couple of months, and it was beginning to grate. Not only was he married, he must have been at least forty, Elizabeth thought. 'Who are you making yourself beautiful for?' he asked laconically, lighting a cigarette.

'My boyfriend.'

'Lucky man. What's he doing for the war effort?'

'RAF, sir. He's on a pass.'

The captain smirked. 'Well, behave yourself. I'll see you in the morning.'

Elizabeth left the office feeling that insinuations had been made against her virtue, and she didn't like it.

David was waiting for her on the steps of the Air Ministry, his RAF coat pulled up around his ears. 'Darling,' he said, taking her in his arms and kissing her. 'I've been here for ages.'

'I'm so sorry,' she said. 'Work... you know.'

'Come on. I'm taking you out for supper and then dancing.'

The ballroom at the Dorchester Hotel on Park Lane was in full swing by the time the couple arrived. Hundreds of people gyrated to the hotel's resident jazz band, Lew Stone and his Stonecrackers. As David swept Elizabeth onto the floor, he whispered into her hair, 'I love you, you know.'

'And I love you,' she replied.

Later, as he walked her to Marble Arch tube station in the gloom of semi-blackout, his arm wrapped protectively round her, she leaned her head against his chest. 'Ma asked if you wanted to come back... the spare room's made up.'

'I'd love to, but I've got to be back at the base by six in the morning. I'm booked on the night train to Ipswich.'

'Oh, poor you. You'll be exhausted.'

'It's been worth it though, just to see you.'

At the tube station, they walked down the steps, until they were deep beneath the streets of London.

David wrapped his arms around her. 'This is where we part, I'm afraid,' he said. 'I'm heading east to the station, you're going west.' He kissed her one last time. 'Please take care of yourself, and don't speak to any strange men.' He smiled, and stroked her hair.

'You are silly,' she said. 'You take care too.'

She watched him striding briskly away, and then, pulling up the collar of her coat, she walked to her platform.

2

NOTTING HILL

JUNE 1943

Charles

Charles Carmichael stood on the doorstep of his house, inhaling the heady scent of an early summer's evening – a mixture of flowering roses and newly mown grass. The weather was unseasonably warm, and he was relieved to be out of his stuffy office in central London, and looking forward to a pre-dinner drink at his club – a small men-only club for Catholics a few hundred yards away in residential Holland Park.

He called back to his wife through the open front door. 'Just off to the club, Violet. See you later.'

'All right,' she replied. 'I'll have dinner waiting.'

Charles put on his trilby hat and set off down Clarendon Road, reflecting on his day. As a civil servant in a government department, his job could be tedious, but it suited him. It paid a reasonable salary and his employer had been generous over the years in allowing him time off to indulge his true vocation as a novelist. He had already published eleven crime novels, and was working on a twelfth. After supper, he would spend the rest of the evening, and much of the night, writing.

His mind wandered to the plot of his new novel, set in China in the 1930s; his detective hero, Percy Aloysius Huff, was in a bit of a fix with a Chinese agent called Tu Huang. Immersed as he was in the lives of his characters, he was startled by a female voice from across the road.

'Father?'

Charles heard the word, but ignored it. It was surely meant for someone else, not for him. Anxious to get to his club, he quickened his step. But when he heard the word again, more insistently this time, he turned round.

Standing on the opposite side of the road was a tall, slender young woman wearing the brown uniform of the ATS. In spite of her drab clothing she was attractive, with short dark hair, brown eyes and full lips. She reminded him of someone.

'I'm sorry?' he said. 'Were you trying to attract my attention?'

'Yes, I was rather.' She blushed. 'It's just... you look exactly like... I thought for a moment you might be my father.'

His stomach churned slightly, and he swallowed. He felt both shock and panic – emotions he had experienced many times before when faced with evidence of his complicated past. Removing his trilby hat, he took a fresh white handkerchief from his coat pocket and wiped his forehead. He needed time to think. Perhaps he could put her off, just for a while, and work out what to do. 'I think you must have made a mistake, young lady.' He replaced his hat, and bowed slightly, before setting off once again down Clarendon Road.

But the girl was not to be fobbed off. She crossed the road and tugged at his sleeve. Charles felt his lungs contract – a hangover from being gassed in the first war – and he began to cough violently.

'I'm sorry,' she said, 'I didn't mean to upset you, and I assure you I don't mean to be impertinent, but, you see, you look very like a photograph of my father.'

His mind was a blur and his leg throbbed; the district nurse had attended him that morning, and had removed several small pieces of shattered bone from his left leg. Twenty-six years before, he had nearly lost his leg while serving in the British Army in Belgium, and bits of metal and shattered bone were even now being picked out of the wound with sharp little tweezers. He winced at the memory.

'Your name *is* Padraig Carmichael, isn't it?'

He flushed, more embarrassed than annoyed, like a child who had been caught out telling a lie. 'I don't use that name any more. I'm Charles Carmichael now.'

'Then you *are* my father,' she said delightedly. 'My name is Elizabeth Carmichael. I am your daughter.'

Charles gasped. He had last seen his daughter when she was just a baby, and now here she was standing opposite him. His mind was reeling; he was aware of his leg throbbing, and a vice-like pain in his chest. Over the years, when faced with awkward situations, his instinct had always been to run. He felt that same urge now. 'I'm sorry,' he said, 'but I have an appointment. I'm already late.' He set off down the road, walking as fast as his leg would allow, away from the young woman.

The girl chased after him. 'After all these years, don't you want to talk to me... to get to know me?'

He stopped and swung round to face her. He was in pain – both physically and emotionally – and a hint of irritation slipped into his voice. 'How did you find me?'

'I didn't,' she replied defensively. 'I mean, I wasn't *trying* to find you. I live over there at number forty-three.' She pointed towards a house on the opposite side of the road with a grand classical facade; it was literally just yards from his own. 'I was just on my way home, and saw you walking down the steps of your house, and I just knew... I recognised you instantly. I don't know how long you've lived there, but Mother and I moved in exactly a year ago this month. It's extraordinary that we've never met before.'

Mention of her mother made him reel back. 'You mean Madeleine? Does she live there with you?'

'Yes, of course. I'm sure she'd love to see you again.'

It was the sort of thing people say, but Charles knew that it couldn't be true. Madeleine's last words to him had been fairly explicit: 'Get out of my life and don't come back.'

'I'm not so sure about that,' he replied enigmatically. 'Your mother and I parted a long time ago, and not under the best of circumstances.'

Elizabeth smiled nervously. 'Look, it's rather awkward talking to you in the middle of the street like this. Perhaps I could pop over sometime for a chat?'

The thought horrified him. Charles had spent the previous twenty years burying the early part of his life. The last thing he wanted was to drag it all up again. Besides, he had never told Violet about his daughter. 'I'm not sure,' he said. 'I may be going away shortly.' That at least was true – his department was threatening to move their personnel out of London for the rest of the war, but Charles had so far resisted the push. 'Perhaps we can write to one another.'

'But you only live across the road, surely—'

'Look!' he said firmly, determined to take control of the situation. 'Drop a note through the door. Mark it for the attention of Charles Carmichael, Personal – and we'll make an arrangement. All right?'

This seemed to settle the matter; she smiled faintly, and nodded. He tipped his hat politely, tried to form a smile at the edges of his own mouth, and hurried away along the road, as fast as his throbbing leg would allow.

. . .

When he arrived at his club, the doorman, an elderly gentleman who had also fought in the Great War, took his hat and coat. 'Good evening, Mr Carmichael. How nice to see you again.'

'Good evening, Swain. How's the leg?'

The pair shared a common injury – an old war wound that would not heal.

'Oh, much the same, you know, sir. The wet weather does it no good.'

'Quite,' replied Charles. 'Well, good to see you again.'

He went through to the members' bar, sank down in an armchair and ordered a large whisky. As soon as it arrived on a small silver tray, Charles grabbed it and downed it in one.

'Another one, sir?' asked the waiter.

'Yes please.'

The man sitting in the chair opposite glanced up from his copy of *The Times*, his eyebrows raised slightly at such apparent indulgence.

'Just a small one,' added Charles, anxious that the man would mistake him for a lush. That would never do.

He tried to gather his thoughts. It seemed incredible that his daughter had found him after all these years. Had it been a coincidence, as she had said? If it were, it was a remarkable one. He settled down to read the evening paper, but couldn't concentrate. A friend joined him in the bar, and they made idle conversation for a while, but eventually he made his excuses and left.

Charles arrived home later that evening, still in a state of slight agitation. Downstairs in the sitting room, his wife, Violet, was playing the piano. It was a beautiful boudoir grand she had purchased recently with a small inheritance, and she played very well for an amateur. Although it was a charming piece by Schubert, he could take no pleasure in it. The girl across the road had unsettled him. Listening to his wife play, he realised that reacquainting himself with this young woman would only cause problems. No good could come of dragging it all up again. Besides, Violet had recently told him she was pregnant with their first child. He had to admit he had been surprised by the news, as they rarely shared a bed. But he knew she was pleased – thrilled even – and he was keen to keep the peace. The last thing she needed was an upset.

At half past ten, he went upstairs to his bedroom. Within months of marrying Violet, the pair had agreed to have separate bedrooms. The rationale was that, as a writer, he needed space and time for his work. His day job meant that spare time was limited to evenings, and he often wrote late into the night. The furnishings were simple – a single bed against the wall, a maple wardrobe, a bookcase and a large maple desk that stood in the window, on which was placed his beloved typewriter.

Sitting at the desk, Charles took a key from his pocket and opened the bottom right-hand drawer. Buried beneath a pile of manuscript paper was a set of diaries. He had started keeping a diary when he was seventeen, after a teacher at his grammar school had told him he had talent as a writer. His teacher's faith in him had lit a spark that had never been extinguished. If it hadn't been for the Great War he would have tried for a scholarship to university; Oxbridge, his teacher had told him, was a possibility. Now, he rifled through the leather-bound volumes until he found the one marked 1918. He flicked through the pages, his eye finally falling on an entry dated 28 June.

Today amidst the hell that is Ypres, I met someone... a young woman with dark hair, midnight blue eyes and a full mouth. She is attractive, beautiful even...

He paused. That was why Elizabeth had looked so familiar. Apart from the eye colour, she was the image of her mother.

Her name is Madeleine, and she is a nurse with the RAMC. I rather think she may be an angel.

As he thought back to that young man, so full of love, he smiled. When they'd first met, Madeleine's devotion to him had been like a soothing balm after nearly four years of war. But sadly, any relationship that begins with a lie is doomed to failure. And Charles's life was so full of lies, he wondered at times how he had ever survived.

3

Elizabeth

The encounter with her father both disturbed and confused Elizabeth. The man she had hero-worshipped her whole life had materialised at last, but things had not played out as she had always imagined. Since childhood she had fantasised about their reunion, picturing it like a scene from a film. She would run towards her handsome father, and he would sweep her up in his arms, telling her how much he loved and missed her. He would explain that he had no desire to leave her, but his work – doing something heroic perhaps– meant they had to be parted. It was nonsense of course, but this fantasy had sustained her through her childhood and teenage years.

Sadly, the harsh reality of their first meeting had been as far from that fantasy as could be imagined.

Tears of disappointment welled up as she walked home and turned up the path to her own house. Slipping her key into the lock, she wondered if she should announce to her mother that she had just met her long-lost father. But as she let herself into the hall, she heard Madeleine chatting to another woman in the sitting room. Elizabeth hung up her gas mask and hat on the hall stand; checking her face in the mirror, she wiped her eyes and opened the sitting room door.

'Oh, there you are,' said Madeleine. 'Look who's turned up. You remember Bunty, from Uxbridge.'

'Yes, of course,' replied Elizabeth, her heart sinking at the prospect of making polite conversation all evening. 'How nice to see you again.'

'She's staying for supper – isn't that nice?'

'Yes, lovely. I'll just go and wash my hands.'

Upstairs in her room, Elizabeth changed out of her khaki uniform. She sat in her satin slip on the edge of the bed and cried silently. She wanted nothing more than to curl up in bed and weep. But she knew she must put on a brave face. Sitting down at her dressing table, she dabbed powder onto her face and touched up her lipstick. Finally she put on a simple summer frock and joined her mother in the sitting room.

When Bunty finally left, Madeleine announced that she was going to bed. 'It's been a very long day, darling. We were so busy at the salon. And now one of the girls has announced she's pregnant. I'll have to advertise for a replacement, and goodness knows how I'll find someone – everyone who is able to work is doing something for the war effort. I might even have to work there myself. I'm too tired to clear away – could you do it?'

'Yes of course.'

'You were very quiet tonight,' said Madeleine. 'Are you all right?'

'Yes, I'm fine. I'm just tired too.'

'They work you too hard at the War Office. Do you mind washing up?'

'No, I said I would. You go to bed.'

Washing the dishes in the quiet of the basement kitchen, Elizabeth thought again about her father. It seemed incredible that he was living just a few yards away. And why had he been so reluctant to talk to her? This man, who had taken on an almost mythical quality in her life, had turned out to be so disappointing. Perhaps that was why her mother had parted from him. She wished suddenly that David were here, but he was in Suffolk, and getting hold of him on the phone at the base was always tricky. Perhaps she would write to him, and ask his advice. Uppermost in her mind, apart from her own disappointment with her father, was whether she should mention him to her mother. For one thing, Madeleine might bump into him in the street. And after everything she had said about him over the years, she would surely be devastated to find she had bought a house opposite the man who, as she had intimated, 'was not all he seemed.'

Elizabeth went upstairs to bed. Unable to sleep, she went over their encounter, trying to explain her father's distant behaviour. It was obvious he had been shocked to see her again; this was no surprise, she realised, and he would naturally need time to adjust to the idea that his daughter had reappeared so suddenly in his life. He had also advised against informing her mother – at least for the time being. So, she would do as he had suggested and write him a note to arrange another meeting.

The following morning, she crossed the road, walked up the steps to number 18 and slipped an envelope addressed to 'Mr Carmichael, Personal' through the brass letter box. She tried to peer through the ground-floor window, but it was heavily curtained. Crouching down on the pavement, she could see into the basement. Unlike in their own house, this appeared to be the sitting room. Her imagination began to run riot as she pictured him living there all alone, and for a moment she felt a wave of sadness. Elizabeth stood for a while outside, hoping for a sight of him, but the ground-floor curtains remained firmly closed. Checking her watch, she saw it was already quarter past eight. She must hurry, or risk being late for parade.

In the note to her father, she had explained that she wasn't sure how her mother might take Charles's reappearance in their lives, and asked him to contact her at her office. She wrote down the War Office phone number, with the captain's office extension. She was not allowed private calls at work, but she could think of no alternative.

Over the next few days, she was on tenterhooks. Whenever the phone rang she expected to hear her father's voice. But a whole week went by without him calling. She had just begun to give up hope when, one afternoon, as she was typing a long and particularly complex letter, she answered the phone.

'Captain Valentine's office – Lance Corporal Carmichael speaking.'

'Lance Corporal?' said the voice on the other end. 'I'm impressed.'

'I'm sorry – who is this?'

'It's Charles Carmichael, your father.'

Her heart missed a beat. 'Hello... Father. How nice of you to call.'

'Sorry for the delay – I had to go away for a week or so.'

'I see. I'm so glad you telephoned, but I can't speak for long.'

'Of course. Look, I wondered if you were free to meet for a drink. Perhaps this evening?'

'Yes, I'd love to.'

'I only just realised as I dialled, you're on the same Whitehall exchange as myself. We must work fairly close to one another. Where are you based?'

'The War Office.'

'Do you know The Clarence pub on Whitehall?'

'Yes, I know it well.'

'Six o'clock?'

'Perfect. See you then.'

The pub was busy. Elizabeth stood at the door trying to peer over the throng of drinkers, searching for her father, her stomach fluttering with anticipation. Finally, above the hubbub she heard her name being called. 'Elizabeth – over here.'

Her father was beckoning from a table in the corner. She pushed through the melee, and finally stood before him. 'Hello,' she said shyly.

He smiled faintly. 'I got you a sherry – amontillado – is that all right?'

'Yes, fine thanks.'

He made room for her on the narrow bench seat, and she sat down, inhaling a delicate odour of tobacco and beer.

'Well,' he began, raising his pint glass. 'Cheers.'

'Cheers.' She sipped the sherry. 'Mmm, this is nice.'

'Good.' He smiled. 'My wife, Violet, prefers fino, but it's an acquired taste I always think.'

'Your wife...' said Elizabeth, taken aback. 'So you're married?'

'Yes. We met just before the war.'

'I see.' She hadn't imagined a wife, and struggled to process the information.

'Look, Elizabeth...' he began awkwardly. 'This isn't easy. I just wanted to say – I'm sorry.'

'What for?'

'For not being there as you grew up. When your mother and I... when we divorced, well...' He glanced down into his beer, as if searching for the right words. 'I'm sorry you got lost, as it were. But your mother, she wasn't keen to maintain...' He seemed to run out of steam and came to a halt.

'I understand,' she interjected hurriedly. 'You don't need to explain. Mother can be...' She too paused, anxious not to misrepresent her mother. 'She can be quite forceful.'

He laughed. 'Quite. At the time, she thought it better if we made a clean break of it. What intrigues me now, though, is how you recognised me. You said something about a photograph?'

'Yes. There have always been two photographs on the mantelpiece: one of you when you were in the army, and the other in civvies holding me as a baby. That's my favourite.' She blushed slightly.

Charles reached over and squeezed her hand. 'My dear girl...'

She blinked away the tears and smiled at him. 'It's all right.'

'Do you know,' he said, 'I think I might have the same photograph.' He reached inside his jacket pocket and took out his wallet; scrabbling inside its various compartments, he finally removed a dog-eared black and white picture and laid it on the table.

'It is the same one!' said Elizabeth delightedly. She had a sudden flash of her fantasy reunion – running to her father and being lifted up in his strong arms. The fantasy may not have materialised, but the fact that he had kept her picture close to his heart all these years went some way to salve her earlier disappointment. 'Oh Dad, that's so lovely.' Then, blushing, she added: 'I'm sorry, I probably shouldn't call you that.'

'Why ever not? I am your father, after all.'

They smiled at one another.

'Why did you and Ma divorce?' she asked eventually. 'If you don't mind me asking.'

'Oh, lots of reasons. I'm not an easy man to live with, you know. I was young when we met, immature, searching for who I was. We met at the end of the Great War. I'd been injured quite badly, and your mother nursed me. We fell in love – it was as simple as that. But relationships formed in such circumstances often don't survive real life.

'After the war I needed a job. I was ambitious – probably rather pretentious too, I suspect. I had ambitions to be a writer, but first I had to make a living. I joined the Board of Trade – as a paper-pusher, you know, nothing very high-powered. But shortly after your first birthday, they offered me a posting to China. It was a like a dream come true for a young man like me. I asked Madeleine to come with me, of course, but she wasn't keen. "China's no place to bring up a baby", was the thrust of it. I was supposed to only be away for a few months. In the end, I stayed for nearly a decade. Your mother served the divorce papers to me in Peking.'

Elizabeth smiled. Her mother was nothing if not decisive.

'When I got back from China, Madeleine and I had long since already lost touch.'

'You didn't think of looking for us?' Elizabeth tried to keep her voice neutral.

'I realise it sounds odd – cruel even – but, no. Your mother had made it clear in her final letter that she never wanted to see me again. I'm sorry if that upsets you.'

'I grew up imagining all sorts of things about you. I romanticised you, I suspect. Of course, I didn't even know if you were alive. As I said, Mother was always very reticent about you. So, you took on an almost mythical quality – like a character in a novel.'

'That's ironic,' he said, smiling. 'There was me writing novels, basing some of my female characters on your mother, while you were imagining me as the hero of a story of your own.'

'What sort of novels do you write?'

'Mysteries... detective stories. My time in China had provided me with so much material that, when I got back, I took two years' sabbatical leave from my job and moved to the Isle of Wight. I wrote six novels in that time – had them all published.'

'How marvellous. In all my wildest imaginings I never dreamed you might be a famous writer.'

'Hardly famous, my dear,' said Charles, smiling. 'But enough about me... I want to know all about you.'

As Elizabeth filled him in on her early life – her schooldays in Uxbridge at the girls' school, her stint at secretarial college, meeting David at a dance in Ealing – Charles gazed at her, admiring her clear complexion, her dark hair and dancing eyes.

When they finally parted in the street, he kissed her on the cheek. 'I'm so glad you spotted me. You must come and meet Violet – she's a good sport. Come next week – Thursday perhaps? Does that work for you?'

'Yes, thank you, I'd like that.'

'Good.' He hesitated. 'I should have asked... your mother – is she quite well?'

'Oh, yes... very well.'

'Did she ever marry again?'

'No.' Elizabeth smiled. 'She's married to her business and is very successful.'

'I'm not surprised, and I'm glad for her. So, six o'clock sharp, all right?'

'All right.' She kissed him once more.

He smiled affectionately, putting a finger to where her lips had grazed, his eyes glistening slightly.

'Well, goodbye then, Dad.' She turned to leave, but suddenly stopped and swung round to face him again. 'Just one last thing.'

'Yes,' he said.

'The photograph of you at home is annotated with your name and mine: "Paddy and Elizabeth". Why did Mother call you that? I mean... your name is Charles, not Paddy.'

Charles flushed slightly. 'It was a nickname, that's all. I was Paddy, she was Maddy – just a nickname.'

'I see... well, goodbye.'

As she walked away down Whitehall, she glanced back. Her father was crossing the road, leaning heavily on his stick.

She presumed his limp was the result of a wound from the Great War. She was suddenly overcome by a strong desire to protect this man. Although she was entitled to be angry with him for deserting her for all these years, she couldn't bring herself to feel any negative emotion at all. Instead, she felt merely joy – that at last, in the midst of war and turmoil, she had finally found her father.

4

Violet

Violet was preparing breakfast for Charles. An egg sat ready in a cup on the table, with a slice of toast already buttered. The kettle wheezed, and she picked it up from the gas ring and poured steaming water into the teapot. Her husband was normally in a rush in the morning and didn't like to be held up by domesticity.

The small kitchen where they ate most of their meals was in the basement of their two-storey flat, overlooking the garden. A tiny lobby led on one side to the bathroom and on the other to the sitting room, which ran the entire width of the house at the front. If she was honest, Violet thought the flat's layout was not ideal. Their two bedrooms were on the ground floor, off the main hall and stairway of the house. This meant that the tenants in the two flats above theirs effectively walked past their bedrooms whenever they came or went. Violet had lost count of the number of times she had come up from the basement bathroom at night, wearing her dressing gown, only to be met in the hall by one or other of the men who lived in the flats above.

Violet had done her best to make the sitting room attractive. The new piano that sat in one corner of the room added a certain grandeur. The other furniture consisted of a pair of small upright sofas upholstered in beige velvet, and one comfy armchair for Charles, all arranged around the coal fire. There was little space for anything else, apart from a card table and four upright chairs that sat in the opposite corner of the room. On the rare occasion they had friends over for supper it doubled up as a dining table, covered with a plastic liner and linen cloth. A door in the corner of the room led to a small, dark yard, which contained the coal-hole and their dustbins. It was not an attractive view, and Violet often wondered if she should whitewash the yard walls to brighten it up. It would have the added advantage of reflecting some light back into the otherwise gloomy room. From the two windows, all you could see of the street above were the black metal railings on the pavement, and people's legs as they walked past.

Violet placed the hot teapot on a mat on the kitchen table and poured herself a cup. She had a good view of the garden from the kitchen, and she spent much of her time there. Next to the back of the house was a narrow brick terrace, which she had arranged with pots filled with hostas – one of the few plants that flourished in the shade. From the terrace a set of steep steps led up to the lawn. The garden was for the exclusive use of the basement flat, and Violet knew the other tenants were rather jealous. Sometimes, when she sat on the lawn in a deckchair, she was aware of their hostile stares from upstairs windows.

An ash tree dominated the far corner. As Violet never tired of pointing out to Charles, the tree was really too big for the space. It cast its shade over their own lawn and that of their neighbour, who frequently complained. The Carmichaels had asked the landlord to have it trimmed back, but so far he had ignored them. But in spite of its imperfect layout, the garden was one of the primary reasons they had taken the flat. 'Flats with a garden are like hen's teeth round here,' Charles told Violet. 'Besides, my club is close by.'

As with so many things between Charles and Violet, no further discussion was permitted, and the couple had moved in.

Violet had met her husband in the summer of 1939, on the eve of war. She had just graduated from University College, London with a first in mathematics, and that morning had been for an interview for a job as assistant to a famous statistician. They had got on well, but the man had been non-committal. On her way home to Peckham, she had stopped in the Lyons Corner House on the Strand for a cup of tea. As she sat down, she noticed a slightly older man – rather handsome, with a neat moustache and dark hair slicked back above his high forehead – casting furtive glances in her direction. Violet had little experience with men, despite having been one of only two girls in her year at UCL, but something made her smile at this stranger. He took this as an invitation to join her, which she initially found rather impertinent, but she was soon under his spell. He told her funny stories in a variety of accents and made her laugh. He worked for a government department, and had lived in China during the 1920s. He also admitted that in his spare time he wrote novels.

'What sort of novels?' she asked excitedly.

'Detective stories.'

'Like Agatha Christie?'

'Yes, like that.'

'How marvellous.'

To the young ingenue, Charles seemed impossibly glamorous. He was so different from her – worldly-wise, witty, talented and charming.

They had met from time to time that summer, and, once

they got to know one another a little more, Charles had shared something of his background.

'My people are pretty low down the pecking order,' he had said, as they walked one early evening in St James's Park. 'My father is a stoker for the electricity board.' He glanced at Violet checking for her reaction, waiting for her to wrinkle her nose in disgust perhaps. But her expression remained impassive, and so he continued. 'He and my mother hardly ever read a book, whereas I couldn't read fast enough. I sometimes wonder how I could have been their child. In fact, I used to fantasise that I might have been adopted. I'm so different from both of them. I have a sister too. She did well at school – won prizes and so on – but she's never really lived up to her potential. She's married to a policeman – he's a good man, but dull as ditchwater.'

'I'm in a similar position myself, I suppose,' said Violet. 'I don't really fit in with my family either. My parents own a bakery and my two brothers and my sister all work for the business. But I always knew it was not for me. I got into grammar school and then university – the first one in my family to do so.' She looked up and smiled at Charles. 'But unlike you I know I'm not adopted – I look just like my siblings.'

He stopped and turned towards her, placing his smooth, elegant hands on her arms, pulling her towards him. 'I think we have rather a lot in common, you and I.' When he kissed her it made her head spin. 'Oh Charles,' she said, as he pulled away. 'How lovely you are.'

'You didn't mind?' he asked.

'Of course not. I liked it.'

Afterwards, she took his arm and they walked together towards a pub he knew on the edge of the park, near St James's Palace. He bought her a gin and lemon – not a drink she was familiar with – and they sat in a dark corner together holding hands.

'I'm much older than you, you know,' he said, sipping his beer.

'I realise that.'

'I mean, much older – almost twenty years. And I've got a gammy leg from the Great War... it gives me jip constantly. You really deserve a younger man.'

'I think I know what I need,' she replied, smiling.

'I'm difficult to live with,' he said. 'My job takes me away sometimes. And if I have a novel to finish, I've been known to write all night.'

'I wouldn't mind that. I'm quite difficult to live with myself. I practise the piano constantly, and I'm learning the flute. So we're almost even in the irritation stakes, don't you think?'

Their romance progressed and, on a chilly February morning in 1940, Violet found herself signing a marriage certificate in a register office off Marylebone High Street, wearing a dove-grey suit – all she could get on her wartime ration – and an absurdly florid hat that her mother had bought for her at the Army and Navy Stores. Violet hadn't the heart to refuse it, but had taken it off as soon as possible. That hat – a hideous floral monstrosity, and quite unlike her normal style – dominated every wedding photograph.

'Morning, Violet.' Charles came into the kitchen for breakfast, looking rather haunted, she thought.

'I made you a boiled egg and a slice of toast,' she said brightly. 'I hope they're not too cold now. Tea?'

'Yes please.' He sat down and opened the newspaper, while she poured the tea.

'Don't leave the egg too long,' she urged him. 'It might go hard, and it's my last one.'

'You have it then,' he snapped, pushing the plate towards her.

'No, I want you to have it. You have work to do, and you can't go out on an empty stomach.'

'Oh, stop fussing,' he said, rising from the table and downing his cup of tea in one. 'I'm late anyway. I'll get something at the office.'

He paused at the door. 'Oh, I forgot to say... someone is popping in later – this evening in fact – for a drink.'

'Oh yes, who?' Violet was used to entertaining Charles's friends; they were mostly old colleagues or friends from the club. An interesting, amusing bunch, they would often play cards, and occasionally they would ask her to play the piano.

'No one you know. A girl.'

'A girl?' Violet couldn't keep the surprise out of her voice.

'A young woman... my daughter.'

He glanced at her, his face racked with anxiety. It had been a struggle to tell her – she could see that.

'Your daughter? I didn't know you had a daughter.'

'Of course you did. She was born after the last war. I'm sure I mentioned it.'

'No, Charles, you have never mentioned it. I knew you'd been married – although I seem to remember you omitted to tell me about that too. I only found out because it was on our marriage certificate.'

She recalled her shock on seeing the letter 'D' for 'divorced' next to Charles's name as they signed the certificate. The consequent conversation between them in the taxi on their way to the pub for their wedding breakfast had been their first row. She had wept, she remembered, and told him she felt humiliated. He had not reacted well, saying she was making a fuss. It seeded doubts about her marriage for the first time, and was not an auspicious start to their relationship.

'Water under the bridge,' Charles muttered.

'But Charles... a child. Has she suddenly contacted you? How did you meet?'

'I've not seen her for decades. She was a baby when my first wife and I broke up. The girl's grown up now... twenty-something. I'm not sure, exactly. As for how we met – I bumped into her a little while ago in the street.'

'In the street? How extraordinary.'

'Yes, wasn't it? Anyway, she wants to see me for some reason.'

'I imagine she wants to see you because you're her father.' Violet almost felt sorry for the girl. 'Is she nice?'

'I don't know. I suppose so. We only met briefly. Look I must go. Humphrey's expecting me for a meeting at ten. See you this evening.' He smiled faintly at her, his eyes wandering down to the neat bump hiding behind her maternity smock. At five months pregnant, she was just beginning to show.

Violet spent the rest of the day in a mild state of shock. *A daughter*, she kept repeating to herself, as she went about her chores – washing up, preparing a casserole with the last of the meat ration for Charles's dinner. It seemed extraordinary that in three years of marriage he had never once mentioned this girl. How was it possible that he had lost touch with his own daughter? Violet had so many questions, but knew from experience that, when probed, Charles was likely to clam up. Finally, her head throbbing, she went to her room to lie down. She closed the curtains and lay on her back in the semi-darkness, feeling the baby fluttering inside her. Perhaps another daughter would be born – a child who would now always be in the shadow of Charles's first child. Unable to settle, she got up, straightening the eiderdown on her bed, and put away the previous day's dress. Then she went out into the corridor to tidy Charles's room. As she locked her own door behind her – something she felt compelled to do in order to keep the other tenants from prying – she mused once again on how unsatisfactory this apartment was. How had she ever allowed Charles to persuade her to move here? It was quite unsuitable for a family.

She tried the brass handle of Charles's door, but, of course, it was locked fast. The key was on the hook downstairs in the kitchen. She went back down the steep staircase and returned with it. Once inside, she opened the curtains, made the bed and hung up his clothes. Charles was working on a new novel, and sheets of typed paper lay in drifts on the desk. He didn't like his papers being disturbed, but she couldn't resist glancing at a couple of paragraphs. It was good – well written, if a little florid in style. Violet ran her hand along the bookshelf, checking for dust, admiring the sheer number of his novels. They were always mysteries. Many were set in China, and had evocative titles like *Chinese Nights*, and *Passenger to Peking*. But recently, he had created another leading character – a detective named Percy Aloysius Huff, who solved crime in novels with thrilling titles like *A Dagger in the Heart* and, Charles's personal favourite, *The Man with No Name*. The title was ironic, Violet thought, for it could have described Charles himself. He wrote using a pen-name: Charles P. Devereux. When she had asked him why, he replied simply, 'The office wouldn't like me to use my real name – muddies the waters. Better this way.'

'But why Devereux?' she persisted.

'I suppose because it has a romantic ring to it.'

He had never explained what the 'P' stood for.

His ambition, she knew, was to give up his day job completely and become a full-time writer. But with a new baby on the way, she wasn't sure that would ever be possible.

She reflected for a moment on the news he had given her that morning. Why had he hidden the information about his daughter? In three years of marriage, he had never once mentioned it. Now she wondered... had he and this girl really just met by chance? It seemed too unlikely – in London of all places. What were the odds? As a mathematician, with a head for statistics, she knew the answer. About a million to one. She ran her duster over the glass top of his desk, then down across the smooth drawer fronts. Something made her pull on one of the drawers, but it was locked tight. Why did he lock his desk? What other secrets might he be keeping from her? It suddenly seemed unsettling, and she began to wonder if she knew her husband at all.

5

Charles

Leaving home that morning, Charles reflected on the conversation he had just had with his wife. All in all, given the shock of discovering they were living opposite his long-lost daughter and first wife, he had come out of it relatively unscathed. Fortunately, Violet was not the sort of person to make a fuss. One of the things that had originally attracted him to her was that she kept her emotions in check and her thoughts to herself. By contrast, Madeleine had been more passionate and outspoken. They had argued constantly, and made love frequently. In the end, the relationship was unsustainable. But he was glad she had created a good life for herself. The fly in the ointment was her close proximity. Madeleine knew things about his past – things he had hidden from his present wife, from family, friends and acquaintances. Her potential reappearance in his life put at risk the complex network of lies he had been forced to create. Like a piece of knitting, he feared, it might begin to unravel.

. . .

It was five minutes to ten when Charles entered the office of his departmental head. Humphrey Ashworth stood with his back to the window, and Charles coughed to alert him to his arrival.

'Ah, Charles, good. Do sit please.'

'Thank you, sir.' Charles leaned his stick against a chair and sat down.

'I want you to do a spot of birdwatching for me, Charles.'

'Oh, yes.'

'Oswald Mosley...'

'He's safely under lock and key, isn't he?'

'Not for much longer. He's not well apparently – phlebitis – and they're planning on releasing him in a couple of months.'

'I hadn't realised.'

'We need you to... keep an eye, you know?'

'Of course. No problem.'

'You and he... got on quite well, yes?'

'Yes, in a master/servant sort of way. He saw me as a sort of pathetic acolyte, I suspect.'

'Your information was invaluable in getting him locked up. Did he ever suspect you were an informer, do you think?'

'I doubt it. He always had me down as a bit of a duffer – you know, working-class lad made good. A romantic dreamer... that sort of thing.'

'You played the part well, I suspect. I presume there's no risk anyone else in the organisation revealed your real role in the affair – that awful creature William Joyce, for example? Or Lord Haw-Haw, as they now insist on calling him.'

'No, I don't think so. I kept Joyce close – or as close as I could, particularly after Mosley expelled him in 'thirty-seven. He felt rather aggrieved, I recall, and set up his own party with a man called John Beckett – the National Socialist League, which was more in keeping with the German model. I went to a few meetings, and as far as Bill Joyce was concerned we were good friends. We had things in common – Ireland for one. And we played cards regularly all through the thirties.'

'Yes, I forget sometimes you were in Ireland.'

'Only briefly, at the start of the Great War.'

'Going back to Joyce,' said Humphrey, 'it's a bally shame we had no idea he was on the move in 1939. There was talk of detaining him, you know, but he escaped to Germany just in time – got out in August, just before Hitler invaded Poland.'

'Yes, I feel a bit guilty about that,' replied Charles.

'Oh, why?' Humphrey studied Charles over his spectacles.

'I should have seen it coming.'

'Well, we all missed it – not your fault.' Humphrey waved his hand with an air of dismissal.

'That's generous of you, but the last time I saw him he said something that should have alerted me that he was planning his departure.'

'What did he say, exactly?' Humphrey turned his grey-eyed gaze on Charles.

'We'd been playing bridge, and when Bill left he stood in the doorway and said, "Whatever you hear about me in the future, remember I have always loved England".'

'Ha!' exclaimed Humphrey. 'What a load of bollocks. He's got a funny way of showing it – spewing out his vile propaganda for Goebbels as Lord Haw-Haw. Still, you're right. His comment was prophetic. I did wonder at one point if you might have been the one to tip him off, Charles. His timing was immaculate.'

'Humphrey, I can assure you I never gave us away – never. But I do admit to feeling responsible. I should have understood the implications of what he said and warned you right away.'

'Oh, well, can't be helped,' said Humphrey. 'You weren't the only one to underestimate the little traitor. Someone should have raised the alarm when he applied for a British passport. I mean, what was a US citizen doing wanting a British passport?'

'He must have lied on his application – he was born in New York.'

'Quite. But no point in going back over old mistakes,' said Humphrey, reaching across his desk. 'Here's the file on Mosley. Make discreet contact when he gets out of prison – play up the old friends card, you know the sort of thing. I suspect he'll keep his head down for a while, but we need to make sure he doesn't start up again. He's a slippery fish. Can you resurrect your old cover?'

'Yes, I think so.'

'Run it by me again.'

'Fred Devereux – senior clerk, Board of Trade. Fought in the first war, spent time in China – so far so honest.'

'Good, well go back to that. You'll have to come up with a good story for what you've been up to over the last few years.'

'Shouldn't be too difficult. Fred Devereux was not very ambitious.'

'We'll resurrect your legend, in case he decides to check up on you.'

'Very good, sir. Is that everything?'

'For now, yes.'

Charles stood up to leave.

'How's the wife?' asked Humphrey.

'Oh, very well, thank you sir. Expecting our first child.'

'That's brave – at your age.'

'Yes. Well, I suppose it's to be expected if you marry a woman twenty years your junior.'

'She's still in the dark about what you really do, I hope.'

'Oh yes. Violet is the perfect wife for someone like me. She's enormously intelligent – a top mathematician, in fact – but with very little curiosity.'

'She's German, isn't she?'

'Yes, sir. Well, second generation. Her parents emigrated to England before the Great War.'

'She speaks the language?'

'Fluently... she and her mother often chat in German – less so now though. Rather bad form, I suppose.'

'Perhaps we should recruit her,' said Humphrey, smiling.

'Maybe you should,' replied Charles, laughing, not quite sure if Humphrey was joking or not.

'Well, good luck, Charles. Keep me in the loop about Mosley.'

'Will do, sir. Oh, and about the move out of London, is that still on?'

'I suspect so. But we'll put it off as long as we can.'

Charles's office was a tiny room on the fourth floor of the SIS's headquarters at No. 54, Broadway. It contained just a small desk and a chair and had one window which overlooked an inner courtyard. The window was permanently stuck – painted in, Charles suspected, by some thoughtless decorator.

The room was airless, so he removed his jacket, hung it on the back of his chair, loosened his tie and top shirt button, and began to read through Mosley's file. It was all pretty familiar – he had written most of the information himself.

Charles had first come across Mosley in 1931, two years after he returned from China. His assignment was to 'keep an eye' on a new party that had just been launched by the politician Sir Oswald Mosley. And so began a near decade-long infiltration, during which he attended meetings and rallies, and ingratiated himself with Mosley and his band of Blackshirts.

As a man brought up in the working class, Charles easily passed as a disenchanted young man who had fought bravely for 'King and Country' in the Great War and now felt disillusioned.

In some ways, he understood the frustration of the Party faithful and their anger at the way society was geared to the elite. The people who profited from the Great War were not the ordinary men and women of Great Britain, but the bankers, moneylenders and armaments manufacturers. Many of the young men he had met in the trenches had felt disenchanted. But Charles did not share their anger. As a loyal member of the Service, he never once wavered in his devotion to duty. For while his wife and family were ignorant of so much in his past and his present, his employer knew everything about him – they were essentially his confessor. And as a Catholic, he relished the opportunity to confess to someone in private – 'atoning for his sins', he reminded himself. The Service alone understood the reasons for the double life he led and the lies he had to tell. Ultimately, they had been his saviour, and he owed them everything.

6

Violet

Violet tidied the sitting room, plumping the cushions and even polishing the piano, desperate that Charles's daughter would find no fault with their home. In spite of her inner feelings of anxiety, she wanted to present a picture of domestic calm. When Charles returned from work, he sank down into his favourite armchair, nodding appreciatively at the silver tray laid with two sherry decanters – one fino, the other amontillado – alongside three glasses, and a little bowl of savoury biscuits he knew she had been saving for a special occasion. Violet was standing by the window, wearing a pale blue maternity smock, her dark hair pinned up, revealing her long white neck. She had even applied a slick of red lipstick.

'You look very nice,' he said. 'And thanks for arranging the drinks – that was thoughtful.'

'That's all right. We must make your daughter welcome. What's her name, by the way?'

He glanced at her anxiously. 'Didn't I say? She's called Elizabeth.'

'That's a nice name,' replied Violet.

'Look, I'm sorry about this morning,' Charles went on. 'It must have been a bit of a shock, hearing about her like that.'

'I simply don't understand why you hadn't mentioned it before. I'm certain you've never told me about her. It's not the sort of thing a wife forgets, you know.'

'I know, and it must seem odd to you – and I apologise. I suppose I had blanked it from my mind. It was all such a long time ago... just after the last war. We married in haste, Madeleine and I, and divorced in the same fashion. Somehow the baby got lost in it all.'

'The thing that disappoints me most is that I just can't understand how a man can desert his wife and young child.'

He flushed. 'Desert them? That's a bit harsh.'

'Well, what would you call it? It's unsettled me, Charles, I can't pretend it hasn't. It makes me wonder... might you abandon me too when our baby's born?'

'Of course not. Oh, come on, Violet. You and me – it's quite different.'

'Is it? Why?'

'It just is... I can't explain.'

They were interrupted by the insistent ringing of the doorbell. Charles quickly rose from his armchair, looking nervous. Violet felt a sudden rush of sympathy for him. Glancing up from her place by the window, she observed a pair of slim legs standing at the front door. 'I'd better go and let her in,' she said.

The young woman standing on the doorstep was dressed in the uniform of the ATS and wore her dark hair swept up in a fashionable style.

'Hello there,' she said, 'I'm Elizabeth Carmichael. You must be Violet.' She held out her hand and shook Violet's enthusiastically. 'I say, it's jolly nice of you to invite me. Oh, you're pregnant. I don't think Dad said.'

'*Dad*', thought Violet. '*Dad!*'

'Anyway, it suits you. You're absolutely blooming... isn't that what they say?'

'Yes, I think so,' replied Violet, disconcerted by the girl's friendliness. 'Look, do come in. We're downstairs in the sitting room.'

Charles was standing in front of the fire, holding a glass of sherry. He smiled faintly as Elizabeth approached him, and held out his hand. 'Hello again, Elizabeth.'

'Hello, Dad,' she said, shaking his hand, before pulling him towards her and kissing his cheek.

Violet was surprised by this sudden show of intimacy. 'Do sit down, Elizabeth. Sherry?'

'Oh yes, rather,' replied Elizabeth. 'Amontillado, if you have it?' She glanced at her father, who nodded.

The two women sat opposite each other on the little velvet sofas, glasses in hand. It struck Violet suddenly that she and Elizabeth must be almost the same age. In another life, they could have been friends; now here she was playing the part of 'stepmother'.

'It's a jolly nice house,' said Elizabeth, looking around the room. 'What fun, having the sitting room in the basement. We have our kitchen down there. I spend my whole life running up and down the stairs. It's a nightmare.'

'Where do you live?' asked Violet.

'Oh, didn't Dad say? Just over the road – at number forty-three.'

Violet paused. 'No, he didn't mention it. So, you and... your husband live there?'

'Oh no, I'm not married – at least not yet.' She smiled. 'Me and Ma – my mother – we moved here a couple of years ago.'

'You... and your mother?' Violet glanced anxiously at Charles, who studiously ignored her gaze.

'Yes. Mother has a hairdressing business in Notting Hill Gate. You must come in one day, Violet – we'll do you a special rate.'

Violet touched her hair self-consciously. She had never bothered much with hairdressers, but now she feared her hair had been found wanting.

'Your mother,' Violet began, 'is obviously quite the businesswoman.'

'Ma, oh yes, she's awfully clever. She's got her eye on another salon now in the West End. It's terribly grand. It will mean a lot of hard work, and poor Ma has a bit of arthritis – those stairs at home don't help. We have four floors, including the attics, which is lovely of course, but takes its toll. David – he's my boyfriend – he says once we're married, he can take over the management of the business, and we might all move out of London... out of the smoke, you know. Find a single-storey house in the countryside. He's awfully nice to Ma.'

There was so much to process, Violet hardly knew where to begin. As she listened to Elizabeth prattling on, it occurred to her that she and Charles had moved to Clarendon Road just a few months before his ex-wife. The coincidence was extraordinary. Was either party aware of the other's existence? Was that why Charles had been so keen to live here?

She glanced across at Charles, who sat in rapt attention as his daughter filled the silence with her gay, happy chatter. She could tell how proud he was of this pretty, intelligent girl, and she wondered how he could have left this child and her successful mother. He could be living in luxury now, in a large house up the road, writing his books in a designated study in the attic perhaps, instead of living in a tatty rented flat and working all hours for the government. She even wondered if he might be regretting his actions of twenty years earlier – wishing he and Madeleine had stayed together.

Violet was suddenly aware that Elizabeth had fallen silent.

'So, you're engaged?' she asked, trying to keep the conversation going.

'We're not actually engaged yet, but I'm sure it won't be long before we are.' Elizabeth smiled happily. 'Dear David. He's a dream. In the RAF, of course – but ground crew, thank heavens, so no danger of immediate death... except by drinking too much beer.' She giggled. 'Those boys – they do put it away.'

'And you're in the ATS?'

Elizabeth nodded. 'I'm at the War Office – secretarial. It's worked out rather well actually because I'm able to live at home. So much better than living in digs. Have you seen the billets they put people up in?'

Violet shook her head.

'Well, trust me, you wouldn't want to spend half an hour in one, let alone all night. When's the baby due?'

'September,' replied Violet, her head beginning to throb. This young woman had a remarkable ability to leap from one subject to another – it was hard to keep up.

'What do you think it will be?'

'I really don't know.'

'Maybe another girl, like me. How exciting. I'll have a little sister – wouldn't that be funny?'

Violet felt a delicate kick – the baby making its voice heard, perhaps.

'Or a brother,' Elizabeth continued. 'Either would be lovely.'

'Another sherry?' asked Charles, proffering the decanter.

'Yes please,' replied Elizabeth. 'I can't be too long – Mother will have dinner waiting. You must both come over sometime,' she said, looking from one to the other with her deep- brown-eyed stare.

'That would be lovely,' replied Violet. Charles, she noticed, had already downed his sherry and was pouring himself another.

The conversation staggered on, Elizabeth seemingly unaware of the awkwardness of the situation. But eventually she stood up and put her glass down on a side table.

'Well, I suppose I'd better be going.' She smiled broadly, and Violet and Charles got to their feet. Elizabeth held out her hand to Violet. 'Jolly nice meeting you. Good luck with the baby.'

Turning to her father, she kissed his cheek. 'It's awfully nice to see you again, Dad. I do hope we can get together soon.' As she looked up at him, Violet saw the vulnerability in her eyes... the years of pain of being separated from her father. She hoped Charles would be kind.

'Yes, of course,' he replied. 'It's been lovely to meet you properly. Your mother should be very proud.'

'What a nice thing to say,' said Elizabeth. 'Have you noticed – I look just like you. Same mouth, same nose, same eye colour. Ma's always said so, and now I can see she was right.'

Charles smiled. 'Chip off the old block,' he replied, patting her shoulder. 'To be honest, I thought you reminded me of your mother.' He looked wistful suddenly.

'I'll see you out,' said Violet.

Back upstairs in the hall, Elizabeth looked around her. 'I hope you don't mind me asking, but are these your bedrooms?' She pointed at the two doors off the hall.

Violet nodded. 'Not the most convenient arrangement.'

'No, I can imagine... people strolling past. Still, maybe you'll move – after the baby's born.' She smiled and kissed Violet's cheek. To Violet's surprise, it brought tears to her eyes. It was such a tender thing to do.

'Yes, maybe,' she said. 'But your father is rather wedded to this place. His club is round the corner, you see, and we have the garden.'

'Yes, of course, I understand. Well, I'll see you again.'

As she stood on the steps waving her new stepdaughter goodbye, Violet found herself shouting, 'Give my best to your mother,' as if they were old friends.

'I will!' Elizabeth shouted back, before disappearing up the path of her own house just a few doors away.

Back in the sitting room, Charles was in his armchair, staring into the fire. Violet stood behind him and touched his shoulder. He reached up and patted her hand. As she came round and knelt before him, tears spilled down his cheeks.

'Oh darling, don't cry.'

He took a handkerchief from his pocket and wiped his face. 'It just brought it all back, you know?' He tried to smile, but she could sense the agony behind it.

Violet laid her head in his lap, stroking his hand. Finally, she looked up. 'I thought she was lovely, and very beautiful. She does look like you, but perhaps a little more exotic. I suspect her mother was quite attractive too.'

'Madeleine... yes, she was.' He paused. 'But you know, looks aren't everything.' He stroked Violet's hair. 'You're a good girl, Violet – so loyal. I don't deserve you.'

'Don't be silly,' she replied. 'I'll go and light the oven and heat up the casserole I made earlier. You must be hungry.'

He smiled again, and nodded. 'Ravenous.'

Standing in the kitchen, Violet reflected on the evening. She had every right to be upset. And yet, somehow, in spite of this rather surprising addition to her family circle, she felt quite calm. Elizabeth struck her as a genuine, good-hearted person – not a meddlesome creature who would destroy their lives. But what surprised her most was Charles's reaction to his daughter. Violet had seen a more emotional, vulnerable side to his nature.

Perhaps, in spite of the close proximity of his ex-wife, this new relationship might turn out to be a blessing in disguise.

7

September 1943

Violet

As it turned out, Elizabeth's proposed invitation to dinner failed to materialise. Privately, Violet was relieved. The thought of being in the same room as the first Mrs Charles Carmichael was a nerve-wracking prospect – she sounded far too glamorous and successful. Besides, as Violet's pregnancy entered the last trimester, she was struggling with high blood pressure and swollen ankles. The family doctor ordered her to rest for the final two months. 'I insist you go to bed each afternoon,' he told her. 'If you don't, I shall have no choice but to admit you to hospital.'

Violet broke the news to Charles one evening over dinner. 'He absolutely insists I rest. I'm sorry, because it will make life tricky. I won't be up to going out in the evenings, and might not even be able to produce supper, or entertain your friends.'

'I understand, my dear,' Charles said kindly. 'You must do whatever Dr Roberts thinks is best.'

But as the summer wore on, Charles's sympathy turned to irritation. A decent evening meal became a rare luxury. Instead of a comforting casserole, or sturdy pie, he often came home to a plate of salad with tinned sardines, or slice of spam. Dining every night in one's club would look bad. Instead, he took to eating on the way home at a small Italian trattoria in Notting Hill Gate, arguing it would 'save Violet the trouble'. Violet didn't complain, but ate her simple supper alone in the basement kitchen.

One evening, after she'd cleared away, Violet decided to ring her mother. Lena and her husband Heinrich had come to Britain from Germany over thirty years before, and neither had ever lost their German accents. Their first bakery shop in the East End had been attacked during the Great War, when anti-German sentiment was at its peak. But they had weathered the storm and a few years later moved the business to Peckham. They lived in a flat above the shop, and their only outdoor space was a back yard, which housed their storeroom and the outside lavatory.

'How are you, liebling?' asked Lena, on the other end of the phone.

'Tired, Mutti. I'm under doctor's orders to rest each afternoon. Poor Charles hasn't had a decent meal for weeks. I find shopping so hard – I just can't carry everything I need, and I'm absolutely exhausted by the time I get back from the market.'

'You must borrow my wicker shopping trolley,' her mother insisted. 'I'll bring it over on Sunday afternoon.'

Lena arrived the following Sunday in a heatwave. She parked the cumbersome trolley in the hall, next to the front door, and Violet led her mother out into the garden, where they sat under the shade of the ash tree, drinking lemonade.

Glancing up at the house, Violet noticed the jealous stares from the flats above. Fortunately, her mother was oblivious.

'You're so lucky to have this garden, liebling,' Lena told her daughter.

'Yes, we're very fortunate – it was what originally attracted us to the flat.'

'Is Charles not joining us?' Lena asked.

'Not today, I'm afraid. He's working on a new novel, and he's got a bit of a deadline.'

'That's a shame – we hardly ever see him these days.'

'No, I'm sorry. He's just so busy with work.'

'Oh well, it can't be helped. Papa and the others send their love. Perhaps after the baby's born we can all meet up.'

'Yes... yes, of course.'

The pair chatted for another hour or so, mostly about Violet's older brothers. One of them had decided to leave the bakery business and set up nearby as a butcher.

'It makes good financial sense,' said Lena. 'There isn't enough money in the business to support them both. And thank God bakers and butchers are reserved occupations. We couldn't cope if they had go away and fight – the business would collapse.'

'Is it awkward – being German, and not being seen to fight for the British?' asked Violet. She rarely thought of herself as German. Like her brothers, she had been born in London, and considered herself English. But she knew her parents' history, and how they had endured anti-German sentiment during the first war.

'No,' her mother replied. 'We are part of the community now. And people accept that my sons can't fight. Without bakers and butchers, where would people buy their bread and meat?' Lena smiled. 'Well, I'd better be off,' she said, standing up. 'It's a long journey back to Peckham, and the buses are awful on a Sunday. What with the bomb damage, the roads are up all over the place.'

'It was kind of you to come, and thanks so much for the trolley.' Violet led her mother up the garden stairs, through the communal hall and past Charles's room, which echoed to the sound of typing.

As she waved Lena goodbye, Violet had a flash of irritation that Charles had not taken the trouble to spend a little time with his mother-in-law. At its most basic level it was just rude, and implied a complete lack of interest. In his defence, he rarely took the trouble to meet up with his own family either. Since their wedding, they only ever saw his parents at Christmas, and then only briefly. He and Violet would travel to their house on the Green Line bus, and would scarcely have time for a cup of tea and piece of cake before Charles would make their excuses and leave. He was always on tenterhooks in the presence of his parents, as if he were frightened of what they might say. She wondered if he were embarrassed by their lack of education. He had risen from the working class and had succeeded in becoming solidly middle class, seamlessly adopting the manners and speech patterns of his new peers. The one family relationship he maintained was with his sister. There was a closeness between them, Violet often thought, as if they shared a secret.

Unfortunately, Charles's sister was not particularly friendly towards Violet, being remote and distant, and often seemed to be jealous of her brother's new wife. Not, of course, that there was any impropriety between them, but it was clear the pair had a special, almost intimate relationship, which Violet interfered with.

Violet had occasionally suggested that Charles's family should visit them in Clarendon Road, but he always demurred. 'My mother struggles with public transport,' he would say, or 'my brother-in-law is an awful bore.'

Eventually, Violet had stopped asking. It was as if Charles preferred to keep his relationships in separate compartments. It made the reappearance of his first wife and daughter even more disturbing. She felt sure it must have upset his equilibrium.

Feeling tired, she went back into the garden and poured herself another glass of lemonade. As she closed her eyes, she prayed he would make a better father to their child than he had been to Elizabeth.

One morning, in the dying days of summer, Violet emerged from her house, bumping her shopping trolley awkwardly down the steps. Although heavily pregnant, she was looking forward to a walk through the quiet streets of Holland Park to Portobello Market. Here she would buy whatever vegetables were available, and queue up for the butcher and baker.

She threw her house keys into the bottom of her basket along with her purse and ration card, and put on her sunglasses. As she did so, her gaze travelled across the road to number 43. To her surprise, a woman emerged from the house, resplendent in a pale lilac suit and matching hat. Pulling on leather gloves, she walked purposefully down the chequered path and out into the road, heading towards the Holland Park Avenue. She must have been in her late forties, Violet thought, but her hair was still dark, and she had the slim figure of a girl. Violet knew instinctively that this was Madeleine, Elizabeth's mother.

To her relief, Madeleine seemed not to notice the heavily pregnant woman pulling the trolley on the opposite pavement. Violet turned to watch her walking away. There was an awkwardness about her gait, almost a limp – perhaps the arthritis Elizabeth had mentioned. Violet rarely thought ill of anyone, but she found herself mildly relieved at this sign of aging. In every other respect, Madeleine appeared to be everything Violet was not: beautiful, elegant and successful. What

Violet couldn't understand was why Charles had ever left her. It really made no sense.

It was a Friday morning and the market was heaving with people. Violet joined the long queues at the greengrocer's stalls and the bakery, her legs throbbing, her forehead moist with sweat. Her last port of call was the butcher's shop, where she lined up with twenty or so others. She bought a few rashers of bacon, and a small piece of scrag end, which she would try to turn into something nice for Sunday lunch. As she loaded the paper parcel onto the top of her basket, she felt a sharp pain in her lower abdomen. Leaning against the handle of the trolley, she breathed deeply.

'You all right, dear?' asked a woman next to her.

'Yes, I'm just hot, I think.'

'All right – well take care, won't you. Got far to go?'

'No, just Clarendon Road.'

'Mind yourself, then,' said the woman.

On her way home, she decided to visit the antique shops on Portobello Road and look for a birthday present for Charles. Once the baby was born there would be little time for such expeditions. The sun was at its zenith, so she walked along the shady side of the street. As she paused at a jeweller's window near the top of the row of shops, her eye was caught by a pair of cufflinks – silver with an etched border. She was about to go into the shop and ask if they could be engraved when the baby kicked, taking her breath away. Suddenly, she wanted nothing more than to get home and lie down. She hurried up Portobello Road, and was just turning into Westbourne Grove when she heard a loud rumble overhead – like an enormous angry wasp – followed by silence. Moments later there was a huge explosion that knocked her off her feet. She landed on her back, cracking her head on the pavement. She lay for what seemed like hours, but in reality was probably just a few minutes. As she recalled afterwards, a man rushed out of his shop and cradled her head in his lap. Violet remembered him talking to her, but she couldn't hear what he was saying – her ears were ringing too much.

She woke up in Charing Cross Hospital. Charles was sitting by the bed, reading a newspaper.

'Hello,' she said quietly.

'Hello, Violet. How are you, dear girl?'

'All right, I think. I don't really remember much.'

'You're lucky to be alive... as is he.'

His gaze wandered to a cot next to the bed. A little leg flew up in the air.

'Oh!' She clutched her abdomen. 'How... I mean... what?'

'You were unconscious when they brought you in. They decided to give you a Caesarean. It was a miracle really. I got a call at the office – they found your ration card in the trolley, and tracked me down. They thought the baby might not survive. But he's a strong little chap.'

He stood up, leaned over the cot and picked up the mewling baby. Swaddled in a cheap hospital blanket, he appeared tiny in Charles's large hands.

'Oh, how wonderful! A boy... our little boy.' Violet burst into tears. 'Give him to me, please?' She held out her arms for him.

'Now, now, Mrs Carmichael,' said the nurse, coming into the room. 'No holding baby yet. That tummy won't like it. Stitches, you know.'

'But I want to feed him,' said Violet, now aware of a tingling sensation in her breasts.

'He's already had a few bottles, I'm afraid. If you want to

feed him, one of us will hold him for you, but it won't be easy. Babies get lazy if they're bottle-fed first.'

'I'd like to feed him,' said Violet firmly.

'Very well,' said the nurse. 'Perhaps your husband can help me.' She turned to Charles. 'She'll need to be pulled up the bed, and propped up with pillows – all right?'

Charles nodded uncertainly, and jiggled the mewling baby in his arms. He looked uncomfortable, as if he didn't quite know which end of the infant was up.

'Right, Mr Carmichael, put the baby down before you drop him,' said the nurse, 'and then put one arm round your wife's back and with the other hold her left arm. We're going to pull her very gently up the bed. Ready? Right... one, two, three, pull.'

Once Violet was correctly positioned, the nurse rearranged the pillows. She then took the baby from the cot, and placed him gently on Violet's abdomen. 'Now, unbutton your nightie.'

'I'll just...' Charles began awkwardly. 'Call of nature,' he said, rushing out of the room.

'Typical man,' said the nurse. 'No trouble getting you pregnant, but can't handle the consequences.' She gently lifted the baby into position. 'Now hold the baby's head to your breast, and let him lock on. He'll soon find the nipple, but he may not latch on immediately. Just keep forcing his head back on, like this, you see?' She pushed the baby's head firmly towards Violet's breast. The baby whimpered and turned his head away. But the nurse was not to be defeated and turned it back again, squishing the baby's mouth against his mother's chest. Finally the child gave in, and latched on. Violet was overcome by an extraordinary feeling of elation. Over the next few days, as her milk rushed in, she was able to block out the pain from the operation, and instead immerse herself in the pleasure of her baby's little pink mouth sucking on her breast.

. . .

Charles visited dutifully each evening, after his trattoria meal. Once or twice he brought her a sample of the food – a little square of lasagne wrapped up in brown paper, or a slice of doughy bread covered in cheese and tomato.

'Mmm, it's delicious,' she said. 'What is it?'

'It's called pizza. I rather like it too. We'll go to the restaurant when you're better,' he said. 'How's the baby today?'

'Oh, he's marvellous – and so greedy.'

'And you... you're OK, are you?'

'Yes, Charles. I'm fine, really.'

'I still can't believe you survived.' He gazed at her lovingly. 'You're a tough little thing.'

'I don't understand what actually happened. It was a bomb, I suppose?'

'Yes, it was a bomb all right. A V1 rocket, in fact. It landed in a mews just off Portobello – at the back of Pembridge Villas. If you'd gone another twenty yards, I'm not sure you'd have made it. It's unthinkable.' He took her hand and kissed it.

She searched his face, and thought she saw tears in his eyes. 'Would you have been upset?'

'Of course I would, you silly girl. I do love you, you know.'

'I just meant... I sometimes think you'd be quite happy living on your own. I worry about how you'll cope with a baby in the house – disturbing your routine and so on.'

'Oh Vi, I know I'm a difficult sod – I'm selfish, that's the problem. But I mean well, you know. And I will make an effort – for you and the boy.'

'Will you?'

He nodded.

'We can't keep calling him "the boy",' she said. 'What name will we give him?'

'I have a couple of ideas, but what do you fancy?'

'Well, I thought at first that Charles would be nice, but it can get so confusing when a child is named after their parent.

So then I wondered about Frederick, your middle name. I suspect I will call him Freddie.'

'All right, if that's what you'd like – Freddie it is.'

Violet smiled delightedly. It was a rare moment of triumph. 'Have you seen Elizabeth again?'

He flushed. 'We had a quick drink the other day. Nice girl.'

'What about her mother – have you seen her?'

'Madeleine! Oh no, definitely not. I have no desire to see her. That would be a step too far.'

'I saw her, you know, on the day of the bomb. I was coming out of the house on my way to Portobello and there she was. She's very glamorous. Really quite beautiful, I thought.'

'Did she see you?'

'I don't think so. Anyway, even if she did, I don't suppose she knows who I am.'

Charles studied his wife's face. 'You're a clever thing. I think you're right. Elizabeth told me she'd decided against mentioning my existence to Maddy. "Bit too close for comfort", she said.'

'Maddy', thought Violet. '*Is that what he called her... when they were together?*'

'But she'd like to see *you* again,' he went on. 'Elizabeth, I mean. And she's keen to meet the baby, of course.'

'Her little brother.'

'Yes... about that. I think it would be best if the child grew up not knowing she was his half-sister. No need to muddy the waters and confuse the poor boy. She can be an old friend or something. You and she are about the same age, so there'll be no questions.'

'How will that work, exactly?' asked Violet, her head beginning to throb at the awful complexity of it all. 'Isn't it better to be open and honest from the start?'

'No,' said Charles firmly. 'I've discussed it with Elizabeth, and we've agreed. She'll be known as Aunty Elizabeth from now on.'

Something in Charles's tone made it clear the subject was closed. Violet disagreed, but she knew better than to argue. What she did know was that this secret would one day come back to bite them. Secrets always did.

8

November 1943

Charles

It was already after nine o'clock in the evening when Charles and Violet finished supper. Violet had struggled to get the baby settled, and their casserole, such as it was, had burned slightly round the edges.

'I'm so sorry about this,' said Violet as she dished up. 'That oven has a mind of its own.'

'Not to worry,' said Charles. 'We'll share a bottle of stout – that will cheer us up.'

After supper, Charles poked the fire in the sitting room, and threw on another scuttle-full of coal. 'That'll stay in all evening,' he said, sinking into his favourite armchair. He opened a copy of *The Times*, while Violet fiddled with the dial on the radio.

'Just put the Home Service on,' said Charles, folding his newspaper in half.

'I'm looking for the Third Programme. I saw there was a concert on tonight.'

'Fair enough,' said Charles. 'Who's playing?'

'The London Philharmonic. They're doing Beethoven's Fifth.'

'How very Teutonic,' muttered Charles.

The radio signal was weak and, as Violet turned the dial, her ears picked up the high-pitched, upper-class tones of the man the newspapers called 'Lord Haw-Haw'.

'Jairmany calling, Jairmany calling...'

'Oh my God,' she said. 'Is that who I think it is?'

'Yes. Turn it off,' said Charles gruffly.

'No, let's listen to what he has to say.'

Charles looked over his newspaper at Violet. 'Are you serious? We know what he'll say. That we're losing the war, and that life will be better under Hitler.'

'I suppose so. I just wonder how an Englishman could be such a traitor. It beggars belief,' said Violet.

'Well, for a start he's not English.'

'Isn't he?'

'No, he was born in New York, of Irish descent. Lived in Ireland for a while.'

'But he sounds like an upper-class Englishman.'

Charles laughed. 'He'd love that description. He's nothing of the sort.'

'How do you know so much about him?'

'I met him a couple of times before the war. His real name is William Joyce.'

'Really? You met that awful man?'

'He wasn't actually that awful. He was quite clever – went to Birkbeck College – and he was a magnetic speaker.'

'How did you meet him?'

'Oh, I don't know... someone at the club introduced us, I suspect.'

'That club...' muttered Violet. 'You aren't a fascist, are you, Charles?'

'Of course not!' he barked. 'Now do find that ruddy concert and let's change the subject.'

A couple of weeks later, on the train from Paddington to Kingham in Oxfordshire, Charles reflected on this conversation about William Joyce. He was on his way to visit Oswald Mosley, the fascist leader, who, along with his Nazi sympathiser wife Diana Mitford, had just been released from jail on parole. After a brief stay with his sister-in-law Pamela Mitford, Mosley had moved into the Shaven Crown Hotel in Shipton-under-Wychwood in the Cotswolds.

The train journey would take a couple of hours. Charles had found an empty compartment at Paddington, and was just settling in, doing the *Times* crossword, when the train came to a juddering halt. He went out into the corridor and found the guard. 'Where are we, and how long are we going to be stuck here? I have an urgent appointment – government business.'

'We're just coming into Reading, and as for how long we'll be, I have no idea, sir. Looks like they found a bomb on the line. Could be a while.'

Sighing, Charles retreated to his compartment. He took his bag down from the sagging luggage rack above and removed Mosley's file. He might as well refresh himself about his target. The assignment to reconnect with Mosley got him thinking about that period in his life. Charles was one of several agents who had been tasked with infiltrating Mosley's operation. In 1932, he duly began to attend meetings of the British Union of Fascists. At his first meeting, a young speaker took to the stage. His name was William Joyce. A slender man, with fair hair, he spewed vitriol in the most magnetic manner. Charles had been shocked but transfixed.

He introduced himself after the meeting, and Joyce invited Charles to join him for a drink in a nearby pub. Mosley himself had declined the invitation, Charles recalled. A baronet, Mosley was not a 'pub' type of man. He was a true, blue-blooded aristocrat, and Charles couldn't help wondering why he had been drawn to fascism. He was rich, and had married well. Why jeopardise all that for a vision of Britain that was so at odds with the national mood?

Charles and Joyce sat in the corner of the bar. They talked about Joyce's early life.

'My family moved back to Ireland when I was three. We lived in Galway. I grew up passionate about the Union. I always believed Ireland should be part of Great Britain. When I was fifteen I was recruited by the British Army.'

'How extraordinary – what as?'

'A courier. In fact, I was nearly assassinated by the IRA one day on my way home from school. My recruiter – a nice man, I remember – was so worried about my safety, he sent me over to England. I went to school in Worcestershire. Had a better education than I'd have had in Ireland. It enabled me to go to university. You could say that assassination attempt was the making of me.'

'I was in Ireland for a while,' said Charles, doing his best to create a bond between them. 'In fact I joined up there – the South Irish Horse.'

'Oh, a fine regiment. What took you to Ireland?'

'Curiosity,' replied Charles. 'I'd left school, wanted to travel a bit, loved Irish writers. Then the war began, and I joined up.'

Charles closed the Mosley file and stared out of the grubby carriage window at the run-down terraced houses beside the railway line. They reminded him of the house he had been brought up in – two up, two down, with no inside bathroom. It had not been a comfortable life but, looking back, his parents had been content with their lot, and were good God-fearing people. It would never have occurred to either of them to lie, whereas for Charles lies had been part of his daily life; in fact, they were an essential part of his survival.

The train began to judder, then slowly pick up speed. Charles opened the carriage window and leaned out. Billowing smoke and cinders hit him full in the face. The guard put his head into the compartment. 'On our way now, sir – false alarm. Where are you heading?'

'Kingham,' replied Charles.

'Be there in an hour.'

At Kingham station, Charles took a taxi to Shipton-under-Wychwood. On the short journey, driving rain turned to sleet. 'There'll be snow by evening time, you mark my words,' muttered the driver.

Charles arrived at the hotel in time for lunch, hoping to find his quarry in the dining room so their meeting would look like a coincidence. Mosley was effectively under house arrest – those were the terms on which he had been released. Charles had been warned to expect a police presence at the hotel, and was not surprised to see a uniformed bobby standing outside as rain turned to sleet.

'Morning, officer,' said Charles as he went through the front door. 'Rotten day for it.'

The policeman tipped his hat.

In the bar, huge logs crackled merrily in the medieval fireplace. Feeling chilly, Charles warmed his hands for a moment, rubbing them expectantly.

'What can I do for you, sir?' asked the barman.

'I wondered if I might have a spot of lunch – is the dining room open?'

'It is – we've got shepherd's pie on today.'

'Excellent,' replied Charles. 'I'll have a quick pint of your local ale before I go through.'

'Of course, sir. You sit down and warm yourself by the fire, and I'll bring it over.'

The wood-panelled dining room was dark and smelt of woodsmoke from the fire that smouldered in the inglenook fireplace. Charles chose a corner table, from where he had a good view of the room, and ordered soup and the shepherd's pie. He thought about ordering a glass of claret, but it wouldn't fit with his undercover role as Fred Devereux, working-class lad made good. Glancing out of the window, he noticed the sleet had turned to snow and was settling on the lawn. He took out a copy of the *Daily Mail* he had bought that morning. If Mosley came in, he would appear to immerse himself in it. It was vital that Mosley should believe Charles's presence was a pure coincidence.

He was just finishing his lunch when Mosley arrived, with his wife Diana on his arm. Charles deliberately concentrated on his paper until the couple were seated. Only then did he allow himself a peek at the infamous pair. There was no hint of prison pallor on Diana's delicate porcelain features. Tall and willowy with huge blue eyes, she sat down languorously at the table and took a cigarette from a silver case. Her husband reached across and clicked a silver lighter; she drew on her cigarette, exhaling airily.

They seemed utterly wrapped up in one another. They kept their voices low – gentle, intimate exchanges – so Charles couldn't decipher what they were saying. The waitress arrived and took their order. She never smiled, Charles noted, and he wondered if the staff were altogether happy at giving houseroom to a traitor and his wife.

When the waitress brought Charles the dessert menu, Mosley looked across the room towards him. He whispered something to Diana, who shot Charles a wary look. Mosley got up, right hand outstretched.

'It's Fred, isn't it?'

Charles looked up from his paper, feigning surprise. 'Yes. Good Lord... Sir Oswald, how marvellous to see you again, sir.' He leapt to his feet, and shook Mosley's hand.

'Yes, what a coincidence,' replied Mosley.

'I had read you'd been released, but I had no idea where to,' said Charles, adding in a whisper, 'I am so pleased for you.'

'I got out a couple of weeks ago. What brings you here?'

'Me? Oh, I have a cousin who lives nearby, in Chipping Norton. He invited me down. I thought I'd try a few local hostelries while I was here. Someone recommended this place. I'm so glad you're out now, sir.'

'Thank you. It's nice to see a friendly face. Most people are rather...' Mosley paused, '...mistrustful.'

'I see. How unfortunate. It's a shame they don't understand that you were only acting from love of your country.'

'Quite. Look, would you like to join us?'

'Oh, I don't want to intrude. Besides, I've nearly finished, and you've just started.'

'Well, how about coffee then – in the lounge afterwards. It would be good to catch up on old times, yes?'

'I'd love that. Thank you, sir.'

As Mosley retreated to his table, Charles smiled at Diana, who narrowed her eyes, exhaled cigarette smoke and turned away.

When Charles had finished his lunch, he walked past Mosley's table. 'See you in there, sir,' he murmured. Mosley nodded.

In the lounge Charles settled into a comfortable armchair and picked up a copy of *The Times* lying on a table. Perusing the headlines, he read that President Roosevelt was meeting Churchill and

Stalin in Tehran. His colleagues had already alerted Charles to the meeting, so it came as no surprise. He tried to imagine the conversation between the three leaders, and wished just for a moment that he were part of it. To be in the room when great matters of state were being decided would be an exhilarating experience, especially for someone as low down the pecking order as he was.

He ordered a pot of coffee and waited for Mosley. He felt rather pleased that, so far, his plan had paid off. Mosley had been surprisingly friendly; Charles was amazed he had even remembered him – they could only have actually met two or three times. Perhaps the years in jail had made him desperate for any sympathetic face. Now, all Charles had to do was convince Mosley that he was a loyal acolyte, and then sit back and wait for him to 'sing'.

9

December 1943

Elizabeth

Snow was falling thick and fast, and the tube was running late. Slipping and sliding towards the War Office through the slush, Elizabeth was relieved she had left home with time to spare. Bad weather was not considered a suitable excuse for lateness in the army. To her relief, the huge clock dominating the entrance hall showed that it was just five minutes to nine.

Running up the imposing staircase, she admired the magnificent Christmas tree. Elizabeth and some of the other secretaries had been detailed to decorate it a few days earlier. It had provided one of the few light-hearted moments in an otherwise gloomy December.

After parade, she set to work in her office, typing up the minutes of a meeting that had been chaired by Captain Valentine the previous day. For once there had been some optimistic news:

Following on from Tehran Conference, agreement has been reached for planned invasion of Europe, codename Operation Overlord.

Preparations are being made for a meeting on 31 December between General Dwight D. Eisenhower, hereafter referred to as Commander of Supreme Headquarters Allied Expeditionary Force (SHAEF), and General Bernard Montgomery, commander of 21st Army Group to discuss amphibious landings, codename: COSSAC.

Elizabeth finished her typing and left the papers on Captain Valentine's desk. He was due to be out of the office all day in a series of meetings, which meant Elizabeth could catch up on a lot of work.

At five-thirty, she put the cover on her typewriter. She had arranged to meet her father after work for a pre-Christmas drink at The Clarence pub.

Charles was waiting for her in the corner of the bar. 'Over here, Elizabeth,' he called out as she rushed in out of the cold.

She shook the snow off her hat and removed her trench coat. 'Golly, it's freezing out there.'

'Well, drink this,' he said, handing her a glass of barley wine and a whisky chaser. 'Those will warm you up.'

She sipped the whisky and choked slightly.

Charles laughed. 'Not used to it?'

'Not really, but I can feel it warming me up.'

'It's Irish – my favourite. Been busy today?'

'Very.'

'Interesting busy?'

'Dad, you know I can't tell you anything.' She smiled. 'But I will say this... there is a bit of optimism around the place. The Americans joining in, and all that.'

'Mmm... I read a report about that too,' replied Charles. 'So don't worry, I think we share the same secret. This is the year when the balance of power will change in the Allies' favour – at least we have to hope so. Cheers.'

'I'll second that.' She chinked her glass against his, then added, 'Have you been busy too?'

'Oh, the usual, you know.'

'What is "the usual"? I've never really understood what you do.'

'My dear girl, if you really understood what I did you'd be bored to tears. Trade in wartime – moving goods around for the nation – is deadly dull.'

She smiled. 'It must be such a change from when you were young?'

'How do you mean?'

'During the war – the Great War, I mean. Young men like you were thrown into such awful situations. I was just thinking about you today, in fact. Being in the forces must have been so different from nowadays. Our troops are always on the move, but you were stuck in the trenches, weren't you? You must have felt so trapped. You never talk about it – I don't even know which regiment were you in.'

'I was in the South Irish Horse. It was a cavalry regiment.'

'I didn't know you rode?'

'I don't. We weren't all on horseback, you know.' He chuckled. 'I was just a private – a sniper – nothing fancy.'

'Why an Irish regiment?'

'Oh...' he paused, and sipped his whisky, '...I just happened to be in Dublin when the call to arms came. Young men then, we just joined up where we could.'

'What took you to Dublin?'

'I wanted to be a writer. I was on a bit of a pilgrimage, I suppose. So many of my literary heroes hailed from there – Congreve, Sheridan, Swift, Wilde.'

'You were very young to be travelling.'

'Not really – I'd finished school. I can't exactly remember how old I was.'

'Oh Dad, you are funny. And what was it like... in the trenches?'

'Ghastly. A sort of hell, if you really want to know.'

'I'm sorry.' She leaned across and touched his arm. 'I didn't mean to pry, but I'm so proud of you and I'd like to understand what you went through.'

'I did nothing special.'

'You told me once that your leg was badly injured, and you were gassed.'

'Oh yes... that.'

'You make it sound like nothing, but I'd like to know exactly what happened. Tell me, please?'

'All right, if you insist. I was a sniper out in no-man's-land one night. Bloody Hun got me in the leg. But you know, Elizabeth – what I experienced was nothing special. Millions of young men lost their lives, and millions more were injured and ended up with terrible life-altering injuries. I saw it all when I was in hospital. The bravery of some of these men, in the face of all their pain and suffering, was remarkable... inspirational.' His eyes filled with tears, and he took out his handkerchief and blew his nose.

'I'm sorry,' she said, touching his shoulder. 'Let's talk about something else. How's Violet and the little one?'

'Oh, doing well. He's growing fast.'

'I'd love to see him sometime.'

'Yes, of course. We'll arrange something after Christmas. Are you doing anything special?'

'Not really. David's on duty, so it will just be me and Mother. Still, I'm looking forward to it. Just knowing that I will clock off at half past five on Christmas Eve and have thirty-six hours away from work will be heaven – my boss is such a letch. It's becoming rather a bore.'

'Really? You shouldn't let him get away with that sort of thing.'

'Oh, I don't. He wasn't in today, thank heavens.' She glanced down at her watch. 'Oh, Lord, it's half past six already. I really ought to get going. Give my love to Violet and the boy.'

'I will.'

'And thank you for the drink. I have to admit, it has warmed me up!' She kissed her father on the cheek and stood up, pulling on her coat.

'Not too tipsy I hope,' Charles said. 'That barley wine is quite strong. And take care getting home – the pavements are lethal.'

'I will, Dad. Goodbye.'

On the morning of Christmas Eve, Elizabeth arrived at her office just as Captain Valentine was on his way out.

'Ah, Corporal. Looking lovely as ever.'

Elizabeth smiled politely. 'You just off somewhere, sir?'

'Yes, I've a meeting down the road this morning, so you'll have to cope without me.'

'Very good, sir. Is there anything you'd like me to get on with?'

'There are a pile of letters on your desk. I hand-wrote them – can you get them typed up for me?'

'Of course, sir.'

'Oh, and this afternoon I'll be attending an officers' pre-Christmas get-together.'

'A party, sir – how lovely.'

'It will be mostly business, Corporal,' snapped the captain. 'I'll see you later.'

. . .

By lunchtime, Elizabeth had finished her typing, and found herself at a loose end. Musing on her last conversation with her father, it suddenly occurred to her that there might be records of his time in the trenches. He had seemed so vague about it all when they last met, and she wanted to know more. Perhaps he'd won a medal, or there might even be a report of his heroism out in no-man's-land. She covered her typewriter, left a note for Captain Valentine in case he returned early and went down to the records office in the basement. The clerks were nowhere to be seen, but there were streamers and Christmas decorations hanging from the ceiling, and she could hear laughter as she approached the reception desk. Glancing through an open door into a side room, she could see a group of men swigging from glasses of beer – having their own unofficial party.

She coughed loudly to attract their attention.

One of the clerks approached, wiping his mouth slightly with the back of his hand. 'What can I do for you, Corporal?'

'I've been asked to find a service record for a soldier in the 1914–18 war.'

'You've had a wasted journey, love. No First World War service records are kept in London any more – not since the big fire.'

'What big fire?'

'The records used to be kept in Arnside Street, but the whole lot got destroyed back in the Blitz. Over two million records were lost. What was left has been taken out of London to Surrey. You could try there, I suppose. Anyway, who wants records of the Great War?'

'Oh, it's a security matter,' she muttered. 'It doesn't matter.'

'If you say so. Happy Christmas.'

'Yes... Happy Christmas.'

. . .

She was tidying her desk and preparing to leave for the day when Captain Valentine returned to the office. Judging by the way he was walking, he was thoroughly drunk.

'Ah, the lovely Corporal,' he murmured as he stumbled through her office to his own, leaving the stench of booze and cigarettes behind him. A few minutes later, he called through to her, 'Could you come in here a minute? I'd like to dictate a letter.'

'Very good, sir.' Sighing, Elizabeth picked up her notebook and pen. It was nearly half past five, and she'd promised her mother she'd be back in time for supper. She found the captain lounging on a sofa in a section of his office he used for more informal meetings. He patted the place next to him. 'Sit here.'

'No, sir, I'm better over here,' she replied, perching on his visitor's chair opposite his desk.

'What's the matter, Corporal? You're not frightened of me, are you?'

'No, sir.'

'Well, come and sit here then. I insist.'

She sat down reluctantly next to Valentine, leaving a good space between them. But he slithered across the sofa, and put his hand on her knee.

'Captain, please don't,' she said, moving as far away from him as she could.

'Stop playing so hard to get,' he replied. 'I know all about girls like you.' Suddenly, he shoved his hand up her skirt until he was touching the flesh above her stockings, all the while leaning across her, his face pressed against hers.

'Captain... please stop it.' She tried to pull his hand away, but he was stronger than her. Moments later, he had swung his other hand behind her back, and pulled her towards him. He kissed her roughly on the mouth, then murmured into her hair, 'Oh Elizabeth. I've wanted to do that for a long time.'

He kissed her again, this time forcing his tongue into her

mouth. She gagged, and tried to push him away, but he was too forceful. She dug her nails into his neck, but this only seemed to spur him on. 'You like that, do you?' he murmured.

He pushed her down onto the sofa and pulled up her skirt, his hands inside her underwear, forcing his fingers inside her. She felt him hard against her, and was aware of him fumbling with his zip.

She knew now that she must fight. With her skirt up around her waist, her legs were free, so she forced one leg up and into his crotch as hard as she could, at the same time biting his neck with all her might. He reared back. 'Ah, you little bitch.'

Somehow, she found the strength to push him off, then managed to roll off the sofa and onto the floor. But as she attempted to crawl away, he grabbed her leg and pulled her towards him by her ankle. She was helpless now, lying face down on the floor, spreadeagled – she was at his mercy. He forced her skirt up, pulled her underwear down and threw himself on top of her. Her heart was racing, her mind blank.

Suddenly, a shrill noise penetrated her consciousness. It was the air-raid siren. There was the sound of running feet in the corridor outside and someone threw open the door to the outer office. 'Everyone out!' a man shouted.

Somehow, Elizabeth found her voice. 'Help,' she cried out, quietly at first, then louder. 'Help me.'

Elizabeth felt her attacker roll off her, and then the sound of him zipping his trousers. She looked up to see an army clerk, wearing the stripes of a corporal, standing over her. She was face down on the floor with her skirt around her waist, her knickers halfway down her thighs.

The corporal knelt at her side. 'You all right, miss? Let me help you up.'

She was shaking so much, she couldn't move. The young man lifted her off the floor. When Elizabeth was upright, he discreetly turned his back, and stood between her and the captain while she pulled up her underwear and rearranged her skirt.

'Thank you,' she said, quietly when she was properly dressed. Her heart was still pounding fast, and she felt almost dizzy from the rush of adrenalin.

'I think we'd better get you out of here, don't you, miss?'

He took her firmly by the arm and marched her out of the office, down the corridor and into the basement shelter. Once there, he settled her between two other secretaries.

'Perhaps you two could keep an eye on this one,' he said to the girls. 'She's had a bit of a shock.'

Before he left, Elizabeth grabbed his hand. 'Thank you – thank you so much.' The adrenalin had finally dissipated, and tears began to spill down her cheeks.

The young corporal crouched down next to her, and whispered in her ear: 'I'll come and check on you later, and escort you back upstairs, all right?'

When the raid was over, he was as good as his word, and accompanied Elizabeth to her office to collect her bag and hat. Valentine was nowhere to be seen.

'I wonder,' began the corporal, as they locked up the office, 'and please say if you think I'm being too forward, but would you like a drink? You've had a bit of a shock.'

'Thank you. I would, if you have time?'

The nearest pub was The Clarence on Whitehall, where Elizabeth often met her father. The corporal sat her down at a table near the door and returned from the bar with a pint for himself, and a glass of brandy. 'Get that down you. You're white as a sheet.'

'Thank you.' She sipped the brandy and felt it coursing through her veins. She sighed. 'I'm all right, really. Thankfully, you arrived just in time... or, at least, Jerry did.' She smiled bravely. 'No real harm done. Just wounded pride.'

'Well, I'm glad about that, at least. But you must report him. Valentine has got a bit of a reputation for that sort of thing. You must speak to your commanding officer.'

'I couldn't. You know what they're like. They'll only take his side, say I imagined it.'

'I'll speak up for you, and tell them what I saw.'

'Then you'll get into trouble – dobbing in a senior officer.'

'I don't mind.'

'It's a lot to ask.'

'Well, think about it. I work just down the corridor from you in Major Williams' office – he's the quartermaster. My name is Danny, by the way.' He smiled.

'Nice to meet you, Danny. I'm Elizabeth.' She took his hand, and squeezed it. 'So, how did you end up at the War Office?'

'I was a journalist in a former life. I joined the army to fight, but it turned out they were desperate for typists. I keep asking for active duty, but they say I'm too useful where I am. If we move into Europe next year, I might be lucky and get over there.'

'Well, it's lucky for me that you're not over there.' She smiled. 'You saved me today. I don't know how to thank you.'

'No need,' he said. 'Another drink?'

'I'd better not. Mother's expecting me.'

'Will you tell her what happened?'

'No. I don't think so. It would only upset her.'

Suddenly, she heard her name being called out. 'Elizabeth?'

She looked up. Coming towards them was her father. 'Oh, Dad, it's you.'

'Hello there,' he said, looking down at them both. 'I'm not interrupting, am I?'

'Oh, no – there was a raid and... well, this young man was very kind.'

'Yes – we were all in the shelter for a while this afternoon, too,' said Charles. 'Can I buy you both a drink?'

The corporal stood up. 'Not for me, sir, thank you. I ought to be going. I'll leave you now, miss. Glad to help. And remember my advice, all right?'

'All right, Danny... and thank you again.'

Charles turned to his daughter. 'You look rather pale. How about that drink?'

'All right – thank you. But just a quick one. Ma's expecting me.'

'What'll it be? Another brandy?'

'No, thank you. I don't really like it.'

'Sherry then?'

'Yes please.'

He returned a few minutes later and put the drinks on the table. 'Cheers.'

Elizabeth chinked her glass with his.

Charles smiled at her, his soft brown eyes searching her face. 'What's the matter, my dear? Young ladies don't normally drink brandy so early in the evening – especially when they don't like it.'

'Something rather horrible happened today, which upset me rather.' She felt tears welling up again.

'The raid, you mean?'

'No, not that.'

'Something to do with that young man?'

'No, quite the reverse, in fact. He was my knight in shining armour.'

'Ah... the letch then?'

Elizabeth had mentioned 'the letch' at their last meeting, and was touched that her father had remembered. Suddenly she wanted to open her heart to him. As tears spilled down her cheeks, she blurted out, 'I wasn't going to say anything to anyone. I'm so ashamed.'

Charles reached across the table and took her hand, squeezing it. 'Darling, you don't need to feel ashamed of anything, especially with me. I've done enough shameful things to last a lifetime.'

Elizabeth took a sip of her drink, followed by a deep breath. 'You know I told you last time that I work for a man named Captain Valentine.'

Charles nodded and sipped his pint.

'He's been flirting with me for weeks, months really. I hate it. He's old enough to be my...' Blushing, she paused.

'To be your father?' Charles smiled. 'Go on.'

'Well, this afternoon there was a party for the officers, and he came back to the office very drunk.' She took a further gulp of her drink, and wiped her eyes with her handkerchief.

'Oh, my dear,' said Charles, 'I can imagine the rest. Don't tell me if you don't want to.'

'I really believed he was going to rape me, Dad,' she whispered. 'It was so close... but that corporal just now – who bought me the brandy – he was walking past the office at the time, getting people out of the building in the raid. If he hadn't come in...' At that, her self-control collapsed, and she sobbed. Charles wrapped her in his arms and rocked her.

'Well, then,' he said after a while, 'thank God he did come in.' He removed a clean handkerchief from his top pocket and handed it to her. 'Here, dry your eyes.'

He waited a few moments while she collected herself. 'This cad Valentine is a problem that won't go away, trust me. So we must do something about it – perhaps get you transferred.'

'Oh no, I couldn't do that. You know what it's like working for the army – we go where we're sent. Besides I like it there. I just don't like *him*.'

Charles mused for a while. 'There may be something I can do.'

'What?'

'I can speak to someone. I'm not without contacts. Men shouldn't get away with that sort of thing. In the meantime, just don't let yourself get into a confined space with him. Make sure office doors are kept open at all times. He'll go one of two ways – either become emboldened, in which case you must speak out, or he'll shrink back and pretend nothing happened.'

'Gosh, I suppose you're right. You're so understanding – I am grateful.'

'Darling girl, what else could I be?'

She glanced down at her watch. 'Oh Lord, it's after six! I really must fly. Ma will be cross. I promised her I'd be early as it's Christmas Eve.' Flustered, she stood up, pulled on her hat and slung her gas mask over her shoulder. 'Damn!' she said, glancing out of the grubby windows. 'It's started to snow again.'

'You haven't a coat?'

'No. In the rush, I must have left it in the office. I'm not sure I can face going back now. *He* might be there.'

Charles reached into his pocket and produced a crisp one-pound note. 'Take a taxi.'

'Oh, Father, that's far too much.'

'It's all I've got. Besides, let's call it an early Christmas present. Buy yourself something.'

She leaned down and kissed his cheek. 'Thank you. You're very kind. I do appreciate your being so understanding. What are you and Violet doing for Christmas?'

'Oh, the usual. Unendurable family visits involving endless cups of tea and Christmas cake in overheated rooms – all appalling agony from my point of view, and from hers too, I suspect. Neither of us are exactly sociable.'

'And how's my little brother?'

'Doing well, thank you. He's being christened just after

Christmas. I didn't invite you. I hope you don't mind – too many questions.'

'No, of course. I completely understand. Besides, we agreed, didn't we? I'm Aunty Elizabeth, friend and neighbour, from now on. But I hope it goes well. And kiss him for me.'

As she stood in the street, waiting for a cab in the snow, Elizabeth reflected on her father's reaction to Valentine's behaviour. It was as if he intuitively understood how she felt. And, interestingly, she felt calmer and more able to deal with the situation. She was determined that Valentine would not get the better of her; and, as long as she could confide in her father, she felt sure she would be able to face the challenge.

10

Charles

Tears came into Charles's eyes as he watched his daughter leave the pub. Elizabeth's stoicism was remarkable, but her frightening experience stirred dark memories in him. As he put on his coat and hat, troubling images that he had spent decades burying flashed up in his mind. 'Stop it,' he muttered to himself. He felt murderous on his daughter's behalf. His instinct was to beat Valentine to a pulp. He wouldn't, of course – after all, he was middle-aged with a bad leg. But he would do all he could to destroy the man – of that he was certain.

He left the pub and walked through the snow towards St James's. He had arranged a meeting with Humphrey that evening – a debrief about Mosley. The pavements were slippery with slush, and snowflakes gathered around the brim of his hat and the collar of his coat. When he arrived at the Broadway, he smiled at the brass plaque that was nailed to the door, announcing that he was about to enter the Minimax Fire Extinguisher Company. He doubted it fooled anyone. Inside, he shook out his coat and hat, and went upstairs to the first floor, leaving a trail of water droplets behind him.

Humphrey was deep in thought, studying a file on his desk, when Charles entered.

'Ah, Charles,' he said, looking up. 'Good to see you. Come in, sit down. What a filthy night.'

'Yes, it's started snowing again. It is rather miserable.'

'Let me get you a drink. Whisky?'

'Thank you, that would be grand.'

'Hang your coat up, and let's sit by the fire,' suggested Humphrey, indicating a pair of battered armchairs. He walked over to a drinks tray, where he poured out two glasses of malt whisky from a cut-glass decanter.

'Cheers,' he said, handing a glass to Charles and settling into an armchair. 'So, I hear you met Mosley?'

'I did, sir.'

'How was he?'

'Reticent, I should say. Yes... reticent.'

'Interesting. Go on.'

'We spent the afternoon together – he was at a hotel in the Cotswolds with Diana.'

'Ah, the legendary Mitford beauty. Were you seduced?' Humphrey smiled.

'No,' said Charles, laughing. 'Although I do see the attraction.'

'How did he react to seeing you?'

'With surprise, of course. But he bought my story – staying with a cousin in Chipping, doing the sights, came to the hotel by chance. He also seemed pathetically grateful to see a friendly face. Insisted I stayed and had coffee... chewed the cud a bit. We discussed Bill Joyce, actually.'

'Oh, yes? And what's his take on the little rat?'

'Oh, he's shocked. Furious, in fact. Called the man a traitor.

"I would never have brought him on, if I'd known what he was capable of," was the gist.'

'Interesting. What are his plans?'

'He seems keen to keep his head down. They're talking of moving house soon, somewhere in the West Country. Not sure hotel life is that easy – the staff are not exactly welcoming. And I suspect he feels he's living in a goldfish bowl.'

'Will you see him again?'

'I hope so, although he's hardly likely to invite me down for the weekend, you know. I'm not quite part of his social circle. But I did ask if there was anything I could do for him. Intriguingly, he suggested I take a message or two for him – should the need arise.'

'Excellent. It might be a trap, of course. Do you think he rumbled you?'

'It's possible. I hope not.'

'Well, when he reaches out, do as he asks. Let's see if he gives you anything interesting.'

'Of course, sir.'

Humphrey put his empty glass down on the coffee table. 'I think that's everything. What are your plans for Christmas?'

'Oh, the usual. Family visits – and we're christening our son.'

'Oh, marvellous. Where?'

'Farm Street Church.'

'Very respectable. I hope it goes well.' Humphrey stood up. 'Well, if there's nothing else.'

'There is just one thing, sir...'

Humphrey sat back down. 'Yes?'

'I don't know if you know, but I have a daughter – she's in the ATS and works at the War Office for a Captain Valentine.'

'Yes, I think I've seen something about that in your file. You've become reacquainted recently, I understand.'

Charles smiled. Of course, the Service knew everything –

especially about its own operatives. 'Yes, we met by chance, in the street of all places.'

'How extraordinary,' said Humphrey. 'What were the chances of that, I wonder?'

'I know. It struck me at the time as remarkable, but I do believe it was a genuine coincidence. Anyway, the point is, Valentine has been making a bit of a nuisance of himself. Not to put too fine a point on it, he almost raped her this afternoon. She's most awfully upset – I've just come from seeing her. She's nervous of speaking out of course, but I won't have it, sir. There must be something we can do.'

'Nasty business – Valentine, you say. Leave it with me. I'll see if we can move him sideways. She's all right, is she, your daughter?'

'Miraculously, yes. There was an air raid at the vital moment. A young ATS clerk was getting everyone out of the building and interrupted the bastard.'

'So, at least we have Herr Hitler to thank for something.' Humphrey smiled, amused at his own joke. 'Well, have a good Christmas, Charles.'

'Thank you, sir. See you in the New Year.'

Crossing St James's Park in the blackout, Charles felt a certain satisfaction. His job was a curious mix of intrigue, fear and boredom. But just sometimes, it did pay to be in His Majesty's Secret Service.

11

Elizabeth

The snow was settling on the pavements as Elizabeth's taxi drove down Holland Park Avenue. Turning into Clarendon Road, she had a moment of guilt that, while she was travelling home in comfort, her father was possibly struggling back on public transport. Now, she wondered why she hadn't offered to share the taxi. As they passed number 18, she peered down into the basement. The flat appeared to be in darkness. Clearly her father had not yet returned.

'Four and six,' said the taxi driver, drawing up outside number 43.

'I'm afraid I've only got this,' said Elizabeth, handing him the one-pound note.

'You got nothing smaller, love? I haven't got the change, and you're my last fare.'

She peered into her purse and brought out half-a-crown. 'That's all I've got.'

He held his hand out. 'That'll have to do. Have the rest on me. Happy Christmas.'

'Oh, that's so kind. Happy Christmas to you too.'

She clambered out of the taxi, her feet sinking into several inches of snow. The garden path was perilous, and she stood on the steps outside the front door, brushing snowflakes off her shoulders and tapping her shoes dry.

Letting herself into the house, she felt her resolve to be brave evaporating. As she took off her hat and shook it over the mat, she had vivid flashbacks of Valentine's hands grasping at her body, of his hot drunken breath on her face. She shuddered, reliving the feeling of his hand sliding up her skirt, pinching the flesh at the tops of her thighs. 'Stop it!' she muttered to herself, and breathed deeply for a few minutes, trying to regain control. Standing by the hall table, she stared at herself in the gilt-framed mirror. In the lamplight she looked pale and haggard; her mother was bound to see that something was wrong. She pinched her cheeks to get a little colour into them, and smoothed down her hair. There were sprigs of holly round the mirror's frame, but their cheerful red berries were in sharp contrast to Elizabeth's mood. She had no Christmas spirit whatever; instead, she felt lonely, frightened and dirty.

'Elizabeth, is that you?' her mother called from the sitting room.

'Yes, it's me. Sorry I'm late. Work held me up.'

'Never mind. I've got a lovely surprise for you.'

Elizabeth sighed. Presumably, another one of her mother's old Uxbridge friends had invited themselves for dinner. She hung up her gas mask, set her face in a fixed smile and entered the sitting room.

Standing by the fireplace was her fiancé, David.

'David! Oh, David, darling.'

Elizabeth burst into tears and ran to his open arms. She buried her face in his chest, inhaling the scent of his uniform.

'Hey, what's all this, sweetheart? Tears? That's not like you.'

'I'm sorry,' she mumbled. 'I've just had quite a hard day. Why didn't you tell me you were coming?'

'I didn't know until this morning. I got a last-minute pass. Got to be back on base by Boxing Day. One of the chaps lent me his car – an old roadster. Wasn't that kind of him?'

Elizabeth looked up at him, tears pouring down her cheeks, the fear she had felt a few moments earlier evaporating.

'Now then,' said David, 'no more tears, darling. I thought you'd be happy to see me.'

'I am happy – you have no idea how happy.' Elizabeth wiped her eyes with a handkerchief.

'Well,' said Madeleine, 'I'll leave you two together. I've got a fish pie in the oven, and I don't want it to spoil. David, pour the girl a drink. They work her far too hard at that place – she looks white as a sheet.'

The couple remained locked in an embrace for another minute before David released her. 'Darling, I'm worried about you. Your mother said you'd been working long hours.'

'Oh, no more than anyone else. She doesn't understand. Now, how about that drink?'

David walked over to the drinks tray. 'What do you fancy?'

'Sherry. Amontillado if there is one.'

'That's new – not known you drink that before. You're normally a Dubonnet girl, aren't you?'

'Oh, someone introduced me to it. I rather like it.'

He handed her the small crystal glass brimming with amber liquid. 'There you go... get that down you. But you do look pale, darling. Come and sit by the fire.'

They sat opposite one another, and sipped their drinks.

'It is lovely to see you,' she said quietly.

'What's up? You look so upset. Is someone being mean to you?'

'Not really. My boss is a... bit of a tartar.' '*Why can't I just tell him the truth?*' she thought.

'That must be hard. Got to stand up for yourself. Don't let him push you around.'

'I know, and I will. Anyway. I'm off now till Boxing Day, like you. So we've got thirty-six hours to forget all about it.'

'I've got something for you,' said David, 'hold on there a minute.'

He went out into the hall, and returned a few minutes later with a small box wrapped in brightly coloured paper. 'Here, Happy Christmas darling.'

'Oh, David, I've not got you anything – I didn't know I was going to see you.'

'I know, it doesn't matter. Being here with you is all the present I need. Go on, open it before your mother comes back.'

'Goodness, David, what on earth is it?'

'Nothing naughty, I promise.' He laughed.

She removed the velvet ribbon and the paper. Inside was a dark-blue leather jeweller's box. Lifting the lid, she found a ring embellished with three small but perfectly cut diamonds. 'David! Is this what I think it is?'

He smiled, took the ring from its velvet box and placed it on the third finger on her left hand. 'Will you marry me, Elizabeth, and make me the happiest of men?'

'Oh, David, of course I will.' She burst into tears, as her mother appeared in the doorway.

'Goodness, what's wrong?'

'Nothing, Mother, nothing at all. I'm just happy.'

'Well, you've got a funny way of showing it.'

'David's asked me to marry him. Look...' She held out her hand and the trio of tiny diamonds sparkled in the light.

'Oh, how marvellous. David, I'm so pleased. We both love you so much.'

David stood up and embraced his future mother-in-law. 'And I love both of you too.'

. . .

Christmas flew by in a whirl of pleasure. David was loving and attentive. Even Madeleine, normally so brisk and efficient, seemed mellowed by the announcement of their engagement. On Christmas Day they enjoyed a delicious meal of roast chicken, and afterwards listened to the radio and played cards in the sitting room.

At ten o'clock David stood up. 'I'm sorry to break up the party, but I probably should head up to bed. I've got to get going before dawn, and it's a five-hour drive back to base. But before I go, I just want to say how happy I am.'

He leaned down and kissed Madeleine and then Elizabeth. In the doorway, he turned and gazed at them both. 'Ever since I met you, you've been like family to me. You know I'm an only child, and both my parents died before their time. You two are everything to me, and I'm so grateful. I shall remember you both, just as you are now, over the next few months. Goodnight.'

Elizabeth woke with a start the following day. It was still dark and, peering at the clock on her bedside table, she saw that it was just after three. Suddenly, she had a desperate desire to see David before he left.

Hauling on her dressing gown, she ran downstairs, praying she was not too late. David was standing in the hall, already wearing his greatcoat. 'Hello there... what are you doing out of bed?'

'I wanted to say goodbye.'

'We did that last night.'

'I know, but I don't know when I'll see you again.' She fell into his arms, and he kissed her, stroking her hair.

'You're freezing,' he said, wrapping her inside his coat. 'I love you, Elizabeth. Shall we get married as soon as we can?'

'Yes please – when you're next on leave perhaps?'

'All right. I'll talk to the CO.'

'Will you try and ring me sometime – I do miss the sound of your voice.'

'I will, I'm just not sure when.' Reluctantly he let her go. 'I must go. Look after yourself. And don't let that scoundrel at work grind you down. Fight back, remember.'

'I will, and please drive carefully. The roads will be icy.'

'Stop worrying. Now go back to bed. I love you.'

Elizabeth lay in the dark, dreading the coming day. The thought of encountering Valentine again was terrifying. She tried to recall her father's advice – to keep the man at arm's length. It had all sounded so plausible before Christmas. Now it seemed impossible. Unable to sleep, she finally got up, washed her face and hands, went down into the basement kitchen and made herself a cup of tea. She ate a couple of leftovers from the larder – a cold sausage and a slice of Christmas cake – before going upstairs to put on her uniform.

At the War Office, she was surprised to find her office locked. She returned to reception. 'Good morning. May I have the key to Captain Valentine's office – it's room 208.'

The clerk at the desk turned round to check to the rows of keys behind him.

'I'm afraid the key to 208 is not there, miss. I'll just check.'

He left the desk and disappeared into a back office, before returning a few minutes later. 'Somebody's coming to speak to you.'

Disconcerted, Elizabeth waited in reception. It was already ten minutes to nine and she was due on parade at nine. A few minutes later an ATS officer materialised.

'Ah, Lance Corporal Carmichael. I understand you're locked out. I thought someone would have told you by now.

You've been reassigned.'

'Oh, have I, ma'am? I didn't know.'

'The decision was taken over Christmas. You'll be working for Major Williams now, in procurement. It's just down the hall from your old office, room 245.'

Walking along the dark corridor towards her new office, Elizabeth felt both relieved and confused. Why had she been moved? What had been said, and by whom?

She knocked politely on the door.

A man's voice called out: 'Come in.'

She opened the door to a large outer office complete with two desks. Sitting at one was the young corporal who had rescued her a few days earlier.

'Danny! What a lovely surprise.'

Danny leapt to his feet. 'Good Lord… hello. How can I help you?'

'Well, I've just been sent here by the CO. This is my new posting, apparently.'

'Wonders will never cease,' said Danny, laughing. 'We've been asking for an extra pair of hands, and it seems the powers that be have finally listened.' He took Elizabeth's coat and hung it on a peg by the door, along with her gas mask. 'Did you have a nice Christmas?'

'It was lovely, thanks. I got engaged.' She held out her hand, and the tiny diamonds on her ring finger sparkled.

'Oh, that's wonderful,' said Danny. 'Congratulations. He's a lucky fella.'

'I'm a lucky girl. So where do I sit?'

'This is your desk,' said Danny, pulling out a chair for her. 'We had another girl here until the beginning of December, but she left to have a baby. Anyway, I'm really pleased it's you.'

'So am I. Look, aren't we due on parade any minute? It's

nearly nine.'

'Yes, of course, and I'll introduce you to the major when we get back. You'll like him – he's firm, but fair, you know?'

In the doorway, she turned to Danny. 'I just want to thank you again for what you did the other day. I dread to think what would have happened if you hadn't been there.'

'Don't mention it. I've been working all through Christmas, and I've not seen the old bastard. His door has remained firmly shut.'

'Maybe he's on leave,' replied Elizabeth.

'Maybe.'

'Either way, I'm surprised that I've been moved. I didn't say anything to anyone. Did you?'

'No, I promised you I wouldn't.'

'How odd,' she replied.

As they walked towards the parade ground, Elizabeth recalled her father's words at their last meeting: 'I'm not without contacts.' Perhaps it was he she had to thank for her liberation from 'the letch'.

Her mother had once said of Charles: 'People are not always what they seem.' Could it be that her father was more influential than he led everyone to believe?

12

Violet

Baby Freddie's christening took place between Christmas and New Year. At Charles's insistence, the venue was Farm Street Parish Church in Mayfair.

'I discovered it soon after I converted to Catholicism,' he told Violet. 'It's a magnificent church – Gothic in design, and it's where all the top Catholics go.'

'You can be a bit of a snob, sometimes, Charles,' said Violet, smiling. 'But if that's what you'd like, I'm happy to go along with it. I just wonder why the baby has to be christened a Catholic at all. I'm a Lutheran, don't I get a say?'

'You don't even go to church, Violet, so clearly your faith is not important to you. Whereas my faith is part of who I am. It's what saved me.'

'From what?' asked Violet.

'Everything,' he replied enigmatically.

Violet knew better than to challenge him further. Besides, the church in Farm Street sounded very appealing.

Her parents were very impressed. 'Mayfair!' said Lena,

when Violet gave her the news. 'Very grand. I'll need a new hat, but I'm not sure I've got the ration points for one.'

'You can wear mine, if you like, the one you bought me for my wedding.'

'Oh, but you'll be wearing that, surely?'

'No, I don't really suit hats. You can have it.'

The christening party was made up of Violet and Charles's immediate families and a few friends – mostly men from the club, two of whom had agreed to be godfathers.

Violet wondered if Charles would invite Elizabeth. She knew he had met up with her a few times. It didn't upset her exactly, but she felt slightly excluded from this new father/daughter relationship. The evening before the christening she plucked up the courage to broach the subject.

'Is Elizabeth coming tomorrow?'

'No, I thought best not. It would only provoke curiosity.'

'I see. Do you mind... her not being there?'

Charles looked across at his wife. 'Not at all. It's our day, yours and mine – and the boy's, of course. It's nothing to do with her.'

Now, cradling her baby by the font in the magnificent Gothic church, Violet was relieved Elizabeth had been excluded. Her own parents would have been curious about this mystery woman, and she would have felt compelled to lie, which would have spoiled such a happy event.

The baby was baptised with three names: Frederick, after his father; Henry, after Violet's father; and lastly – Padraig.

'Why Padraig?' Violet asked Charles. 'You're not Irish.'

'No, but I like the name. And I was in an Irish regiment. I had a friend called Padraig in the army. He was a nice lad.'

'You've never mentioned him before.'

'Haven't I? Look, does it matter? I like the name – what's wrong with it?'

'Why not the anglicised version, Patrick, or another family name? Perhaps we could name him after one of his godfathers – Simon and Jack are both fine names. Or we could choose the name of someone we admire – Winston, for example.'

'Don't be absurd,' said Charles. 'I want Padraig. It has... significance.'

In the end, Violet gave up. 'After all,' she said to her mother after the ceremony, 'no one ever uses their middle names anyway. It will only appear on his marriage certificate or passport.'

After the ceremony, the party moved to a private room on the second floor of Charles's club in Lansdowne Road. The club, grandly titled The Knights of St. Columba, had been established in an impressive three-storey house, backing onto a large garden – and just a few hundred yards from the couple's flat in Clarendon Road.

The guests were shown into a panelled room, complete with chandeliers and a couple of magnificent life-size statues. As it was lunchtime, sandwiches had been arranged on silver platters and laid out on a large table in the centre. Violet had kept the top layer from their wedding cake for just such an occasion, and this had been sliced up and also laid out for the guests. To one side were glasses of sherry and beer.

The guests ate and drank, and the conversation flowed. Charles chatted mostly to his club friends, while Violet did her best to include the family members. They appeared a little in awe at the grand surroundings.

'What a wonderful place,' murmured Charles's mother. 'Do you come here often, Violet?'

'Oh, no, not me. It's a men-only club.' Violet smiled. 'The men prefer it that way.'

'Oh, that's a shame,' said Charles's sister.

'Oh, I don't mind. They just drink and play cards. And there's a small chapel too – it's very much Charles's thing, not mine.'

When it was time to leave, Charles's family approached him. His father shook his hand. 'Proud of you, boy. You've done well for yourself.'

'Thank you, Dad.' Charles kissed his mother and sister fleetingly on the cheek. 'Take care of yourselves.'

'Perhaps you might call in one day, Charlie,' said his mother hopefully, clinging to her son's hand.

'It's hard to find the time, Mum,' said Charles. 'The war... you know.'

'You've still not told us what you're doing,' said his mother.

Charles tapped the side of his nose. 'Government business, I'm afraid – all a bit hush-hush, you know.'

Violet thought this remark was unkind. As Charles often said, 'It's not as if I do anything important.' He was a clerk in the Department of Trade – surely he could tell his mother what he did. It was really just another way of excluding her from his life.

'Best not to ask, Mum,' said Charles's sister gently.

'Maybe I can bring the baby up to see you one day,' Violet said brightly. 'We enjoy a nice day out. We could get the bus to Enfield.'

'Oh, that would be lovely,' said Charles's mother. 'We'd like that, wouldn't we?'

Her daughter nodded enthusiastically.

After the families had left, the two godfathers lingered at the bar, chatting to one another. But even they, finally, prepared to leave. 'Well, we'd better be off too,' said Simon, shaking Violet's hand. 'Thanks for asking me and Jack to be godfathers.'

'No, thank you,' said Violet. 'Charles always speaks so highly of you both.'

Jack also shook her hand, before turning to Charles. 'We're coming back here later. Round of bridge, we thought. Fancy joining?'

'Yes, marvellous – thanks.'

As Violet and Charles wheeled their infant son home in his pram, she felt a tinge of disappointment. She had hoped they might spend the evening together celebrating this significant day in their son's life. 'Must you go out?' she asked, as they bumped the pram up the steps of their house.

'Just a game of cards – you don't mind, do you?'

'No, not really. I just thought, given what a special day it is, that we might... you know – go out for a drink or meal or something.'

'Who would babysit?'

'Maybe we could ask your daughter?'

'Elizabeth? I doubt that. She'll be at work.'

'Never mind, then,' said Violet resignedly.

Charles disappeared into his own room, and she soon heard the tapping of the typewriter. Trying to suppress her disappointment, Violet put the baby down for a nap in his cot in her room. The room was chilly, and as she tucked little Freddie into his covers she realised his nose and fingers were icy cold. She dressed him in a woollen bonnet, booties and mittens, and turned on the gas fire. Feeling suddenly exhausted, she went downstairs to the sitting room. This too was freezing cold, and she spent some time preparing the fire, making a base in the grate of scrunched-up old newspaper, before going out into the basement coal-hole and bringing in a scuttle full of coal. Once it was laid and lit, she went out into the kitchen to wash her hands and make herself a cup of tea. By the time she returned to the sitting room the fire was well alight. She lay down gratefully on the sofa and covered herself with a woollen rug.

She must have fallen asleep, because she woke to find

Charles standing over her, gently shaking her shoulder. 'Sorry to disturb,' he said, 'but I'm just off. Back around nine.'

'What about supper?' she said, struggling to her feet.

'Don't bother. I'll eat something at the club. See you later.'

No sooner than the front door had closed, the baby started to cry. Violet ran upstairs, calling to him: 'I'm coming, I'm coming.'

The room was like an oven, and the child was hot and red in the face. Turning down the fire, she lifted the sobbing baby out of his cot and carried him downstairs to the bathroom, where she laid him on the lino floor to change his wet nappy. 'There, there, sweetheart... all nice and clean now.'

Jiggling him in her arms, she carried him into the kitchen and inspected the larder. There was a small amount of Cheddar left on a plate – enough to make herself cheese on toast. But first she would feed the baby. She poured herself a glass of milk, sat down at the kitchen table, opened her blouse and let the child latch on. He drank in desperate gulps. 'Hey, slow down, little chap – you'll get wind if you're not careful.'

He finally had his fill, and she laid him in the carrycot on the kitchen table, while she made her own supper. Then she carried the plate of food and the baby into the sitting room. Sitting down on the sofa, the baby at her feet, she was suddenly overwhelmed by a sense of disappointment. It was not in her nature to complain, but she couldn't help feeling that married life was not quite as she had expected. To be abandoned by her husband on an evening such as this seemed unnecessarily cruel. She tried to convince herself that Charles was not being deliberately unkind; it was rather that he couldn't see life through her eyes. Tired, she picked up the slice of cheese on toast and ate in silence, tears of self-pity trickling down her cheeks.

13

Charles

Charles felt a brief pang of guilt as he left the house that evening. Perhaps it had been inconsiderate to leave his wife alone at home, but she always seemed so self-sufficient. It occurred to him then that he had a tendency to take Violet for granted. Her stoicism made it easy for him to ignore her feelings. Comforting himself that he would only be away for a couple of hours, he began to walk down Clarendon Road towards his club. It was long past dusk, and in the blackout the moon provided the only illumination to light his way.

As he passed his ex-wife's house, he noticed bright light spilling out from her sitting room window. A Christmas tree had been erected in the bay window and its tinsel sparkled in the lamplight. He caught sight of Madeleine standing near the fireplace, gazing into the fire. She was wearing a simple blue sheath, her dark hair swept up in an elegant chignon. He had a momentary flicker of something – desire perhaps. Suddenly, she turned round, and for a second he feared she might notice him outside. He quickened his step and ducked behind a postbox.

Glancing back, he saw that Elizabeth had come into the room. She walked purposefully over to the window and closed the curtains.

Grateful not to have been spotted, Charles continued up Clarendon Road towards the club, recalling Elizabeth's own christening more than twenty years earlier. He had not yet converted to Catholicism, and the service had been held at the local parish church in Uxbridge, followed by a reception at Madeleine's parents' house – a tidy semi-detached built in mock Tudor style. Madeleine's father considered himself an entrepreneur. He had been quick to spot the potential of car ownership and had set up a garage and car dealership in the town. Her mother was a housewife and stalwart of the Women's Institute. They had always made it clear that they disapproved of Charles, especially his working-class origins. Charles despised them in equal measure; in his opinion they represented the worst characteristics of the lower middle classes – unimaginative and snobbish. He suspected they had been relieved when the marriage broke up.

At the club, Charles found Simon and Jack leaning against the bar, beer in hand. 'Charles, old man,' Simon called out, 'over here.'

'Pint?' asked Jack.

'Please.'

'I thought it went well today,' said Simon. 'How's the little woman?'

Charles didn't appreciate this description of his wife. Violet was intellectually far superior to both of his friends. 'Rather tired, I think. The baby's quite hard work.'

'Time to put her feet up then,' said Simon. 'You dining with us, Charles?'

'Yes... thought I'd save Violet the trouble.'

'Shall we go through?'

The three men carried their drinks through to the dining room. It was not a grand room, such as would be found in the spacious men's clubs of Pall Mall. Rather it was a small but well-appointed dining room, decorated in shades of beige and brown, with enough seating for fifty. The food was not particularly impressive; both the members and the chef favoured a traditional 'nursery food' style of cooking – pies and sponge puddings were all popular. The three men ate a hearty meal, shared a reasonable bottle of claret and chewed the cud about the war.

'What's the word from inside government, Charles?'

'Well, my department doesn't really deal in the interesting stuff, but I have heard a bit of chatter about General Eisenhower agreeing to run the show in Europe – it's creating a bit of optimism.'

'What are they planning?' asked Simon.

'Can't say, old man – above my pay grade. But suffice it to say, there is a plan, which has to be good news. Forty-four will be the year, I think, for the ground to shift in our favour.'

'Well, that's a positive note to end on,' said Jack. 'Round of bridge?'

'Why not? Just a quick rubber,' said Charles. 'We'll need a fourth, though.'

'I noticed Jonty was in earlier – let's ask him,' said Jack.

In the lounge they found Jonty reading the newspaper by the fire. While Charles and Simon sat down at the card table in the corner, Jack approached him. 'Fancy a game of bridge?'

'Yes, all right,' Jonty replied. 'I'll make up your numbers.'

The four men settled down and began to play. In the third game of the rubber, Charles, seated in the corner facing out, was playing 'dummy'. Effectively redundant while his partner played their two hands, his mind and his gaze wandered. He looked around and noticed someone he didn't recognise, standing by the bar. He was chatting to the barman, and had an unusually loud voice and strong Irish accent – pure Dublin, Charles thought. One or two of the older members glanced across at the interloper with irritation.

'Who is that man?' asked Charles.

Jonty turned to follow his gaze. 'Don't know him, sorry.'

Minutes later, another man joined the stranger at the bar.

'That's Anthony d'Courcy, isn't it?' asked Charles. 'Not seen him for ages.'

Simon glanced up at the pair. 'Yes, he's been away for a while – out East on business.'

After a few moments, d'Courcy led his friend to a pair of armchairs in front of the fire, just a few feet from the card table.

Something about d'Courcy's guest seemed familiar. Charles tried to recall where he had seen him before. Suddenly their eyes met, and Charles experienced a bolt of recognition. His heart began to race, as the stranger stood up and approached the bridge table. 'What's that you're playing?' he asked casually.

The players looked up in surprise – it was not done to interrupt a game of cards. They ignored him, and Jonty, who was in the middle of a particularly crucial manoeuvre, frowned with concentration.

'Bridge, is it?' said the stranger, apparently unaware of his faux pas.

D'Courcy took him by the arm. 'Michael, leave the chaps to their game. Come and sit down.'

The pair returned to their armchairs, but the Irishman kept glancing over at the bridge four. Finally, the game came to an end, and the scores were totted up. 'Game to you two, I think,' said Simon. 'Well played, Charles and Jonty.'

'Thanks,' replied Charles. 'You played well, Jonty. I particularly admired the way you finessed during that final hand. We must play again.'

'Any time, old man,' replied Jonty.

'Well, I'd better be getting along. Violet will be waiting,' said Charles, rising from the table. The Irishman was making him nervous, and he was suddenly desperate to get away.

'All right,' said Jack. 'Give her our best, and see you tomorrow, maybe.'

As Charles hurried out of the lounge, the Irishman suddenly approached him.

'It's Paddy, isn't it? Paddy Devereux?'

'No,' said Charles, trying to push past him. 'I'm afraid you've got the wrong chap.'

'Are you joking?' said the man. 'I know we're both a bit older now, Paddy, but I'd know you anywhere.'

D'Courcy grabbed his friend's arm, clearly embarrassed. 'Michael, what are you talking about? This is Charles Carmichael. He's a long-standing member of the club. I've known him for years.'

The man stared at Charles and began to laugh. 'Charles, is it? No, I don't think so. Sure as eggs is eggs, this man is Padraig Devereux. I'd stake my life on it – we spent three years lying in a trench together outside Ypres.'

Simon and Jack glanced anxiously at one another. Simon silently mouthed, 'Padraig?'

'I know...' whispered Jack. 'And Devereux, isn't that Charles's pen-name?'

Charles didn't notice his friends' confused looks. He was more preoccupied with escaping the situation. His heart began to race, sweat breaking out on his brow. 'I can assure you that you are mistaken, sir. Now, if you'll excuse me...'

He scurried away towards the lounge door, aware of several pairs of eyes fixed on his retreating back. In the hall, he stammered: 'My hat and coat, Swain, please – and hurry.'

The moon had dipped behind the clouds as Charles emerged from the club. The night air was cold and damp, and in the wartime blackout he had to feel his way home by tapping his stick against the garden walls. By the time he arrived, he was breathless and sweating. He unlocked the front door and slammed it shut behind him. Violet found him in the hall a few seconds later, leaning against the door, breathing heavily.

'Charles? Are you all right?' She was in her dressing gown, clutching a hot-water bottle to her chest.

'Yes, just took a funny turn. I'll be fine.'

'Oh dear. Let me help you.' She took his arm and opened his bedroom door. The room was cold, and he shivered as she helped him out of his coat and suit jacket. 'Let's get these trousers off,' she suggested. Once off, she guided him to the bed. He sat down silently, allowing her to remove his socks and shoes.

'Your feet are freezing,' she said, rubbing his cold toes. 'Put on your pyjamas, and get into bed. Here, take this hot-water bottle – I'll get another, and while I'm in the kitchen I'll make you some tea – or cocoa if you'd prefer.'

'Either... thank you.'

Lying in bed, the stone hot-water bottle warming his icy feet, Charles tried to get control of his breathing. It was irregular, coming in little fits and starts, interspersed with violent coughing. Since his exposure to mustard gas in the first war, coughing was an everyday event, but this was different. He felt as if his lungs were trying to expel something poisonous, and was relieved when his wife returned with a steaming cup of tea.

Violet sat on the edge of his bed as he sipped the warming liquid, her face etched with concern. 'You look awful – as if you've seen a ghost.'

'Maybe I have,' he muttered, closing his eyes.

'What was that, dear?'

'Nothing. Thank you for the tea. I'll be all right. It's a cold night and the chill got to my chest. The old problem. Sorry to disturb.'

He leaned back against the pillows, allowing Violet to smooth his brow.

'Well, if you're sure you're OK?'

'Absolutely. How was your evening?'

'Oh, quiet, you know. The baby went down an hour or two ago, so I managed to play the piano. I'm trying to get to grips with that new Schubert piece I bought a few weeks ago. It's got some pretty tricky arpeggios, I have to tell you. But I'm getting there.' She smiled.

'Good girl. You must play it for me – tomorrow perhaps. We can have a quiet night in... just the two of us.'

'That would be nice. I'll make supper – something you really like.'

'I'm sorry I left you alone this evening,' he said, taking her hand and kissing it. 'Selfish of me.'

'Not at all. You had to thank Simon and Jack, after all. How were they?'

'Oh, they were fine. And I won at bridge tonight – playing with Jonty Middleton. Have I ever introduced you to him?'

Violet shook her head.

'Jolly good bridge player. We must invite him over sometime.'

'Of course. Well, if there's nothing else, I'll head off to bed.' Violet kissed him on the cheek, and silently closed the door.

Alone, Charles mused on the events of the evening. He went over the encounter with the Irishman endlessly, realising that it wouldn't be long before Simon and Jack – and all the other members of the club – would put two and two together. He tossed and turned, full of regrets. Why had he used Devereux as a pen-name, and christened his son Padraig so publicly? Why did he have to go out that evening? Why couldn't he have stayed at home with his wife? If he'd simply been more thoughtful and kind, he would never have come face to face with this man from his complicated past. He lay in bed, fitful and anxious, for some time, his mind filled with images from the Great War – the waterlogged trenches, the stench of death all around, the sheer bloody agony of it all. Finally, early in the morning, he fell into a troubled sleep.

14

Charles

The following day, Charles woke feeling weak and feverish. He wasn't actually ill, but more in a state of shock after the events of the previous evening. He felt unable to face the world.

Violet knocked on the door at eight o'clock. 'Charles? Are you all right?'

'Not too great, actually,' he called back. 'Caught a chill last night. Think I'll stay in bed, if you don't mind.'

'Oh, poor you. Shall I bring you some breakfast?'

'Maybe later... going to try and get back to sleep.'

Charles heard her go to her room next door and talk softly to the baby. After a few minutes, she went back downstairs. Only then did he get up and go over to his desk. He felt under the typewriter, and removed a small key, which he put into the lock of the desk's bottom drawer. He opened it to reveal a neatly stacked collection of diaries. He rummaged around until he found a diary marked 1915. He retreated to his bed, pulled the covers up around his chin and flicked through the pages until he reached the entry marked 14 April.

The journey to Ireland from Liverpool was thrilling. I stood alone on the deck of the SS Connemara *as it forged its way through the foaming water of the Irish Sea, and felt liberated. I was getting out of England, and with each nautical mile I felt my spirit lift. I had run from fear, terror and hopelessness. But now I was off on a new adventure. In spite of the dense layers of metallic grey cloud rolling in from the vast Atlantic beyond, I felt giddy with excitement. I breathed in the salty air, enjoying the sensation of spray stinging my skin like so many needles. Overhead, seagulls wheeled, following the ship's path – in anticipation of food being thrown overboard.*

Charles smiled at his youthful literary style. His novelist pretentions were evident even then.

We docked in Dublin at five o'clock. By then, the sun had forced its way through the gunmetal grey clouds, and the sky was an opalescent turquoise flecked with apricot. It seemed somehow prophetic of a new future, filled with limitless possibilities. I walked down the gangplank and stood on terra firma, breathing deeply. The predominant smell was of engine oil, but somewhere out there I could smell bacon cooking. My stomach rumbled – I hadn't eaten since the night before. Jingling the last few shillings in my pocket, I realised there wasn't enough for both food and a roof over my head. If I chose food I'd have to sleep in a shop doorway, or park bench, and I'd had enough of sleeping rough. I would find a boarding house, I decided, have a wash, and tomorrow would look for a job. I threw my rucksack over my shoulder, and set off for the city centre.

It was after six when I found myself in Lower Camden Street. Judging by the quality of buildings, this had once been a place of grandeur and wealth. But the large houses had long ago been subdivided into flats, and their elegant ground floors turned into business premises. As I passed a pub called Cassidy's, a young man with hair the colour of ripe wheat suddenly landed at my feet. He lay on the pavement, stunned for a moment, observed by a large man wearing a leather apron, who shouted: 'And don't come back!'

Charles laid the diary down, smiling at the memory. Judging by last night's appearance, Michael Reilly had hardly changed. His hair was still golden, his eyes still a startling shade of blue. He was surprised he hadn't recognised Reilly straight away. He tried to recall what had happened next.

As he remembered it, he had helped young Michael to his feet. The lad had dusted himself down, then shouted back at the landlord, who was heading back into the pub, 'You're a disgrace! You know that.'

The landlord had turned round and launched himself at the young man, grabbing him by his lapels. 'Say that again to my face,' he shouted.

Before young Charles could stop to think, he took hold of the older man by his shoulders and managed to separate the pair. 'Come on now, no need for this. Leave the lad alone.'

'Mind your own business,' shouted the publican, his face red with fury.

Charles recalled a frisson of fear that the man might be about to hit him too; he had raised his hands in a boxing stance, as his father had shown him as a child. 'Come on then,' he said, 'let's see what you're made of.'

The man scoffed. 'I can't be bothered... I'd bloody kill you. Get lost the both of yous.'

At that, Charles picked up his backpack and nodded at the young man. 'I think we should go while we still can.'

As they walked together down the street, the lad put his arm round Charles's shoulder: 'Bloody well done. That showed a bit of courage.'

'Not really,' said Charles. 'He was all talk. What's he so cross about, anyway?'

'He was banging on about the republican cause – angry that Irish boys are defending the British Empire. My brother's one of those boys and I'll be joining the army soon. It's our duty, and men like that just see this war as an opportunity to make trouble here in Ireland. He had the nerve to call me a troublemaker – me! When it's the republicans who are causing all the problems in this country.'

At the time, Charles had no idea what he was talking about.

The pair walked companionably down the road until they reached a crossroads. 'Well, this is me,' said the lad. 'Thanks again and I'll be seeing you around.'

He strode off down the street without a backward glance. Not really knowing where he was heading, Charles turned in the same direction. A hundred yards or so further on, the lad stopped and turned round. 'You following me, Englishman?'

'I'm sorry... I don't mean to – it's just I'm new here. I'm looking for somewhere to stay.'

'Is that right?' The young man smiled. 'Well, we've a spare room at our place. One good turn and all that.'

'Oh, I didn't mean... I couldn't put you to any trouble.'

'It's no trouble. Come on, you look like you could do with a hot meal. My name is Michael, by the way... Michael Reilly.'

Reilly lived in a small but comfortable house on the outskirts of the city. It reminded Charles of a doll's house he'd once seen in a shop window – four-square, sitting in a neat garden, with a well-painted front door and windows on either side.

In the hall, the lad called out: 'Hey, Mammy, I brought home a Good Samaritan.'

The young man's mother was in the kitchen, peeling potatoes at the kitchen table. Tall and slender, her hair was the same shade of gold as her son's and her blue eyes twinkled charmingly. 'Here you are at last, Michael. I thought you'd left the country.' She smiled, and offered her cheek for her son to kiss. 'And who's this?'

'This is my Good Samaritan, Mammy. He rescued me from that idiot who runs Cassidy's on the Lower Camden Road. I thought we could give him a bed for the night. He's nowhere to stay.'

'Why on earth did you go down the Camden Road?' asked his mother. 'You know it's a den of republican iniquity. A few doors down from there, I've heard, they're training young men to fight for the cause.'

'I know...'

'So why did you go there?'

'I was curious, I suppose.'

'Curiosity killed the cat,' said his mother, drying her hands on a tea towel. 'Well, you'd better sit yourself down, Michael's Good Samaritan. I can't keep calling you that – what's your name?'

Charles knew he shouldn't give his real name – it was too risky. He was a man with a complicated past and, as far as the rest of the world knew, he was no longer alive. If he was now discovered in Ireland, he feared arrest – and even execution.

He cast around for a suitable name. There was a newspaper lying on the table. The lead article mentioned a man called Padraig Pearse – a barrister and Irish revolutionary – presumably one of those republicans they were talking about.

'Padraig,' he blurted out.

'But that's an Irish name,' said Michael's mother.

'Yes, I know. My mother was Irish.' It was a lie, but what could he do?

'Was?'

'Yes, she's dead now, sadly.' Charles felt a stab of guilt as he denounced his mother. What would she make of such deceit?

Although, to his surprise and not a little shame, he found lying quite easy.

'I'm so sorry to hear that,' said Michael's mother gently. 'You poor lad. Michael mentioned you needed a bed for the night.'

'If that wouldn't be any trouble...'

'Michael, take him up to the first floor – he can have Anthony's room.' Then, turning to Charles, she explained: 'My eldest is away in France, fighting the Boche.'

'I see. Well, if you're sure it's all right – I'd be very grateful.'

Michael led Charles upstairs and opened the bedroom door. Charles had never seen such a charming room. Facing the door stood a wide single mahogany bed, its blankets covered with a paisley quilted eiderdown. To one side was an elegant chest of drawers with brass handles. Beneath the window was a table with a jug and basin; silver hairbrushes lay on either side. It was three times the size of his room at home.

'Padraig what?' asked Michael.

'I'm sorry?'

'Your surname... Padraig what?'

'Oh, I see.' Once again, he had to think on his feet. Arriving at the docks that afternoon, he had noticed a sign for 'Devereux Shipping'. It had struck him as a romantic-sounding name, with an air of adventure about it. 'Devereux,' he said.

'Devereux? That's French, isn't it?'

'Possibly,' Charles replied, regretting his choice instantly. 'My father's people... way back, I suspect.'

'It's quite a mouthful, isn't it? Padraig Devereux... quite a lot to live up to.'

It was an odd to thing to say, and yet so apposite. Charles began to wonder if Michael had seen through his disguise already. 'Parents,' he said, smiling. 'They hand out these names without much thought, I suppose.'

Michael laughed. 'Yes, I suppose you're right. There's a bathroom down the hall, by the way. Take a bath if you like.'

'Is it that obvious?' asked Charles, blushing. It had been weeks since he'd had a proper wash.

'No, you're all right. I just thought you might like it. You can use my razor if you like. Come down when you're ready.'

When Charles came back into the bedroom, wrapped only in a towel, he found Michael's mother picking up his clothes from the floor.

'Oh, please, Mrs Reilly, you don't have to do that.'

'Come on now, they could do with a wash. Have you anything else to wear?'

'Nothing clean, if I'm honest, Mrs Reilly.'

'Call me Sinead, please. Now, give all your things to me, and I'll loan you some of Michael's. You're about the same size.'

Charles recalled how he felt, standing in front of the mirror in that comfortable bedroom wearing clean clothes. Gone was the tramp of the previous six weeks. Here stood a good-looking young man with brushed hair and shaved face, wearing a crisp white shirt and grey flannel trousers. Only his tatty shoes hinted at the gruelling journey he had undertaken.

'To be sure, you look very nice,' said Mrs Reilly, as Charles came downstairs into the kitchen. 'But those shoes have seen better days. What size are you?'

'Nine and a half.'

'The same as my husband! Michael, go and get those brown brogues of your father's.'

'Oh, I really couldn't,' said Charles, terrified of Mr Reilly's reaction when he discovered his shoes had been stolen by a tramp. 'He'll be furious, surely.'

'Not at all... My darling husband died nearly ten years ago. For some silly reason I couldn't bring myself to get rid of his shoes. You should take them. They don't fit either of my boys, and they're no use to him where he is, God rest his soul.' She crossed herself.

Michael's mother had been a remarkable woman, Charles recalled. Warm, friendly, but intensely inquisitive. He picked up the diary again:

> *Dinner was a lamb stew with mashed potatoes and swede. After so many weeks on the run, with little to eat, that first proper meal nearly brought tears to my eyes.*
>
> *Michael's mother was full of questions – what brought me to Dublin, who my people were. It was exhausting, and I had to think on my feet. I couldn't tell the truth, obviously, so I lied. I said I'd come to Ireland to 'explore my mother's roots'.*
>
> *Of course, Sinead wanted to know everything then – where they had come from, what they did for a living.*
>
> *Quite honestly, I had no idea – I'd never been to Ireland before, and knew nothing about the country.*
>
> *But there was a map of Ireland hanging above the sideboard in the dining room. Glancing up, I plumped for the first name I saw. 'Her people come from County Wicklow,' I told her.*

Charles recalled the conversation as if it were yesterday:

'Oh, but that's quite close; you could visit that easily,' Sinead had said. 'There's a bus you could take. Do you still have family there?'

Charles remembered his sense of panic. He had not expected such an inquisition. 'I'm not sure,' he'd said. 'My mother wasn't actually born in Ireland, you see... but her people come from here.' He knew instinctively that, if the lie got too complicated, he would lose track and the whole artifice would unravel.

'How old are you, Padraig... if you don't mind me asking?'

He was nineteen – well over the age for joining the army – but he didn't want Sinead to think he was as a conscientious objector, or a republican.

'Seventeen,' he said.

'Does your father know where you are?'

'My father walked out on us a long time ago.' It was another lie, of course, and he began to feel guilty. With each answer he betrayed his parents a little more.

Sinead reached across the damask tablecloth and took his hand. 'Oh Padraig, that's awful sad. I'm so sorry. You seem such a lovely boy. Sounds like you've had to bring yourself up. My own boys know what it is to lose a father,' she went on, clearing the plates. 'My beloved husband died when Michael was only eight. Anthony was ten. They never really got over it.'

'We had you, Mammy,' said Michael, squeezing her hand. 'You've been both mother and father to me and Anthony.'

'That's a lovely thing to say, Michael.' Then turning to Charles, she added. 'So, Padraig, Michael tells me you've been travelling a while.'

'Yes, I worked my way up from London to Liverpool to earn the fare to come over here.'

'That was enterprising of you.'

'In fact, I was going to look for a job tomorrow. I obviously need some money to live on – and to find a place to stay.'

'Well, you can stay here, Padraig. We've plenty of room, after all. And there are lots of jobs to be had if you have a mind to work hard.'

'Oh, I do...'

'Can you read and write?'

Now, nearly thirty years later, Charles chuckled to himself at how surprised Sinead had been by his answer.

'Oh yes,' he remembered saying to her. 'English is my best subject. I am hoping to go to university.'

'University? Well, there's a thing,' Sinead had said, her eyes widening. 'Perhaps you could encourage my lazy son to study a little more. He finishes school this year, but he's not so keen on the books.' She patted her son's hand, and Michael smiled as if he'd heard it all before.

'Michael,' Sinead went on, 'what about that friend of yours from school – what's his name – with the father who owns the posh general store in town. He could do with a nice polite intelligent boy like Paddy here...'

'Mr O'Connell, you mean,' said Michael. 'Sure, I'll take him over there tomorrow.'

After supper, they discussed literature, he recalled. At least when discussing his favourite writers he didn't have to lie – he had read several Irish authors. Sinead was impressed by his knowledge.

'You're a curious fish, young Paddy Devereux,' she said. 'I'm not quite sure how you fit into the world.'

'Perhaps I don't fit in at all,' Charles replied.

'Perhaps you don't,' she said, smiling sweetly.

Charles flicked through the diary once again. He had lived in Dublin for just a few weeks, but it felt like a lifetime.

15 April

Michael took me to Mr O'Connell's shop today. It was the poshest general store I'd ever seen. The man himself was a stout fellow wearing a tweed three-piece suit. He seemed impressed by my education and employed me on the spot!

25 April

I love this city with its grand streets, and colourful people. I can imagine living here for the rest of my life.

This evening, Michael and I went to the pub to listen to the fiddle bands. I've learned most of the words now and can sing along. Sometimes the local lads dance and, if I've had a beer or two, I get up and join them. I never danced in Enfield – I felt too self-conscious. But there's something about the Irishman's generosity of spirit that liberates the soul.

28 April

Today we went to Mass. I find the rituals – the 'bells and smells' of Catholicism – strangely intoxicating. As a Protestant, I am not permitted to either take communion or receive absolution, but as I watch others enter the confessional, or kneel at the altar rail to receive the 'Body of Christ', I find myself yearning for the simple certainty this religion offers. The concept of being forgiven for your sins simply by confessing seems so elemental and pure. I find it has entered my consciousness and lodged there, like a bright white light of hope.

1 May

Although my job is intellectually far beneath me, I get pleasure from it. I enjoy meeting customers, and they seem to like me. It pays well enough, and I have a safe roof over my head. In many ways, I couldn't be happier. My only problem is Sinead's inexhaustible curiosity. She treats me like her own son – cooking for me and doing my laundry. But in return she expects complete openness. She is curious about everything, and her endless questions about my upbringing are becoming troublesome. The more lies I am forced to tell, the harder it is to remain consistent. I feel sure she will find me out one day, and then all will be lost.

13 May

I had an afternoon off today and Sinead insisted on accompanying me to the library. On our way home, we walked together down the quiet street towards her house. The cherry blossom was coming to an end, and was falling onto the ground in drifts like pink snow.

In the house, Sinead asked me if I might join up with Michael once he finishes school in the summer. She hoped I might 'keep an eye on him – stop him doing anything stupid.'

I almost laughed out loud at that. I mean... I was the one who had done something stupid. I had run away, and probably destroyed my family's lives.

Charles, lying in bed, his throat scratchy and sore from his cold, shivered as he read the entry.

I was the one who had destroyed my family's lives.

It was a stark and honest comment – and yet the young man who wrote that diary made it sound like a joke. How could he have 'almost laughed out loud'? What he had done by deserting his first regiment had devastated his parents. He had disappeared, run away to Ireland and broken their hearts. Now he made it seem like nothing – a joke. Was that why he became a Catholic? Since then he had spent so many hours repenting of his sins, and one sin in particular: the profound pain he had inflicted on those who loved him most. Tears came into Charles's eyes as he listened to his son gurgling and chirruping in the next room. God forbid that little Freddie would do the same to him one day.

Violet knocked on his door: 'Are you all right, Charles – is there anything you need?'

He quickly buried the diary beneath the covers in case she came in. 'No, dear, I'm all right,' he called back. 'Going to try and sleep a little more.'

'All right, if you're sure. I'm just taking Freddie downstairs for breakfast.'

Charles retrieved the diary, and continued to read:

In all honesty, it hadn't occurred to me to join up again. After all, I had only just managed to escape the army for the first time. And yet, I thought, why not join up as Padraig Devereux? It would salve my conscience a little, at having deserted once before. And I want to fight. I want to 'do my bit'. That's what no one will ever be able to understand – I didn't leave the army because I was frightened of fighting. I left the army for something far more disturbing.

So I told Sinead I would join up and fight alongside her son. She hugged me then, standing in the hall, and I wanted to cry.

Later, we were standing in the kitchen. Sinead was making tea, chatting about things, as she did, laying out cups and saucers, cutting up slices of soda bread and buttering them. I felt so comfortable with her, so at home. I almost love her like another mother.

But then she suddenly brought up the subject of visiting my 'mother's people' in Wicklow. Panicking, I tried to put her off.

But Sinead insisted on accompanying me, saying she loved Wicklow and wanted an excuse to go there. How do I extricate myself from this situation? I like Sinead very much, but her questions are becoming ever more difficult. Sooner or later I'm bound to give myself away.

Charles remembered how clear-headed he had been. Despite his affection for Sinead and Michael, that evening he made the decision to join an Irish regiment and fight in France. It was a drastic solution to a mounting problem, and logically the only sensible thing to do.

Very early the following morning, he rose and dressed hurriedly in the clothes he had arrived in. He folded up the shirts and trousers Sinead had lent him and left them neatly on the chest of drawers.

His old shoes had long been thrown away, and the only shoes he had to wear were the ones Sinead had given him. He had a moment's guilt about taking them, before realising he had no other option. He took a ten-shilling note from his wallet and laid it on the pile of clothes. The least he could do was pay for them.

Then, sitting down on the edge of his bed, he tore a sheet of paper out of his diary and began to write a note.

Dear Sinead and Michael,

I'm so very grateful to you for all your hospitality and kindness, but I fear I have overstayed my welcome. Also, my desire to do my duty for my country has been weighing heavily on my conscience. I know I said I would wait till the autumn, and go with Michael, but I have read of the shortage of men out in France, and I feel I can wait no longer. Please would you explain this to Mr O'Connell, and ask him to forgive me.

Forgive me too, for not saying goodbye – but I feared you would only ask me to put it off, and I have quite made up my mind.

Michael, you have been such a good friend to me, and I hope we will meet again – perhaps across the Channel.

Sinead, I can never thank you enough for your kindness to

me. Taking in a complete stranger was a remarkable act of charity, which I will not forget.

Until we meet again, I remain yours,

Padraig Devereux

PS – I have left ten shillings to cover the cost of the shoes. I hope this is sufficient.

Still in his stockinged feet, Charles crept downstairs, his rucksack over his shoulder. As he laid the letter on the kitchen table, he looked around. The happy hours spent in that kitchen would stay with him for ever.

In the hall he slipped on his shoes, shut the door quietly behind him and walked swiftly to the bus stop. He had already seen signs to the recruiting office every day on his way to work.

At the reception desk, he gave his name as Padraig Devereux, of no fixed abode. When asked his age, he lied. 'Eighteen, sir,' he announced firmly, as if by erasing the previous year he could start a new life. To his surprise, there was no further inquisition – no proof of identity was even required. In fact, the recruiting sergeant hardly looked up. The stories Charles had read of the shortage of men fighting for their country were obviously true.

After a quick examination by the medic, Private Padraig Devereux was kitted out in the uniform of the South Irish Horse. For the second time he was joining the army to fight for his country. He just hoped things wouldn't end so badly this time...

15

31 December 1943

Elizabeth

It was eight o'clock in the morning on New Year's Eve, and Elizabeth was just pulling on her overcoat, preparing to leave for work, when the doorbell rang. She opened the door and found the telegram boy standing on the doorstep.

'Telegram for Miss Elizabeth Carmichael. Is that you?'

'Yes, that's me.'

The boy handed her the beige envelope and wheeled his bicycle back into the street.

No one in wartime received such an envelope without a sense of dread, and Elizabeth slit it open with shaking hands:

The Air Ministry regrets to announce that Fl. Sergeant David Masters was killed in a road traffic accident on 26 December. Letter to follow.

Her mother found her lying on the tiled floor a few minutes

later. 'Elizabeth, darling... what on earth?' She picked up the discarded telegram. 'Oh no... oh, dear God no. Oh, my darling girl.'

Stooping down, she gathered Elizabeth up in her arms. 'Come, you can't stay down there on that hard floor.'

Somehow Madeleine got her daughter into the sitting room and sat her down on the sofa. Elizabeth began to shake violently.

'You're in shock, darling,' said Madeleine, taking a woollen rug from the chair and wrapping her daughter in it. She then riddled the fire, scrunched up some newspaper and placed some kindling on top. Once lit, she added a small amount of coal.

'The room will warm up in a minute. I'll go and get some tea – strong and sweet – that's what you need.'

She returned a few minutes later carrying a tray. 'Here, darling,' she said, handing Elizabeth a cup. 'Drink it all up.'

Her daughter looked up at her with a bewildered expression. 'How did it happen? Why? Why?'

'I don't know. Perhaps the roads were icy. Oh, I'm so, so sorry. Dear, darling David.'

Elizabeth began to sob uncontrollably, and her mother sat down and cradled her in her arms. 'Oh, dearest girl, I feel completely helpless. I don't know what to say or do. I'd better call your office and explain what's happened.'

She went out into the hall to make the phone call. When she came back into the room, Elizabeth was sitting up rigidly, staring blankly into space.

'They've said not to worry... they understand. You'll get compassionate leave or something.'

'I want Dad,' said Elizabeth. 'I must see Dad.'

Madeleine looked at her, puzzled. 'I'm sorry... what did you say?'

'I want to see my father!'

'Elizabeth, are you quite well?'

'I want to see Dad. He lives over the road at number eighteen... get him please.'

Madeleine stood up, glancing at the photos of her ex-husband on the mantelpiece. 'Over the road?' she muttered to herself. 'He can't be... I don't understand.'

She walked out into the hall, took her fur coat from the rack and pulled on her thick winter boots. 'I'll be back soon,' she called out to her daughter.

~

Violet

Violet was just going downstairs, carrying the baby on her hip, when the doorbell rang.

Opening the door, she found an elegant dark-haired woman standing on the doorstep, wearing a smart mink coat. Violet recognised her instantly as the beautiful woman she had seen in the street the day she was nearly blown up by the bomb. This was Charles's first wife, Madeleine. Startled, but determined to remain calm, Violet smiled. 'Yes, can I help you?'

'I'm looking for Charles Carmichael.'

'I'm afraid he's at work. Can I help?'

'I'm not sure. If you don't mind me asking... who are you?'

'Me? I'm Violet Carmichael – Charles's wife.'

Violet and Madeleine sat opposite one another in the sitting room of the flat, while the baby lay wriggling on a rug that Violet had placed on the floor between them.

'I'm sorry it's so cold in here,' said Violet. 'We don't normally use this room till the evening. If you don't mind, I'll just light the fire.'

Violet lit the fire with a gas poker, then wiped her hands on her apron and sat down on the sofa. 'Now, how can I help you?'

'I'm here because of my daughter, Elizabeth,' Madeleine began.

'Oh yes.' Violet tried to keep her voice calm. Charles had been quite clear that he didn't want Madeleine to know of his existence. Elizabeth, she presumed, must have revealed his whereabouts.

'She's had a terrible shock,' Madeleine went on, 'and has asked to see her father. I have to be honest, Mrs Carmichael – I didn't realise that Charles lived so close. The last I heard, he was in Peking. It's been over twenty years since we last saw one another, you see.'

'Ah, yes, I do see. How awkward.'

'Have you and Charles been together long?'

'Not long, no... we met and married at the start of the war, and moved here two or three years ago – more like three really.'

'And you have a child?' Madeleine looked down at the chubby baby rolling on the floor.

'Yes, Freddie. But you said something about your daughter?'

'Elizabeth.'

'You mentioned a shock?'

'Oh yes – the most awful tragedy. Her fiancé, David, has been killed. She's in a terrible state and asked to see her father.' Madeleine paused uncertainly. 'I have to confess it came as a monumental surprise, as I had no idea Charles was still alive, let alone known to my daughter. I presume they have been meeting secretly. I knew nothing about it.'

'Yes... well, they have met.'

'You knew?'

'Yes, but it's quite a recent thing, you understand. I think they discovered each other quite by chance. She came here once. I thought her very charming – and a great credit to you. I'm so very sorry to hear about her fiancé. Was it a bomb?'

'No... a car accident. He'd been down to see us over Christmas, to ask Elizabeth to marry him. He was killed driving back to the base.'

'How awful,' said Violet. 'What a dreadful thing. Poor Elizabeth.'

The pair sat in silence, considering Elizabeth's predicament.

'When will Charles be home?' Madeleine said eventually.

'Not till this evening. I'll tell him as soon as he's back, of course.'

'Perhaps I could call him at work.'

'You could, but he's not often in the office – he seems to have lots of meetings all over the place. It's probably best if you leave it to me. He's normally back by six-thirty. Can it wait till then?'

'I suppose it'll have to. I really don't know what I'm going to do, she's in such a state.'

'Get her to bed,' suggested Violet kindly. 'The doctor maybe can prescribe something – for the shock.'

'Oh yes, of course, the doctor. I hadn't thought of that. I'm in shock too, I suppose. You'd have thought I'd know what to do... I was a nurse in the war – the last war, I mean.'

'Were you? Elizabeth said you owned a hairdressing salon.'

'Oh, did she? Yes, I got into that when Charles and I divorced.' Madeleine put her handbag on her knees, preparing to leave. 'But you're right – a sleeping pill or something. That's what she needs for a day or two. Just to get her through the worst of it.'

She stood up. 'You've been very kind, Mrs Carmichael. I'm sorry to have disturbed you.'

'Oh, please... do call me Violet, and you're not disturbing me at all.' Violet shook her hand. 'I'll tell Charles as soon as possible, and do let me know if there's anything I can do – really anything at all.'

'Thank you.' Madeleine smiled tightly. 'I'll see myself out.'

That evening Violet waited anxiously for Charles to return home. She was upstairs in her bedroom, settling the baby for the night. Freddie had developed nappy rash, and had been fractious, but he had finally closed his eyes, and his breathing was now even and steady. Praying he would not wake, she was just tiptoeing towards the door when she heard the front door slam shut. Normally her husband would call out as he arrived, but that evening he said nothing.

Out in the hall, Charles was standing breathless by the door. He looked pale, a fine sweat on his brow – just like the evening of the baby's christening when he had returned so distressed from his club.

'Charles dear, are you all right? You're not having another turn?'

'No, nothing like that. Just a bit tired. Been a long day.'

'Come downstairs. I've got a shepherd's pie in the oven.'

He sat at the kitchen table, and she poured him a glass of stout. 'Drink that, Charles. It will do you good.' She poured herself a small sherry.

'Violet, old girl,' said Charles, clearing his throat. 'I've got a bit of news.'

'Before you go on,' said Violet, 'I've got some news for you.'

'Oh, yes?'

'Yes... it's about your daughter.'

'What about her?'

'Her fiancé, David, has been killed, and she's asked for you. Her mother came over today in a terrible state. She was very gracious, I thought. I felt so sorry for her. I thought perhaps you could go and see Elizabeth after supper?'

'Goodness,' said Charles. 'How awful. Poor Elizabeth. She'll be in despair. She adored that young man.'

'Yes... It's terribly sad.'

'Madeleine came here, you say?'

'Yes.'

'How did she seem?'

'Quiet, dignified. But I think your existence had come as a bit of a shock.'

'I see.'

'Do you want some supper?'

'I suppose I should. I was awfully hungry when I got home. Less so now.'

'I'll dish up then.'

She spooned the meat and potatoes out onto two plates and set them down on the table.

'What was your news?'

'Oh, it can wait. Let's eat and then I'll go over the road.'

'If you're sure.'

'Oh yes. I'll tell you tomorrow.'

Later that evening, Violet stood on the doorstep and watched her husband struggling along the slushy pavement and walking up the path of number 43. He rang the bell, and a few moments later the door opened and he disappeared inside. Violet tried to imagine the scene: the couple meeting twenty years after they'd parted. Deciding it would be best if she shut all such thoughts out of her mind, she went back indoors, listened at the baby's door to check he was sleeping, and then went downstairs to practise the piano.

As the evening wore on, Violet struggled to concentrate on her music. Periodically, she checked her watch – nine o'clock, and ten o'clock came and went. Where was he, she wondered. How long did it take to comfort a grief-stricken daughter?

The fire began to die down, and the room became chilly. Normally, she would have gone to bed, but somehow she couldn't bring herself to relax. She threw some more coal onto the fire, and made herself a cup of tea. Settled on the sofa, she tried to do the crossword, but couldn't rid her mind of the image of her husband in the arms of his beautiful ex-wife. She was not a jealous person by nature, and had never had cause to suspect Charles of infidelity, but Madeleine was an attractive woman, and they had once loved each other. Might the spark remain? Might this be the night that Charles and Madeleine were reunited?

16

Charles

Charles stood awkwardly opposite his ex-wife in the hall of number 43.

'Thank you for coming,' said Madeleine. 'Can I take your coat?'

'Yes, thank you. How is she?'

'Devastated. The doctor came and gave her a sedative. She's in bed.'

'Poor girl.'

'Quite.'

'What happened?'

'I took a telephone call earlier from his CO who gave me the details. Apparently, David's car skidded on the ice and slammed into a tree. He'd been here for Christmas to ask Elizabeth to marry him. We'd had such a lovely time. He left before dawn on Boxing Day to get back to base, and was only ten miles away from the airfield. Died instantly, apparently.'

'Well, that's something.'

'His CO told me that David considered us his family – his

parents were dead, you see. It's just the most awful rotten luck.' Madeleine wiped her eyes with a handkerchief. 'Can I get you a drink?'

'Yes please... whisky.'

'Of course, I remember.'

She led him into the sitting room and poured a large measure for each of them into crystal tumblers.

'This is a lovely room,' said Charles, looking around.

'Thank you.'

His eye was caught by the photographs on the mantelpiece. He touched the one of him holding his baby daughter. 'I have this photograph too. I keep it in my wallet.'

Madeleine suddenly burst into tears. 'Oh, Paddy... what an awful mess.'

He put his glass down on a side table and took her in his arms. 'There, there, Maddy. None of that. It's very sad, but I'm here now. I'm here. We'll get her through it, don't worry. I promise we'll get her through.'

After a few moments, Madeleine pulled away. 'I'm sorry,' she said, wiping her eyes.

'Don't be,' he replied. 'You're upset – we both are.'

'Do sit, please.' She pointed to a pair of armchairs on either side of the fire. In spite of its warmth, a chill descended, and their conversation became tentative and stilted.

'I met your wife,' said Madeleine. 'She seems very nice.'

'Oh yes, Violet's a good sport.'

'Charles... is that really the way to talk about your wife? I hope you never referred to me as a "good sport".'

'You... oh, no.' He smiled nervously.

'And a baby... at your age.'

'I know. It was a surprise to me too, but Violet's happy.'

'I met him – he's a delightful child.'

'Did you? Yes, well... he's a baby, and all babies are delightful, aren't they? Look... about Elizabeth...'

Madeleine sighed. 'What's to be done? The poor girl is so unhappy. What can we do, or say?'

'That life goes on. That tragedy recedes eventually. That broken hearts mend...' He gazed at Madeleine, with tears in his eyes.

'Oh Paddy,' she said, reaching over and taking his hand. 'After you left, I thought my heart would never mend.'

'I'm so sorry,' he replied, squeezing her hand and kissing it.

They sat for a while, each reflecting on the missed opportunities in their past.

'Why didn't we do this years ago?' he asked eventually. 'We seemed to go from loving to fighting, with nothing in between.'

'You were always too busy to talk.'

'Was I? I'm sorry. I did love you, you know – desperately.'

'You had a funny way of showing it. Running off to China like that.'

'It was my work, my duty.'

'Surely they could have found you something closer to home. I mean, the Board of Trade have offices everywhere.'

'You don't understand.'

'Don't I? Well, explain it to me.'

Charles gazed at his ex-wife. She was still beautiful, her dark hair streaked with fine silver threads, her skin pale and clear. Her dark blue dress picked up the colour of her eyes perfectly. He yearned to tell her everything there and then. To come clean, to confess, to rid himself of years of secrets and expunge himself of breaking not just Madeleine's heart, but that of his own mother.

He sipped his whisky and breathed deeply. He must steady his nerves and fight the desire to reveal all – no good would come of it. 'Madeleine, it's pretty straightforward – there's no great mystery. My work took me abroad. There was nothing I could do about it.'

She shook her head. 'You made a choice, Charles – a choice that didn't include us. There's no escaping that.'

They sat for a while in silence. 'You called me Paddy earlier,' he said eventually. 'I rather liked it.'

'I still think of you as Paddy, really – that was the name I knew you by when we fell in love. You were never Charles to me. That name came later when you got a proper job and went away. In my mind, I married Padraig and divorced Charles. To me they are two different people – two men, inhabiting the same body. One I loved, the other... I grew to hate.'

Charles began to feel anxious – the conversation was entering dangerous territory.

'I've never understood why you gave yourself that name,' Madeleine went on. 'Why did you join up as Padraig and not as Charles?'

Charles felt his throat constrict. 'A whim,' he muttered. 'An artifice – the romantic notion of a young man escaping his past.'

'What was there to escape? That's what I never understood.'

'My upbringing. I never felt I belonged... not really.'

'But you loved your mother. I saw how you reacted when she found you in that hospital... alive. The way you held her – I thought you'd never let her go.'

Charles knew, with certainty, that he had to stop this discussion. This was precisely why he had dreaded his ex-wife's proximity. Somehow he must keep a lid on these revelations. 'I should go up to Elizabeth.'

'That's right... run away. Whenever one of us gets too close, you bolt. It's who you are, Charles. I just hope you don't do it to that poor woman over the road.'

'I won't.'

'Why? Because you don't care enough, or because she doesn't try to get too close?'

Charles studied Madeleine's face, and saw the contempt

there, the suppressed anger of twenty years. 'Both perhaps.' He put his whisky down on the table between them and stood up. 'I'll find my own way to Elizabeth's room.'

On the first floor he pushed open a couple of doors until he found his daughter's bedroom. Elizabeth was in bed, her pale face illuminated by the glow of the bedside light. She appeared to be sleeping. He went in and sat quietly on the chair at the side of her bed, stroking her forehead. She woke, and smiled briefly, before her eyes filled with tears. 'Oh, Daddy.'

'I'm here, darling. I'm here.'

17

Violet

Violet waited up for Charles until after midnight. Finally, she decided to go to bed. Just as she was slipping into unconsciousness, she heard him coming into the hall. She considered getting up and asking him how it went, but felt that would be intrusive. He would be tired; she certainly was. It could wait till the next day.

The following morning she woke to the sound of her son chirruping happily. She pulled on her dressing gown and bent over his cot. Freddie had removed his socks in the night, and was now sucking the toes on one of his feet.

'Hello there, little one,' she said. 'Where are your socks... your feet are freezing, you silly boy.'

She lifted him up, took a clean knitted romper suit from a chest of drawers and carried him down to the bathroom. Once he had been changed and dressed, she took him into the kitchen, where he lay in his Moses basket on the kitchen table, gazing out at the sky.

The room was chilly, so she lit the gas oven and opened the

door. Warm air seeped into the kitchen. Then she set about making breakfast, boiling a couple of eggs and grilling some toast. Once the tea was made, she placed the pot beneath its knitted cosy and laid it on the Formica table.

Charles appeared soon afterwards. 'Morning,' he said quietly.

'Good morning. How did it go last night?'

He slumped down at the table and poured himself a cup of tea. 'Dreadful – they're in such a state. I felt completely helpless.'

'Oh, I'm sorry. Were you able to offer Elizabeth any comfort?'

'I went up to see her, of course. She was very tired – drugged, I think. Tearful, utterly miserable – can see no future for herself. I tried to tell her – life throws you a googly sometimes and it's how you cope that matters. No one's life is without pain.'

'That was wise advice.'

'Bit too soon for her to take it all in, I suspect.'

'And Madeleine... how was she?' After her wild imaginings of the evening before, Violet braced herself for the reply.

'Oh, much the same. More vulnerable perhaps than I remember. Terribly upset. Poor Maddy.'

'Is that what you called her, Maddy?'

'Yes... I was Paddy, she was Maddy. It was our little joke.' He smiled.

Violet felt her throat constrict, and she began to choke on the piece of toast in her mouth.

'You all right?' asked Charles.

'Yes,' she croaked, slurping a cup of tea. 'Why did she call you Paddy?'

Charles flushed slightly. 'Oh, it was just a pet name... silly really.'

'Is that why our son is called Padraig?'

'No, not really,' said Charles dismissively. 'Oh, I don't know... does it matter?'

'Yes... yes, I think it does. Suddenly I discover that our son was christened using a name your first wife gave you. It's rather upsetting.'

'If that's all you have to be upset about, then really, Violet...' He trailed off, and they sat in stony silence.

The baby began to cry, and Violet picked him up and settled him on her breast, where he slurped contentedly.

She decided to change the subject. 'By the way, what was your news yesterday?'

'Oh, that. My department's moving out of London – somewhere near Oxford. Most of them made the move a couple of months ago, but I managed to put it off because of the baby and so on. They've finally insisted. I'll be leaving in a week.'

She felt a stab of something; what was it? Shock perhaps, or resignation? There was also something worryingly predictable about this little speech. Was Charles deserting her just as he had deserted Madeleine all those years before? She tried to sound calm. 'Why didn't you tell me sooner, when it was first mooted?'

'I didn't want to worry you unnecessarily. I was hoping they would let me stay in London. But it seems the decision has been made. It's war, Violet, and it's my job. What else can I do but comply?'

'I understand. Are we all going?' she asked, already knowing the answer.

'No, I don't think that would be wise – the disruption and so on. They'll find me digs up there – a room somewhere. Harder for them if I have a family. Besides, we don't want to give this place up, do we? Best if you stay here, then I can pop back from time to time.'

'Or we could visit you? Oxford is lovely.'

'Yes, perhaps...'

. . .

As the day of his departure drew nearer, Violet raised the idea of returning to work. 'With you away, I can't bear the thought of just sitting here, doing nothing.'

'Quite right. I agree that staying at home is a waste of your fine brain and first-class education.'

Violet always had a feeling that her husband was secretly jealous of her university degree. When they had first met, he had told her he could have gone to Oxford or Cambridge, had it not been for the 'wretched' war. 'By the time it was over,' he had told her, 'I was too damaged to go back into education. Besides, I needed to earn a living and was lucky to get a job.'

'But it's such a shame,' she had said back then. 'You have such a fine mind. You could have done anything – the law, teaching...'

'Teaching? I don't think so. it's a splendid profession for those who have the aptitude for it, but I'm far too selfish.'

'Selfish?'

'Yes. I'm well aware of my failings, and selfishness is one of them.'

'I'd quite like to be a teacher,' she had said quietly.

'There you are then – you've just proved my point. Teachers must be completely selfless. And you my dear are the epitome of selflessness.'

Now, as she sat watching her husband reading the paper, cup of tea in hand, she realised he had been spot on. He was selfish. But was she really selfless enough to teach?

'I thought I might go into teaching... there's always a shortage of maths teachers.'

'Whatever you want, my dear.'

'And don't worry about the baby – I'll get an au pair or something.'

'Au pair... yes,' he said distractedly, opening another page of the newspaper. 'You'll be a fine teacher, Violet – you know I've always thought so.'

When they'd first met, Violet might have taken this as a compliment, but now she was less sure. Perhaps he had meant she hadn't the character for anything else. What did people say: 'Those who can do, those who can't, teach.'?

The following weekend, Violet and Freddie accompanied Charles to the bus station. Watching her husband climbing aboard the coach, struggling with his cumbersome leather suitcase in one hand and his precious typewriter in the other, she felt some concern for him. His leg had been painful recently, and the district nurse thought the wound was getting worse.

'He really needs more protein in his diet, Mrs Carmichael,' she said.

'I know,' Violet had replied, 'but it's so hard to find enough protein in wartime.'

'Well, do what you can.'

Now Violet worried that, away from her care, his leg might deteriorate. There was always the threat that it would have to be amputated.

Charles finally found his seat on the bus, stowed his luggage and returned to the open door. 'Right, well, I'm settled. Look after yourself, Violet.'

'You too – and take care of that leg. They will send a district nurse to you in Oxford, I hope?'

'Oh yes. I'll register with a doctor when I get there.'

It was cold, and the baby began to grumble.

'You'd better go,' said Charles. 'I don't want you both to catch a chill. I'll write.'

'You will come back as often as you can, won't you? You promise?'

'Of course.'

As the bus drew out of the station, Violet stood alone on the pavement, rocking the baby's pram. A tiny part of her – the pessimist she tried hard to keep at bay – wondered if she would ever see her husband again. He had an elusive quality that meant she never felt as if she had a hold over him. Even when he was physically present, it was as if part of him was somewhere else entirely.

A light sprinkling of snow began to fall, and in the cold air it settled on the icy pavement.

'Come on then,' she said to Freddie. 'We'd better get home, before the snow gets much worse.' And she pushed the pram away up the road, tears spilling down her face.

18

Violet

By early February, Violet had grown accustomed to Charles's absence. He rang her almost every week on Sunday evening. He had started attending Evensong at the Oxford Oratory, he told her. Work was dull, his digs were adequate, and his landlady was a competent cook who did his laundry once a week. Usually, they chatted about domestic trivia – the electricity bill, or Freddie's latest bout of childhood illness. Gradually, she relaxed about her husband being away. He seemed relatively settled and happy, and in some ways her life was easier. Charles's room no longer needed regular dusting. There were no shirts to iron, and no need to produce an evening meal. She had never been bothered much about food – seeing it more as fuel rather than pleasure – and quickly got into the habit of simply snacking. She would breastfeed the baby seated at the kitchen table, while eating something very simple: a slice of toast perhaps, or, if she had enough ration points, a boiled egg or tiny square of cheese. Occasionally, for a treat, she would fry a sausage or two, or ask the butcher for a thin slice of lamb's liver.

She became obsessed with carrots, and would stand gazing out at the garden while munching noisily. Usually she didn't even bother to peel them.

Inevitably, she lost weight – feeding the child seemed to take everything out of her. But her life was calm and not unhappy.

Now, she stood at the kitchen sink washing the breakfast things, gazing out at the muddy garden. It had been raining since Christmas and the lawn lay under an inch of stagnant water. In spite of this, the tips of daffodils, she noticed, were just pushing their way through the quagmire. It was a rare sign of hope.

The baby lay in his Moses basket on the little kitchen table. He too was looking out at the grey sky, waving his hands in greeting to the new day.

The washing up finished, she folded the dishtowel, and hung it over the grill on top of the gas stove to dry. 'Well, that's that,' she said out loud to her son. 'It's rather miserable today, I'm afraid, but I suppose we could go for a walk. Would you like that? To go and look at the ducks in Kensington Gardens?' She made a little quacking noise, and the baby turned his head towards his mother's voice and gummed a smile. He shook his fists excitedly.

'You would like it? Excellent. I'll get our coats.'

In the hall, as she settled baby Freddie in his pram, her neighbour from the flat above materialised. Nigel, a single man in his early fifties, was a clerk in a firm of stockbrokers.

'Hello, Nigel,' said Violet. 'Not working today?'

'No... bit of a cold. Worried it might go to my chest. How's the little chap doing?'

'Oh, very well,' she replied. 'I hope he doesn't keep you awake at night?'

'Not really.'

'That's a relief. We're just off to the park.'

'That's nice. How's Charles? Not seen him around recently.'

'No, he's had to go away – government business.'

'Oh, I see. I'm sorry.'

'It's all right. I've got little Freddie for company.'

'Away for long, is he?'

'I'm not sure. You know what it's like – especially in wartime. No one seems to know exactly what's going on, do they?'

Nigel nodded sagely, and tipped his hat. 'Well, enjoy your walk.'

Violet set off down Kensington Church Street, admiring the antique shops. She pushed the pram through the backstreets, past the grander houses of Kensington, until she reached a side entrance to the park. Her destination was the Round Pond in the centre. The trees were bare, but here and there bulbs were pushing their way through the grass's surface. Elsewhere, much of the park had been dug up and put to wartime use growing vegetables. She passed a couple tending an allotment. The woman was wearing what appeared to be her best suit and a smart trilby hat. It struck Violet as odd. The woman needed some breeches, like the ones worn by land girls.

A distant clock struck twelve and the park began to fill up with people searching for a quiet place to eat their lunch. Office workers too old for military service, in overcoats and trilby hats, sank down onto benches and opened up greaseproof paper parcels filled with sandwiches.

Here and there, younger couples walked arm in arm. Mostly, the men were in uniform, and she felt a pang of sympathy for their wives and girlfriends. It was bad enough Charles living away from home, but to know that this visit from your lover or husband might be his last must surely be unbearable. Suddenly, she thought of Elizabeth. As it turned out, David's last visit *had* been their last – and yet she had thought he was safe in his role as ground crew. Now, Violet suddenly felt an overwhelming sadness for the girl, and wondered if she should call and see how she and her mother were coping. With Charles away, she had quickly recovered her equilibrium about his first wife. It had been childish of her to feel any jealousy. She would drop by later that day, and bring them a bunch of spring flowers.

Also among the lovers and tired office workers were women like her, pushing prams. It was a chilly day, and most of them wore fur coats. Violet pulled the collar of her woollen coat up around her ears, and found herself yearning, just for a moment, for such a coat. What a joy it would be to nestle contentedly in racoon, or even squirrel. Madeleine, she remembered, had worn a dark brown mink coat that awful night she came looking for Charles.

She found a quiet spot – a bench overlooking the Round Pond – and settled herself with the baby's pram beside her. Freddie was propped up against his pillows so that he could see the activity on the pond. Although he wore his thickest coat, a woollen bonnet and mittens, and was tightly wrapped in three blankets, his face was still rosy with cold. But he seemed not to mind, and gurgled excitedly as a pair of ducks waddled in front of him and launched themselves into the water.

'They'll have ducklings soon,' said Violet. 'In a month or two there will be a dozen little ducklings waddling behind their mummy and daddy.'

Among the wildlife, three little boys – aged about seven or eight – were playing happily with their model sailing boats. Violet, whose own childhood had been without such luxuries, watched admiringly. The way the boys rigged their sails, and controlled the boat's trajectory, was impressive. 'Look Freddie –

look at those clever boys. When you're a bit older, I'll buy you one of those... just as soon as I get a job.'

Violet had decided to look for a teaching job in the spring and start work in September. By then, the baby would be one year old, and she would look into employing an au pair. The only problem, of course, was that in their flat the only spare room was Charles's – and she knew he would hate anyone else invading his private space.

Realising this was a thorny problem that could not be easily solved, she tucked the baby into his blankets, took her book from the basket beneath the pram and began to read.

Soon, the peace was disturbed by the sound of marching boots. She looked up the Broad Walk – the long path that led from Bayswater in the north to Kensington Gore to the south – and was surprised to see a large group of men marching towards her. They wore a range of German uniforms, and were being guarded by men in British Army battledress. Prisoners of war, she thought. Violet had heard of the 'POWs in the park', but she had never actually seen them before. To her surprise, they stopped near her bench and began to unroll a huge ball of barbed wire. An army sergeant barked orders at a German, who then passed the orders on to the rest.

Violet, who had been brought up speaking the language by her German parents, was intrigued by the backchat between the prisoners.

'Pull it this way,' one was saying. 'And hurry up, Fritz, or we'll be here all day.'

'What's the rush? It's not as if there's anything better to do,' responded Fritz.

'Stop complaining,' said the first prisoner. 'It's not so bad here. We have comfortable beds to sleep in and food to eat. Better than being shot at by Spitfires!'

Fritz laughed. 'I'll second that.'

It amused Violet to hear her fellow Germans joking with

one another. It was comforting that they felt so at home in enemy territory. It was one of the things she loved about England – the fact that they appeared to be so fair and decent to their prisoners. However, Charles had told her once that there was a secret prison, known as 'the cage', hidden in an elegant house overlooking Kensington Gardens, where the British Secret Service interrogated German prisoners of war. That sounded rather less welcoming.

'Do they torture them?' she had asked.

'Of course! How else do you get people to tell the truth?'

'That's an awful thought,' she had said. 'That in the midst of our genteel city such horror is taking place.'

'War is war,' Charles had said, matter-of-factly. 'It's never pretty. I should know.' He had slapped his bad leg, wincing.

'How do you know about it?' she had asked.

'Oh, office gossip,' he had replied.

She had let it go at the time, but now, thinking about it, it seemed rather odd that he would know such a thing. How could someone who spent his days as a not very high-up civil servant know anything about enemy interrogation? Charles never really told her what he did. It was one of the many things about her husband that was rather a mystery. Maybe after the war, she would finally discover the truth.

19

March 1944

Charles

It was the first day of spring, and the midday sun was just piercing the fog as Charles walked down Clarendon Road. He was in London for a long weekend, and was relieved to be back on home turf. He had spent the previous few weeks observing Mosley, travelling between Oxford and Crux Easton in Hampshire, where Mosley had temporarily set up home. Now, Charles was looking forward to one or two home-cooked meals, and sleeping in his own bed. As he let himself into the hall he called out, 'Hello...' The house felt quiet and empty. He unlocked his room, laid his suitcase on the bed and placed his beloved typewriter on the desk. He ran his hand down the front of the drawers, checking they were all firmly locked.

Reassured all was well, he went downstairs, but there was no sign of either Violet or the baby. He peered out into the back garden, but they weren't there either. Hungry suddenly, he opened the larder and found the heel of a loaf and a slab of cheese. He made himself a slice of cheese on toast under the grill, boiled the kettle for a pot of tea and sat quietly at the kitchen table, eating his lunch.

Afterwards, he put the dirty plate and cup into the stone sink, but didn't wash up – Violet would only redo it. She often complained that his domestic skills were inadequate.

He was tempted to spend the afternoon writing – it had been weeks since he'd had time for any creative work – but he knew he should really visit his daughter. After leaving a note for Violet on the kitchen table, he put on his coat and went outside, the remnants of the fog catching in his throat.

He crossed the road to number 43, and tentatively rang the doorbell. There was no response, and he half-hoped that Elizabeth was sufficiently recovered to be back at work. He was just considering leaving and returning home when the door opened. To his amazement, Violet stood before him.

'Charles! How lovely. When did you get back?'

'An hour ago. What are you doing here?'

'Same as you, I imagine – I came to see how Elizabeth was. Madeleine asked me to call in while she was at work. Elizabeth's in the kitchen. Come down.'

Disconcerted, Charles followed his wife down the stairs to the basement kitchen. She led the way as if this were her second home. Elizabeth was sitting at the kitchen table, dandling Freddie on her lap. 'Dad! How lovely.' She handed the baby to Violet, and rushed over to hug her father.

'Hello, my dear,' he said, kissing her. 'I must say, this is a delightful domestic scene... my wife and two children all together, like one happy family.'

'Isn't it?' Elizabeth smiled. 'Your boy's such a little charmer. Violet's been a godsend recently – keeping me company. It's done me the world of good.'

She smiled broadly at Violet, who blushed a little.

'Would you like some tea?' Elizabeth asked. 'We were about to have some.'

'No, thank you. I had some at home.'

'Have you had lunch?' asked Violet.

'Just cheese on toast,' he replied. 'So, Elizabeth – how are you?'

She stood with her back to him at the sink, filling the kettle. She looked thin, he thought.

'Not too bad, thanks.' She put the kettle on the stove and turned to face him, smiling bravely. 'I'm going back to work next week. They've been very patient, but I think it's time. I need the distraction.'

'That sounds sensible.'

'I'd only been in the new post for a few days before I left again, but Major Williams – that's my new boss – is awfully nice. And Danny – you remember Danny, you met him in the pub – has been very sweet. He's been over to see me a few times.'

'I'm so glad,' said Charles.

'I suspect I have you to thank for my new job, don't I, Dad?' Elizabeth winked at him.

'I don't know what you mean.'

'Yes you do. That day when we met, on Christmas Eve, when you said you had "contacts". Valentine seems to have disappeared off the face of the earth, or so Danny says.'

Charles's face remained impassive... inscrutable.

'What's this about contacts?' asked Violet. 'And who is Valentine?'

'Oh, he was my old boss – there was a bit of unpleasantness and Dad offered to sort it out for me.'

Violet stared at her husband. 'Did he? How marvellous to be so... influential.'

There was an edge to her voice that Charles found disconcerting. Anxious to change the subject, he held his hands out for the baby. 'How's my little chap?'

'Oh, he's doing well,' said Violet. 'The nappy rash is improving. Madeleine thinks it's the warmer weather. She says he'll be crawling by Easter, and we can let him play in the garden with his clothes off.'

Charles had the distinct impression that the world had shifted slightly on its axis. His two wives appeared to have formed a bond, and he wasn't included. 'How nice of her to take such an interest.'

'Oh, Ma loves babies,' said Elizabeth, 'and she adores Freddie, doesn't she, Violet?'

'Yes, she's been very kind. Madeleine's helping me find a nanny so I can go back to work.'

'I see,' said Charles, bouncing his son on his knee absent-mindedly. 'Well, Elizabeth my dear, I'm so relieved to see you with a little colour in your cheeks. I'm proud of you – and of the way you've recovered.'

'As you said that day, Dad, we all have to cope with pain in life and it's *how* we cope that matters. Obviously, I miss David dreadfully, and so does Ma – she adored him too – but we must move on. So many people have lost loved ones in this awful war – I'm not the only one.'

'Very commendable,' said Charles, standing up and handing the baby back to Violet. 'Well, I'd better be going – work, you know.'

'But it's Friday afternoon. It's the weekend tomorrow,' said Violet.

'The war, my dear, makes no allowances for such things,' said Charles. 'I still have a few meetings to attend.' He turned to Elizabeth. 'Perhaps you can pop over one evening before you start back at work. I'll be in London till Tuesday.'

'I'd love that. Can I bring Ma?'

'Of course,' said Violet, before Charles could interject. 'How about Sunday?' she added brightly. 'Come for supper and afterwards we can play cards.'

'Well, that seems to be sorted,' said Charles quietly. 'Violet, I'll see you at home later.'

'Yes, I'll pop down to Portobello Market first, and buy something for supper.'

'I'll see you out,' said Elizabeth.

As the door to number 43 closed behind him, Charles couldn't escape the feeling that his life had suddenly become more complicated. He felt as if he had lost control. He wanted desperately to go to his club, to sit in a comfortable armchair in the members' bar with a small tumbler of whisky and forget all about it. But the fact was, he had not ventured into the club since that fateful night when he ran into Michael Reilly. He'd not spoken to Simon or Jack since then, either. He dreaded to think what rumours were circulating about him.

Irritated suddenly, he briskly headed home, intending to start work on his current novel. But when he reached his house, he felt compelled to keep walking. He needed to make sense of what was happening – to think through the implications of this convoluted new family dynamic. He continued down Clarendon Road, his stick tapping the ground in time with his steps. At Holland Park Avenue, he paused, wondering if he should turn left or right. Instead he crossed the road, and headed south towards Kensington, almost as if his feet were leading the way. Finally he found himself standing outside a fine Edwardian house in Melbury Road. It was red brick with limestone-edged windows. Standing beneath the fledgling blossom of a cherry tree, he recalled the first time he had seen the building. It was 1920 and he had finally been discharged from St Bartholomew's Hospital, where he'd spent the best part of eighteen months.

Tired suddenly, he sat down on a bench opposite the building, the sunshine warming his face and hands. How on earth had he arrived at this point? He had spent the last twenty years covering his tracks, concealing his private life, avoiding discovery. But now the whole edifice he had so carefully crafted appeared to be crumbling.

20

Violet

After Charles had left, Elizabeth came back into the kitchen and found Violet standing at the French windows, staring out at the garden.

'Are you all right, Violet?' Elizabeth asked.

'Me? Oh yes, I'm fine, thanks.'

Elizabeth poured fresh water into the teapot, and then sat down at the kitchen table.

'Don't you think Charles was rather odd just now?' Violet asked.

'Odd in what way?'

'Unsettled somehow. Not himself.'

'Perhaps he's just tired,' suggested Elizabeth, pouring tea into her own cup.

'No... it's more than that. He was rattled. I don't think he likes me and Madeleine knowing one another. I don't know why. I think it's the only civilised way to behave.' Violet sat down opposite Elizabeth. 'Apart from anything else, I like your mother – I think she's charming and resourceful. And I really like you too, of course. We're nearly the same age and I think of you as a friend, Elizabeth, honestly I do.'

Elizabeth reached across the table and squeezed Violet's hand. 'Oh Vi, that's a lovely thing to say. I think of you as a friend too. I just wish Dad could understand and be pleased about it. More tea?'

'Just one cup. Then I really ought to get off to the market.'

'You can leave Freddie with me if you like. He looks sleepy. I can put him down in his pram for a nap.'

'Would you? You are kind. That would make things easier. And I can pick him up on my way home.'

Violet sipped her tea. 'Going back to Charles... I realise I know very little about his life just after the war. Has your mother ever mentioned what he did – his job, I mean.'

'I don't think so. Honestly, we never talk about my father. Until David died...' Elizabeth paused '...do you know, that's the first time I've been able to say that... David-has-died.' Tears came into her eyes.

'You're being so brave, really you are.'

'Well, anyway – until David... you know – Ma had no idea where Dad was. The last she heard, he was in Peking. When I first bumped into him in the street, he did apologise for not getting in touch when he returned.'

'I should think so too,' said Violet curtly. 'What excuse did he give?'

'Oh, too much time had elapsed... that sort of thing. And he had books to write.'

'Oh yes, he's always made time for that,' said Violet bitterly.

'I read one of his books, you know,' said Elizabeth. '*Passenger to Peking*. It's set in China and was awfully good – really exciting, you know. All about a girl who gets caught up in all sorts of thrills and spills. His characters are so richly drawn –

men from the ministry and the embassy, all outdoing evil villains in China.'

'I've flipped through one or two of them,' said Violet, 'but they seem rather melodramatic to me. I always thought his storytelling was an antidote to his real life, which let's face it is rather dull.'

'That's a bit harsh,' said Elizabeth. 'He must have done some really interesting things in China.'

'But he was just a lowly clerk, surely,' said Violet. 'There's nothing interesting about that.'

'I think that's a bit unfair. You can't deny how brave he was in the last war. He told me one or two things he'd done, and I was awfully impressed. Not that he is vain or anything. He always plays down his heroism. Just between you and me, I went looking for his war record once, just to see if he had any medals or anything.'

'Oh really,' said Violet, leaning forward. 'And did he?'

'I don't know. Apparently most of the First World War records were destroyed in a fire. It was jolly frustrating. Anyway, I thought the book was very realistic. I got the impression he had really known those sorts of people out in China. I mean, you couldn't make it up.'

'I'm sorry, I realise I must sound rather nasty and negative. I don't mean to be. I love your father, and admire him. It's just, he's not an easy man to live with, you know. He can be very distant and secretive.'

'Ma said something similar. When he first went to China, it was only supposed to be for a year or so. But when he decided to stay, Ma did her best to persuade him to come home, but he refused. The job, it turned out, was more important than we were. But you know Ma – she's not one to fall apart. She realised the marriage was over, divorced him and got on with life.'

'I sympathise with her. And if I'm honest, Elizabeth, I was

appalled when he told me that he had left you and your mother – really appalled. I told him so too.'

Elizabeth smiled. 'I think you and my mother are rather alike in some ways. I'm so glad we met.'

'So am I, dear.' Violet stood up. 'Well, I ought to be going, or the market stalls will be empty. Are you sure you don't mind looking after Freddie?'

'Not at all. Off you go and I'll see you shortly.'

Violet set off up Clarendon Road towards Portobello Market. She bought a cabbage and a few potatoes and then went to the butcher, where she chose a small piece of ham for that night's supper.

'Anything else?' asked the man behind the counter.

'I need something for a meal for four. What can I have on my ration?'

He surveyed his meat display, and tutted. 'Tricky. I've got a bit of shin of beef. If you cook it long and slow it can be quite tender.'

'That sounds perfect. Thanks.'

Heading back to Clarendon Road, she wondered if Charles would be at home. In all probability he would be hidden away in his room typing. She collected the sleeping baby from Elizabeth and walked back to her own house, bumping the pram up the steps. Inside, she parked the pram in the corner, next to the front door, and knocked on Charles's door. There was no reply. Tentatively, she turned the handle, and to her surprise found the door unlocked. His typewriter was on the desk, and his suitcase lay unopened on the bed. Clearly, he had dumped his things in a hurry and left. Intending to unpack for him, she flipped the catches on the leather suitcase and lifted the lid. As she began to remove his clothes, noting which ones needed a wash, she came upon a small leather-bound copy of Walter

Scott's *Ivanhoe*. Next to it was a notebook. She opened it to reveal pages of random letters and numbers, written in columns. She turned the pages, one after another, but each page was much like the last. The last few pages consisted of an index of some kind, which appeared to relate to *Ivanhoe*. Instinctively, she realised that this was something private. Nervously, she carefully replaced the clothes, folding them as she had found them, closed the lid, flipped down the catches and left the room.

The baby was just stirring in his pram in the hall. He opened his dark brown eyes and smiled up at his mother.

'Hello, darling,' she said. 'Shall we go downstairs?'

She lit the fire in the sitting room, and sat on the sofa with the baby on her lap, brooding over what she had seen. What did those columns of letters mean? Next to her on the sofa lay a copy of *The Times*, with the crossword half-finished. She had abandoned it earlier in the day, frustrated at not being to solve clue number 10: 'Half Mediterranean island's taking on a female's code (6)'.

Suddenly, it came to her. 'Cypher', she said out loud. As she filled in the missing letters, she realised that was what she had just seen upstairs – a cypher of some sort. It was a simple code, where each letter represented another letter. Leaving the baby safely on the sofa, she ran back upstairs and into Charles's room. She opened his suitcase, felt beneath the folded clothes and retrieved the notebook. Taking a piece of paper from Charles's desk, she copied out some of the pages, her heart beating hard, praying he would not return before she had finished. When she had a representative sample of letters, along with the index, she hid the notebook back in the suitcase. As she closed the bedroom door, she heard footsteps outside the house.

Violet ran downstairs, folding the paper as she did so, and into the kitchen, where she hid the piece of paper inside an old biscuit tin at the back of the larder cupboard. Her heart racing, she returned to the sitting room, put the baby back on her lap and picked up the crossword.

At least if Charles came into the room now, all he would find would be his wife poring over a crossword. Whatever secrets he was keeping from her, she was determined to maintain the illusion of innocence. She needed proof before she could confront him.

21

Charles

Sitting in the sunshine opposite the building in Melbury Road, Charles tried to recall the first time he had been there. It had been the spring of 1920, and the weather was unseasonably warm, the sunshine hinting at the summer to come. Standing outside the elegant red-brick building back then, Charles had felt no optimism, no joy. Instead, it was as if he were standing on the edge of a precipice.

'There's no going back now,' he remembered saying to himself. 'You've got yourself into this and there's nothing you can do about it.'

Now, so many years later, he tried to piece it all together – the journey that led to Melbury Road and his secret life.

It all began with the Great War.

He had first joined up in September of 1914. He was eighteen, had just left school, and the war was just a few weeks old. All over Enfield, posters of Lord Kitchener, Secretary of State for

War, stared out at every passer-by. His pose was compelling: he looked you straight in the eye, his finger pointing at every young man, demanding they do their duty and fight, because 'Your country needs you!'

Charles had been kicking a ball around in the park with his best friends, Tom and Jimmy. On the way home, they saw the poster outside the library.

'Let's go and join up,' said Jimmy, 'it might be a lark!'

There was a queue outside the recruiting office that stretched right down the high street. Many of the young men knew each other, and there was a great atmosphere, with lots of laughter and banter. Signing up was a formality. After a cursory medical examination the three friends were in.

They left the recruiting office full of excitement. They were off on an adventure. Jimmy said his mum would be glad to see the back of him, but Charles instinctively knew his mother would be upset.

He came down the alley at the back of the house, and slipped through the back gate and into the yard. He stood for a while watching his mother through the window stirring something on the stove. Her auburn hair was tied up on top of her head, stray locks escaping from the pins. She looked so happy and content, and suddenly Charles felt guilty. He was about to shatter her world. At first, he was tempted to run away, but finally he plucked up the courage to open the door.

'Oh, there are you are Charlie,' said his mother, 'I wondered when you'd be home.'

'That smells good, Mum.' He wiped his feet on the mat and hung up his hat, but his hand was shaking.

'What's the matter?' His mother didn't miss a thing; she had always been able to read his moods.

'I've got something to tell you, Mum, but I don't want you to get upset.'

'Oh Good Lord, Charlie.' Kathleen wiped her hands on her apron, as if preparing herself for action.

'The thing is,' Charles began, 'me and some mates... we've been queuing all day to join a local Pals Battalion.' He tried to keep his voice light and cheerful.

'I don't understand, Charlie.'

'I've joined the army, Mother. To fight the Germans.'

'Why on earth have you done that?' replied Kathleen furiously. 'You're not old enough! You've only just left school. Nineteen is the age, that's what it said in the paper. And even then, it's voluntary.'

'I know, but me and my mates – we wanted to go together.'

'What for? Why do you always have to go along with the crowd? Can you change your mind?'

'I don't want to change my mind. And we joined up together because we want to serve together. It wouldn't be any fun with strangers.'

'It won't be any fun at all!' screamed his mother. 'Don't you understand? This is war we're talking about, not a Sunday school picnic.' She wiped her forehead with the back of her hand, and sank down onto a kitchen chair. 'Oh, I don't know what your father will say.'

'I hope he, at least, will be proud of me,' said Charles, sitting down opposite her. Then, desperate to change the subject, he asked: 'Any tea left in that pot?'

'Yes, of course,' she said distractedly, pouring tea into a cup. 'Oh Charlie, I wish you'd spoken to me first.'

'You'd only have tried to talk me out of it – and I want to do my bit.'

'Why? It's not your war.'

'Yes, it is. And it's the right thing to do...the honourable thing.'

'Did that form master of yours tell you that?'

'If you mean Mr McMasters, as it happens, he suggested I

wait. He wanted me to take my university entrance first. Thinks I could try for Oxbridge.'

'Then why didn't you listen to him?' Kathleen was red in the face now with fury. 'You might think you're a big clever man, Charles Frederick Carmichael, but you're nothing of the kind. You're just a stupid child.'

She leapt to her feet, tears pouring down her cheeks. Charles stood up and came round the table and held her to his chest. 'I'm sorry you feel that way, Mum. But it's something I have to do. Besides, I won't be doing any actual fighting yet. We've got three months basic training first. We all joined the local Middlesex regiment, so I'll only be up the road. And by the time we're ready to go to France, I suspect it'll all be over. Then I can go to university – but for the next few months at least I'll be with my friends. Now, what's for tea, I'm starving.'

When George, Charlie's father, came home, he looked a bit startled when he heard his son's news, but remained calm. 'I'm proud of you, boy,' he said, shaking his son's hand.

'Oh, George,' wailed Kathleen. 'What's there to be proud of? That your only son might get killed?'

'You don't understand, Kath,' said George. 'It's a man's thing.' Then, patting Charles's shoulder, he added quietly, 'She'll come round. Open a bottle of beer, son. I'll join you in a minute – I'm just going upstairs to change before tea.'

But Kathleen didn't 'come round'. She alternated between sulking and weeping.

As the day of Charles' departure grew closer, Kathleen washed and ironed his shirts and polished his shoes. On his last morning, she stood at the back door and handed him a cake wrapped in greaseproof paper. 'In case you get hungry.'

'Thanks, Mum. I love your cakes.'

'I hope you don't mind,' she said through tears, 'but I can't see you off... I couldn't bear it.'

'It's all right, Mum. I understand. And I'll see you soon. I love you.'

A couple of hours later, he marched down the high street alongside his fellow recruits; over five hundred of Enfield's finest young men marching in unison to the sound of the regimental band. Suddenly, he heard his name being called: 'Charlie, Charlie!'

He turned towards the voice and saw his sister, waving frantically. 'Good luck, Bruv,' she called out. Standing next to her, tears streaming down her face, was his mother, waving a sodden handkerchief.

To his surprise, nearly thirty years later, Charles found himself crying. He would never forget that day and the look of despair on his mother's face. And perhaps, if he'd listened to her, and waited for the call-up, so much that had gone wrong in his life might have been different.

22

MARCH 1944

Violet

On Sunday morning, Violet and Charles were sitting at the kitchen table eating breakfast when Charles announced he had to go out.

'Really? On a Sunday?'

'I've got a meeting with someone this afternoon. But first I thought I might go to Farm Street for Mass. I haven't been there for ages.'

'You won't forget we've invited Madeleine and Elizabeth for supper?'

'No, I won't forget, don't worry.'

Violet was keen to put on a good show for her guests that evening, and spent the morning preparing the meal, chopping and frying carrots and onions, before adding the beef. Once it was all in a casserole dish, she added some stout and put it in the oven on a low heat.

She then set about preparing an apple crumble, but found she had run out of flour. The shops would all be shut on a Sunday, and without flour the only pudding she could make was stewed apple, and nobody really liked that.

Cursing her own bad housekeeping, she wondered if Madeleine might have some flour to spare. So she dressed Freddie in his coat and bonnet, put him in the pram and wheeled him up the road to number 43.

Elizabeth opened the door. 'Oh, hello, Vi... how lovely. Is everything OK? We're looking forward to seeing you tonight.'

'Yes, everything's fine. I just realised I've run out of flour. I couldn't borrow some, could I?'

'Of course. Come in. Leave the baby in the hall. Ma's in the kitchen.'

Madeleine was peeling potatoes. 'Hello, Violet. What can we do for you?'

'Vi needs some flour, Ma. Can I give her a pound or so?'

'Of course – I've got plenty in the jar.'

'Thanks so much,' said Violet. 'I was making an apple crumble for tonight, and suddenly realised I'd run out.'

'Why don't you stay for lunch?' said Elizabeth brightly. 'We're having soup – at least we will be if we make it in time.'

'Well, if you're sure, that would be lovely. Charles is out for lunch. But I shouldn't be too long. I've got the beef on a low oven.'

'Oh, the beef will be fine,' said Madeleine. 'It needs at least five or six hours, especially if it's a cheap cut.'

'Is there any other kind these days?' asked Violet ruefully.

'Here, let me take your coat,' said Elizabeth. 'And I'll go and get the baby, shall I?'

'It'll be a pretty basic soup, I'm afraid,' said Madeleine.

'There are so few vegetables around at the moment. It's just potato and onion.'

'It sounds delicious,' said Violet. 'Let me help.'

'All right – can you peel these?' said Madeleine, handing her a knife and a couple of potatoes.

Once the soup was bubbling on the stove, the three women sat at the kitchen table.

'How's Charles?' asked Madeleine.

'All right, I think. Very busy always.' Violet sighed. 'And he's bit distant, if I'm honest – preoccupied, you know.'

Madeleine smiled. 'That sounds familiar.'

'Madeleine... tell me to mind my own business, but I often wondered how you two met?'

'We met out in Belgium during the last war. I was a field nurse near Ypres.'

'Gosh, how brave you must have been,' said Violet.

'Not really. My brother was out there fighting, and I wanted to be part of it. I suppose I knew there was some risk, but the field hospitals rarely got hit – we were several hundred yards behind the front lines. The challenge was trying to keep things clean, and control infection. That and having to starch your uniform in very unhygienic conditions.' She smiled at the memory.

'I admire you, I really do,' said Violet.

'In many ways it was quite fun. We were billeted in the neighbouring villages. I had a lovely landlady called Dominique. She made the most delicious biscuits, I remember, and was very kind to us. Occasionally, they'd host little supper parties for us – at Christmas and so on. I think they were so grateful we were there to help.'

'So when did you meet Charles?'

'He was brought to the field hospital. He was in a pretty

bad way – in and out of consciousness for days. He'd been gassed, but fortunately he'd been wearing his gas mask, or he would have died. He nearly lost his left leg, of course. A case like his was untreatable out there, so after a few weeks he got shipped back and I accompanied him. That was quite common then – nurses being sent back with the wounded. We came back to England on the boat train. The carriages were kitted out with beds just like a hospital. They even had operating theatres on board for emergencies. Once we got to England, Charles was transferred to St Bartholomew's Hospital. They needed nurses with battlefield experience, so they asked me to stay.'

'You didn't want to get back to the front and all that excitement?' asked Violet.

'No, not by then.' Madeleine blushed. 'I'd rather fallen for him, you see.'

'Oh, Ma,' interjected Elizabeth, squeezing her mother's hand. 'I've never heard you talk about him like this.'

'Perhaps I shouldn't.' She turned to Violet. 'I'm sorry, I don't want to upset you.'

'You're not, it's all right. It was me who asked you about it, after all. Oddly enough, I had a similar reaction when I met him. I think I fell for him within hours.'

'He was unlike anyone I'd ever met,' Madeleine went on. 'He was very handsome, of course. And he was clever, and a great raconteur. But I pretty soon realised that he was also rather complicated. All those names for a start.' She laughed.

'What do you mean?' said Violet, 'all those names?'

'Well, when I first met him, he was going under the name of Padraig Devereux.'

Violet started slightly, and shivered as if there was a sudden draught.

'Are you all right?' asked Madeleine. 'You've gone rather pale.'

'Yes, I was just a bit taken aback. That name... it makes sense now.'

'What does?'

The baby wriggled on Violet's lap, demanding attention. 'Oh dear, I think he needs changing.'

'Please go on,' said Elizabeth. 'What makes sense?'

'Well, when we christened Freddie, Charles insisted his middle name should be Padraig. When I asked him why, he wouldn't tell me. Now I understand. The thing is – why did he fight under an assumed name?'

Madeleine shook her head. 'I don't know. I think he thought it was rather romantic. When we got married he put Devereux as his middle name on the marriage certificate. "Charles Frederick Devereux Carmichael". It was such a mouthful.'

'Are you allowed to do that?' asked Violet, always a stickler for rules. 'I mean... he wasn't registered as Devereux at birth, was he?'

'I don't think so. Anyway, no one said anything. Things were a bit slipshod after the war.'

Wheeling the baby back home after lunch, Violet mused on what she had learned. At least she now understood the significance of her own baby's name, but why had Charles joined up as Padraig Devereux? It made no sense.

Towards the end of the afternoon, Violet was setting the table in the sitting room when she heard Charles's familiar cough in the hall. 'Down here,' she called out.

He looked tired and grey-faced, and sank down exhausted into his armchair.

'Are you all right?' she asked. 'You look awful.'

'Bit of a cold, I think. Must have caught something.' He lit a cigarette, and coughed violently.

'I do wish you wouldn't smoke – you really ought to take more care of your lungs.'

'Don't go on, Violet. I think I'll lie down.'

'All right. But don't forget – they're coming at seven.'

'Who are?'

'Madeleine and Elizabeth.'

'Must they?' he sighed, getting to his feet.

'Yes. They're looking forward to it – especially Elizabeth. Please be kind, Charles.'

Just before the guests were due to arrive, Violet looked into Charles's room. He was lying on top of the bed fully clothed. His face was flushed, and she felt his forehead. 'Oh, Charles, you're burning up.'

She telephoned the doctor.

'Open the window, and get him to drink plenty of water. It'll probably pass – it's just a cold, I suspect. But if you're worried, I can pop in tomorrow.'

When the ladies arrived, Violet made his excuses. 'I'm so sorry, but Charles is really not well. I thought he was just tired, but he's got a fever.'

'Oh, poor Dad... can I see him?'

'Elizabeth,' said Madeleine, 'you don't want to catch something. You're about to go back to work.'

'I just want to pop my head in.'

Elizabeth opened his bedroom door and slipped inside, closing it behind her, leaving Madeleine and Violet in the hall.

'Well,' said Violet, smiling. 'I suppose we'd better leave her to it. Why don't you come downstairs while I check on the dinner?'

23

Charles

Charles was aware of someone coming into his room – a gentle footfall on the wooden floor, the scent of jasmine and roses.

He opened his eyes and saw a beautiful girl sit down by his bed; she took his hand. 'Hello,' she said quietly.

He smiled. 'Hello, angel. I missed you.'

'That's nice. I'm sorry you're ill.'

'I'm all right now you're here.'

'I just wanted to see how you are,' she said, surprised by this show of affection.

'Pain... here,' he murmured, touching his chest.

'I'm so sorry. I'm sure it will pass soon.'

'Perhaps.' Charles closed his eyes, and felt the girl withdraw her hand. 'Don't go, Maddy,' he whispered, grabbing her hand back. 'Please don't leave me.'

'Don't worry, I'll be back soon. Try and sleep.'

He closed his eyes again, and heard the door close.

Lying in the darkness, in the throes of his fever, he was back in the trenches... back in the horror of war.

. . .

Within days of joining up as Private Padraig Devereux, Charles was sent to Belgium. His regiment were billeted temporarily in Poperinge – a small town a few miles from Ypres. On their route march into town, they passed a young man in British army uniform tied to a post by the side of the road. The lad was clearly dead, and was riddled with bullet holes.

'What the hell has happened here?' he asked the soldier next to him in the column.

'He must be a deserter,' replied the man, an Irishman. 'The army shoot them, and leave them there for a few days, *pour encourager les autres*.'

Charles didn't speak French, but he understood the man's meaning. 'Oh, I see. Bit grim, isn't it? I mean... no one deserts for fun.'

'No, I suppose not. But they can't let people think it's OK. Otherwise we'd all be doing it, wouldn't we?'

The soldier had laughed, but Charles felt a cold shiver run through his body. He recalled the day when he had fled his first regiment, his heart racing as he ran at dawn from his barracks, praying the guards would still be asleep. He remembered the fear as he emerged on the other side of the barrack wall, running through the woods, tears streaming down his face, his heart pounding in his chest. He thought too of the injustice of it all. He had not deserted out of fear – at least not fear of fighting. His fear was more complex, more dangerous. But the fact was this: if his desertion from his first regiment was ever discovered, he might end up like that corpse strapped to a post.

In those first few days in Belgium, he worried that he might bump into his old pals Jimmy and Tom. Then his new identity as Padraig Devereux would be well and truly blown. But to his relief, he soon discovered their regiment had been sent to Picardy in France – near the banks of the River Somme, a hundred miles or more from Ypres. There was no chance of a casual meeting.

Charles spent the next three years in the trenches. These twelve-foot-deep ditches were dug by the soldiers and provided the only protection from enemy fire. This was where hundreds of thousands of men lived, ate, slept and fought – lives of extreme tedium and filth, punctured by occasional terrifying skirmishes. Some of these involved night-time raids, in which whole battalions would cross into no-man's-land, hurling grenades into the enemy trenches, or attack with bayonets.

The aim was to move the line forward and take enemy territory, but their attempts rarely achieved the desired result. After one such excursion, during which many of his battalion were killed, Charles asked the sergeant major what the strategy was.

The man stared at him with contempt. 'Strategy, lad, strategy? We're destroying their morale, that's what the strategy is. And if I were you, I'd keep my daft questions to myself.'

Charles soon realised that, once you had accepted that you were going to die, you could get through it. As you lobbed a grenade, or, more rarely, engaged in hand-to-hand combat with the enemy, you would tell yourself: 'You're going to die anyway, so fight as if it's your last moment on earth.'

Now, nearly thirty years later, as Charles lay sweating in his narrow bed in his Holland Park flat, his mind flooded with images he had tried for decades to forget. Men, their limbs lost, lying screaming in agony, horses shot from beneath their riders, their beautiful carcasses lying lifeless in the mud, their dark eyes staring up at the sky until the birds picked the sockets clean. Sometimes, if the Boche had deployed their big artillery, horses were thrown up into the sky in the explosions. On occasion their corpses landed in the branches of trees. The first time Charles saw a horse hanging lifeless in such a fashion, he could scarcely believe his eyes. It seemed to defy gravity.

'How on earth did it get up there?' he asked the sergeant major.

The man, a professional soldier who had fought in the Boer War, stared at him witheringly. 'It climbed up there by itself, you idiot. How do you think?'

Back in the autumn of 1915, and six months into his time in the trenches, Charles was washing his socks one morning in a bucket of filthy water, relieved his feet were getting a little air, when he heard his name being called out across the trench. 'Paddy Devereux... as I live and breathe.'

He recognised the Dublin accent instantly, and part of him was pleased. Michael Reilly had been a good friend, after all. But his arrival would also make life more complicated, and more lies would have to be told.

'Reilly, you old dog,' Charles shouted back. 'I wondered when you'd finally turn up. I've been waiting for you.'

They had hugged, slapping one another on the back, laughing.

'How's your mother?' asked Charles.

'Oh, she's well. She said if I found you I was to send you her love. She was mighty cross with you for deserting us.'

'*Deserting*,' thought Charles. It was an odd choice of word. 'Yes, well, I'm sorry about that. But we're together now, and I haven't forgotten my promise to look after you.'

'Ach... I don't need looking after.'

. . .

Somehow the weeks turned into months and then years, with 'Padraig Devereux' and Michael Reilly fighting bravely, often side by side. In some curious way, Charles almost enjoyed it. He relished the sense of purpose and camaraderie. He slotted easily into his new identity. It suited him in some ways to be the orphan boy with a love of literature and the heart of a lion. He volunteered for several dangerous missions into no-man's-land and often went alone at night to spy on the enemy.

But no amount of bravery, no amount of companionship could root out the guilt he felt at the pain he had caused his family.

This guilt was never more in evidence than when the others in his regiment received post from home. As they pored over these letters, sharing the odd titbit with their comrades, some noticed that there were never any letters for Paddy Devereux.

'I'm an orphan,' he would reply calmly. 'At least it means I have no one to worry about. If I'm blown up no one will miss me.'

'Is that why you keep volunteering for these dangerous nocturnal excursions?' asked Michael Reilly, smiling.

'Perhaps,' replied Charles.

'You know, if you died, I'd miss you and so would my mother.'

'Thank you. You're a good friend,' said Charles, slapping Michael on the back.

Of course, he did mind. Charles often thought of his family. He wondered if Tilly had married. He agonised about his own mother, and how she had coped with the news of his death. The thought of her struggling through each day, believing her only son was dead, tortured him. He worried that she might even have *died* from grief, not knowing he was still alive.

. . .

Being an Irish regiment, they had a Catholic padre, who was a comforting presence. Although Charles had been brought up in the Church of England, he had been beguiled by the Catholic faith while in Dublin. He decided to convert to Catholicism.

'Why?' asked the padre.

'I have something to confess.'

'Well, while it's true that God will forgive your sins if you are truly repentant, it's not a panacea. You must first truly believe.'

'I understand, Father.'

Over the next few weeks, Charles studied the Bible and took lessons from the padre in the Catholic faith. Finally, the padre announced he was ready.

'I think it's time for your initiation. You will first be baptised, then confirmed, and will receive Holy Communion. We could start tomorrow, if there's no action planned.'

That night, as Charles and Michael sat in their trench heating up some bully beef over a Primus stove, the CO approached.

'Private Devereux, I have a job for you. Tonight, there will be total cloud cover, and consequently no moon. As such, the conditions are perfect for getting out into no-man's-land and inspecting the enemy trenches. Things have gone a bit quiet over there, and I need to know if they have retreated.'

'Very good, sir.'

'Good man. Finish your supper first, then go.'

'I'll go with him,' offered Michael Reilly.

'No, Reilly, you stay here. This needs to be a solo operation. It needs total silence. You two never stop talking, and I can't take the risk that you might be overheard. It could be fatal.'

The CO took Charles aside, hand on shoulder. 'Crawl on your belly all the way across no-man's-land. Once on the other side, if their trench is empty, make notes of what you see – ammo, equipment and so on. Good luck.'

. . .

After dark, Michael Reilly helped Charles up the makeshift ladder and out of the trench. 'Good luck, my friend,' he whispered. 'I'll be waiting for you.'

'Thanks,' Charles replied. 'If I don't make it... I'm glad to have known you.'

Once out of the protection of the trench, Charles began to crawl on his stomach, past the stinking corpses of horses and the limbs of his comrades, now rotting in the mud. The task looked daunting. Over two hundred yards of ground stretched ahead of him. But he focussed, and began to mouth 'Hail Marys' to himself. The closer he got to the German trench, the more confident he was that it was empty. Tentatively, he sat up on his haunches, alert for the slightest sound. It was eerily silent. He stood up, half expecting to be hit by a hail of bullets, but none came. He walked slowly towards the trench and dropped down inside. Walking along its length, he noted abandoned mugs and pans, a defunct paraffin stove lying on its side, and a pile of blankets soaked with rain and mud. It looked as if the Germans had left in a hurry. Further along into the trench, he found a complex series of 'rooms' dug into the earth, which showed evidence they might once have contained ammunition and weapons, now long gone. He made copious notes before replacing his notebook in his tunic pocket. He made one final patrol up the trench, and was about to climb a ladder and walk back towards the British lines when he found a German soldier lying face down in the mud. Charles prodded him with the bayonet on his rifle, and kicked him gently with his boot, but the man didn't stir.

Confident he was safe, Charles began to walk back to his own lines. Suddenly, from behind, there was a hail of artillery, and the unmistakeable stench of mustard gas. Looking over his shoulder, he saw the shells had landed several hundred yards to the west, and the gas was being blown rapidly towards him. Charles hurriedly put on his gas mask and began to run towards his own trench. But a few yards further on, a shot rang out. It hit him full force in the left leg, and he collapsed, as an agonising pain spread up his body. In spite of the mask, his lungs, which had been exposed for no more than a second, felt as though they were on fire. Terrified that whoever had fired the shot would come after him and finish him off, he lay doggo, pretending to be dead. His lungs hurt so much he could barely breathe.

Drifting in and out of consciousness, he couldn't judge the passage of time, but after a while it occurred to him that the enemy weren't coming. They must have thought they'd killed him.

Rain began to fall, and his uniform, already soaked with mud and blood, became sodden. What struck him was how quiet it was; he felt a sort of peace and began to prepare himself for death. He just wished he had made his first confession to the padre. He could have done with explaining everything properly to God before they met.

As dawn broke, the clouds cleared. Charles managed to lift his head a little, and saw the sun hovering on the horizon like a giant orange orb. Suddenly, he felt a rush of happiness, and wanted desperately to live. Moments later, the silence was broken by an aeroplane engine. Charles made a superhuman effort and rolled himself onto his side, raised his arm and waved. The biplane flew overhead and away, and at first Charles thought they hadn't seen him. But the plane returned a few minutes later and did a loop, flying low, and Charles managed to raise his arm again and wave. The plane flew off, but an hour or so later he found himself being heaved onto a stretcher and back to the British trench.

'Good God, Devereux,' said his CO, when he saw him, 'we

thought the gas might have got you, then we heard the shot – we were sure you were a goner.'

'No sir,' replied Charles weakly.

'Anything to report, Private?'

'The enemy appear to have retreated, sir.' Charles handed the CO his notebook. Then he fainted.

24

Violet

Elizabeth joined her mother and Violet in the sitting room.

'How is Charles?' asked Violet.

'Oh, all right, I think. He was rather feverish and seemed to be hallucinating a little.'

'Oh dear,' said Violet. 'He does suffer so with his chest. I'd better send for the doctor tomorrow.'

'Would you rather we went home?' asked Madeleine.

'Oh no,' replied Violet. 'I mean, there's nothing we can do for him, is there?'

'No, exactly. He just needs to rest.'

After dinner, the three women sat companionably around the fire, glasses of port in hand.

'Would you mind if I asked you a little more about your time with Charles?' asked Violet. 'If it's not too... intrusive?'

Madeleine shrugged. 'There's not much more to tell.'

'How long was he in hospital?'

'Oh, at least eighteen months.'

'Gosh... why so long?'

'He had a very complicated leg injury – for a long time they considered amputation. And he'd been gassed, of course.'

'Yes, he told me that. I wish he wouldn't smoke,' said Violet. 'I worry so.'

'Quite right. His lungs were damaged – although, many were far worse off.'

'You mentioned something earlier about him fighting under an assumed name. How did you find out about that?'

'Oh, do we really want to dig all that up, Violet?' said Madeleine, a little impatiently.

'If you don't mind, I would like to understand.'

'Yes do, Ma, I'm fascinated,' added Elizabeth.

'All right, if you insist. It's a bit complicated. When I first met him in the field hospital, he went by the name Private Padraig Devereux. I used to call him Paddy – just a classic shortening of the name, you know. A lot of the Irish boys were Paddy. Except he wasn't Irish, of course. At least, he had no Irish accent. His real name – his birth name, if you like – was revealed a little later.'

'How?' asked Violet.

'We'd both been back in England for many months, and to our relief, he began to get better. One day he asked if I could send a telegram for him.'

'Who to?' said Violet.

'To his sister. I thought it was a bit odd, because I was under the impression that he had no family.'

'What made you think that?'

'I'd heard it somewhere, or perhaps he'd told me. I can't really remember. He never got any visitors, so maybe I just presumed. Anyway, he insisted I send this telegram.'

'Saying what?'

'I can't recall the words exactly, but I do remember this. He signed it "Bruv". He handed me a piece of paper with the words he wanted sent, and I said, "who is Bruv?"

"It's me, of course," he said. "It's my sister's pet name for me. As soon as she sees it, she'll know it's from me."

'I said, well, why not just put your proper name, then she'll definitely know who it's from.

'He got a bit agitated about that, I remember, and said, "If you won't send it I'll find someone who will". So of course I sent it. I didn't want to upset him.

'Then a few days later, this woman turns up. She was young, just twenty or so. She stood at the end of his bed and burst into tears. In fact, she made such a noise the other patients began to complain. Anyway, I found her a chair, and closed the curtains around them. I thought perhaps she was his girlfriend, and the sister thing was just to put me off the scent.

'She left after an hour or so and then his parents turned up the following day. His mother – gosh, I remember this – she howled like an animal when she saw him. Fell to the ground and actually howled. Her daughter had to comfort her. And Paddy, well, he wept too. I remember that. His father just stood and stared, shaking his head, as if he was seeing a ghost.

'A few days later his sister came back, but this time with her husband, who was a policeman.

'Another month or so went by, and Charles had another visitor. Not a relative this time, I'm sure of that. He was rather brusque, and insisted they shouldn't be disturbed. I suspect he was military.'

'What makes you think that?' asked Violet.

'Oh, something about the bearing. He wore a trench coat and a trilby, I recall.'

'And then what happened?' asked Violet, on the edge of her seat.

'Nothing too dramatic. Within a few weeks Charles was well enough to leave. On the day he was due to go out, he told me that he was in love with me. He said, "Once I get settled, will you marry me?"'

'I'd call that pretty dramatic,' said Elizabeth. 'It's like something out of a romantic novel.'

'Do you think so? Anyway, I said yes. I mean, how could I say no?'

'How indeed,' said Violet.

'We married on Christmas Day,' said Madeleine, blushing. 'The church was full of red flowers and holly – it was very charming. He'd dropped the Padraig thing by then. Told me it was just a youthful fancy – that his real name was Charles. But I still called him Paddy... he was always Paddy to me, you see.

'Anyway, he needed a job, of course, so my father, who owned a garage, offered to start him off selling cars – it was a new thing back then. But Charles wasn't interested. "I've got plans of my own," he told my father.

'We lived with my parents at the start, but a few weeks later – it was the early spring, I recall – Charles came home and said he had got a job working for the government. Board of Trade. My father was very impressed. So that was it... we moved into a flat on the Cromwell Road, I got pregnant, and then within a year or so he was offered this post in China – something to do with import/export. I felt it would be impossible to go there with a six-month-old baby. But Charles said it was a chance of a lifetime. So off he went. I moved back in with my parents, and that was the end of us...'

'Oh Ma... that's so sad.' Elizabeth reached across and took her mother's hand.

'It's all right, darling. We coped, didn't we? But it's so strange that he's now come back into our lives. And Violet, I do want you to know that I hold no grudge against you or him. It was all a lifetime ago, after all. And I'm glad he has found someone he could settle down with. I suspect he and I were never really suited. Falling in love in such dramatic circumstances is bound to fail, isn't it?'

. . .

Later that evening, Violet stood in the hall, saying goodbye to her guests.

'Give Dad my love, won't you?' said Elizabeth. 'I hope he's better in the morning.'

'Yes of course,' said Violet. Then, turning to Madeleine, she added. 'Thank you for your frankness this evening. I do so appreciate it.'

'That's all right,' replied Madeleine. 'Charles is a conundrum that none of us will ever solve, I suspect. I sometimes think he'll go to his grave shrouded in mystery. Perhaps it's best not to dig too deep. Good night, Violet.'

25

Charles

Charles woke to the sound of women talking outside in the hall, and peered at the bedside clock. It was quarter to eleven and his fever had passed. Shivering, he pulled the covers up around his ears.

He listened as his ex-wife made her little speech about him. He couldn't hear everything, but he heard enough to make him anxious. What had she said? 'Charles is a conundrum'. She'd got that right.

The front door slammed shut and he heard the sound of women's shoes clip-clopping up the road. He braced himself for Violet entering the room, but she paused outside his door and then went into her own room. He heard her low voice as she soothed the baby.

Lying in the dark, his mind drifted back to the end of the war, and the day his career had really begun.

After about eighteen months in hospital, he had woken one morning to find a tall man wearing a trilby hat and trench coat standing at the end of his bed. Charles had recognised instantly the bearing of a military man, or perhaps a policeman. Either way, his heart began to race.

'Ah, good, you're awake,' said the stranger.

'I'm sorry... who are you?'

'I would have thought the real question is who are you? Are you Private Padraig Devereux, or could you perhaps be Private Charles Carmichael?'

Charles – or Paddy, as he still thought of himself at that time – felt a shudder of anxiety. His sister and her husband, John, had promised a few weeks earlier that they would 'sort things out'. 'You've fought bravely for your country,' said John. 'I can't believe they'll punish you now. Leave it with me and I'll see what can be done.'

Except now, faced with this fearsome man, Charles worried that his brother-in-law's intervention had simply made things worse. Was he about to be arrested for desertion after all these years?

'May I sit?' asked the stranger. Not waiting for an answer, he turned to the nurse. 'We must not be disturbed. Pull the curtain round, and tell everyone to leave us alone.'

Charles's visitor had a natural authority that he found rather alarming. The man's eyes were now at Charles's level. 'So, how are you, Private?'

'Not too bad, thanks, sir. On the mend, you know.'

'That's good to hear. Now, I need hardly tell you that desertion is a capital offence.'

Charles decided that silence was the best policy. He was determined not to say more than was necessary.

'Having said that,' the man went on, 'we are prepared to make an exception in your case.'

'An exception, sir?'

'Yes... your – how can I put it – your ability to dissimulate, to take on another identity, has impressed us greatly. It takes a certain sort of man to carry off that sort of thing.'

Charles wondered nervously what was coming.

'Your reasons for doing what you did all those years ago don't interest us. After all, you fought with distinction for more than three years. No country could ask more of its young men. And you were nearly killed performing an act of extreme heroism out in no-man's-land. Your CO speaks very highly of you, you'll be glad to know.'

The man removed a notebook from his pocket, flipped it open and began to read: 'Private Devereux is a highly resourceful, ingenious, intelligent man, afraid of nothing and no one.' He snapped the book shut. 'It's rather a flattering description. Are you pleased?'

Charles shrugged.

'So, Private, no one could accuse you of cowardice. What I want to know is if you would be prepared to continue that heroism on behalf of your country.'

'I might,' said Charles, aware that his leg was beginning to throb. 'But I am injured, you know. Not quite the man I was.'

'Yes, yes, we know all that. I've seen your medical records. As it happens, we recruited quite a few injured during the last war. They were invaluable in Belgium – a man with a crutch is rarely challenged, particularly if they speak French. Do you speak French?'

'No,' replied Charles.

'Pity. Now, of course, I needn't shy away from pointing out that you deserted your first regiment which, as I said before, is a capital offence. However, there is something you can do to wipe the slate clean.'

'And what is that, sir?'

'You can work for us.'

'And who are you, sir?'

'We, Private, are the SIS – the Secret Intelligence Service.'

~

Charles must have fallen asleep, because he woke to find Violet standing over him, holding a tray.

'How are you?' she asked. 'I've brought you some breakfast – an egg and soldiers.'

'That's kind. I'm much better, I think. The fever's gone. Still got a bit of a cough, you know, but nothing I can't manage.'

'Will you stay at home today?'

'Possibly. I was supposed to have a meeting later. I'll see how I feel.'

'Well, don't overdo it. If you don't mind, Freddie and I are going out for an hour or two. Will you be all right on your own? I've left some of the casserole from last night for your lunch. Just pop it in the oven for half an hour.'

'Will do... see you later.'

After Violet left the house, Charles got up. He ate his breakfast sitting at his desk. His cold seemed to be receding, and he decided to get on with his day as planned. He was due back in Oxford that evening, but first he had a meeting with his boss at number 54, The Broadway. He washed and dressed, then packed his suitcase, intending to go to the station directly after his meeting. The manuscript for his latest novel, *Chinese Chapter*, lay invitingly on the desk, but regretfully he placed it in a buff-coloured folder and put it in his suitcase.

He then wrote a note to his wife, which he left on the kitchen table.

The suitcase felt heavy as he walked towards Holland Park tube station. It might have been more sensible to leave his things at home and collect them later, but he was keen to avoid an interrogation from Violet. From what he had overheard the previous evening, he felt sure his wife was on to him in some way. Years of training had given him a sixth sense about that sort of thing.

Emerging from Green Park tube station, Charles decided to walk to Broadway through the park. The sun was shining and, in spite of the heavy suitcase, he felt the need for fresh air. He crossed the Mall and entered St James's Park. The flower beds had been dug up at the start of the war to construct a network of underground air-raid tunnels. The whole area had turned into a sea of mud, which was a terrible eyesore. Worse, he knew the tunnels filled with water when it rained, making them almost useless in a raid.

The elongated pond at the centre of the park glittered in the sunlight, tempting Charles to sit on a bench and admire what was left of the view. Lighting a cigarette, he was startled to hear his name called out. 'Charles, how are you, dear chap?'

He looked up, but couldn't identify the man against the bright sun. 'I'm sorry,' he said, 'do I know you?'

'I should bloody well hope so... it's me, Simon.' The man moved away from the sun's glare, and his face came into view.

'Simon! Apologies – the sun was in my eyes. How nice to see you.'

'It's good to see you too. Gosh, it's been months. It was December, wasn't it? The baby's christening.'

'Yes, yes.' Charles got to his feet and the two shook hands.

'So, where have you been, Charles? We've missed you at the club.'

'Oh, you know, work.'

'Really? You normally manage to combine work with pleasure. Speaking of which – do you have time for a quick snifter?'

'Well, I'm on my way to a meeting,' said Charles. 'I'm not sure...'

'Oh, go on. There's a pub just round the corner – it's two minutes away.'

Somewhat reluctantly, Charles followed Simon to the Two Chairmen, which displayed a sign saying *the oldest pub in England.*

'You get a table,' suggested Simon, 'while I get the drinks. Pint?'

'Please,' said Charles.

'Something to eat?'

'Yes, perhaps a sandwich,' said Charles, realising he would need something to eat before his meeting that afternoon.

The pair sat in a dark corner, nursing their drinks.

'So how have you been?'

'Busy,' replied Charles. 'I've been moved up to Oxford, hence not being around.'

'Oxford? What on earth for?'

'Lots of government departments have been moved out – space and so on.'

'And Violet?'

'Oh, she stayed at home. Better that way.'

'And how's my godson?'

'Doing well, thank you. The little lad is growing fast.'

'I must pop in and see him.'

'Do, please. Violet would like that.'

There was an awkward silence.

'Charles...' Simon fiddled with the beer mats on the table.

'Yes.'

'About that night at the club with Michael Reilly?'

Charles flushed. In spite of his best efforts, he had never been able to conquer his response to embarrassment. 'Yes...'

'It was all a bit odd,' Simon went on. 'Reilly was so convinced he knew you, and... well, it was strange that he mentioned two names that do actually mean something to you – Padraig and Devereux. I mean, after all, you'd just christened your son Padraig, and Devereux is your damn pen-name.'

'Yes, I do see how it must all seem rather odd.'

'So, what's it all about? Why the mystery?'

Charles racked his brains. He couldn't possibly reveal his

secret now. But his training had taught him long ago that, in order to be convincing, a lie needed to contain a seed of truth.

'The thing is, Simon, it's a bit hush-hush.'

'Oh, I see. Well, I don't want to put you in a difficult position... but now you've rather whetted my appetite.'

Simon looked deeply in Charles's eyes, with an expectant look and Charles realised he would have to give him something.

'I have met Reilly before – during the last war. But at that time I was involved in some undercover work for the government, about which Reilly knew nothing. The Irish republicans were very active then, if you recall. They tried to take advantage of the Great War to end British rule.'

'Oh, so was Reilly one of them – a republican?'

'Not exactly. It's more complex than that, but I'm not allowed to talk about it. All part of my past, you understand – but I did sign the Official Secrets Act, and I am still a government employee. So, if it came out... well I'm sure you understand.'

'Oh, my goodness, of course, national interest and all that.' Simon smiled broadly and emptied his pint glass. 'Do you know, Charles, that's such a relief. There have been all sorts of mad rumours swirling around the club. I didn't know what to say or think. But I should have realised, knowing you as I do, that you couldn't have been involved in anything disreputable. Not you. Oh, my dear chap, that is a relief.'

The pair sat in silence for a moment, as both reflected on these revelations.

'Just one thing, old man,' Simon said eventually. 'Do I have your permission to stifle some of the worst rumours? Try and put it about that there was nothing underhand – all above board, King and country, and all that. That it was a misunderstanding on Reilly's part – who's a bit of a drunk by all accounts. He's been banned from the club too. Anthony d'Courcy was jolly embarrassed about the whole thing.'

'Yes, all right. Please do scotch the rumours if you like. Just don't overdo it,' said Charles with an inner sigh of relief. 'By the way, is Reilly still in London, do you know?'

'Don't think so. He was only over here on business, which is how he met Anthony, who invited him to the club. He's back in Ireland, I think.'

'I see. Thank you, Simon.'

'Not at all, old chap. Hopefully see you at the club soon. We've all missed you.'

'I'd like that very much. When I'm next down from Oxford.'

'Good. And let's hope this wretched war is over soon and we can all return to normal. The park is looking like a bloody quagmire.'

'Quite...'

Walking away from the pub towards Broadway, Charles reflected on this chance encounter. He hoped he had said just enough to stifle the rumours. At least now he could go to the club without fear of an embarrassing encounter. But he had a flash of guilt about denying his friend Michael Reilly, who had been such a good and loyal companion in those harsh years of the war. Charles hoped he would find it in his heart to forgive the betrayal.

26

MARCH 1944

Violet

The conversation with Madeleine the previous evening, and the strange notebook she had found in Charles's suitcase, had piqued Violet's curiosity. Determined to find out more about Charles's past, she had arranged for Elizabeth to babysit that morning. Now, she wheeled Freddie in his pram up the road, and rang the bell of number 43.

'Morning, Violet,' said Elizabeth, opening the door. 'Thank you for last night – lovely supper.'

'Oh, you're welcome. Are you still OK to have the baby?'

'Of course. How long will you be?'

'Oh, just a few hours. I should be back just after lunch. There are two bottles of formula in the pram, and if he seems hungry perhaps you could mash up some cooked carrot or apple. Is that all right?'

'Absolutely. Now off you go. See you later.'

Elizabeth wheeled the baby into the hall, and shut the door. Violet headed for Holland Park Avenue and the Green Line bus stop. Her destination was Enfield and Charles's sister, Tilly.

The bus arrived in the town centre just after eleven o'clock. Violet set off to walk through the suburban streets towards her parents-in-law's house. When Tilly and John had married, they initially moved into her parents' small terraced house. A few years later they had moved to a three-bedroom semi-detached in a quiet suburban road. Approaching the house, Violet admired the tidy front garden with its neat path leading to the front door.

She rang the bell, hoping her mother-in-law would be out – it would make the conversation easier.

To her relief, it was Tilly who opened the door. She retained the slight cockney twang her brother had long since extinguished. 'Violet! What a nice surprise. Come in. Is everything all right?'

'Yes, fine. I'm so glad you're in. It's so tricky to make arrangements without a telephone.'

'We don't feel the need for one. I rarely go out these days. Come in. I'm in the front room, writing.'

'Writing?'

'Yes, didn't my brother tell you? I've started writing short stories. I've already had three accepted by women's magazines.'

'No, he didn't say. How marvellous – two writers in the family. Well done.'

The front room had been set up like a study with a desk in the window. As with her brother, a typewriter took pride of place.

Violet peered at it. 'Oh, it's an Imperial, just like Charles's. Very grand.'

'It was John's present to me for our wedding anniversary. It will be thirty years next year,' said Tilly. 'I can hardly believe it. He was going to wait and give me the typewriter then, but I begged him to let me have it early.'

'Quite right,' said Violet.

'Would you like some tea? Or coffee? It's only Camp coffee, I'm afraid.'

'Tea is fine. Are your parents here?'

'No, they've gone away for a few days – to Suffolk, on the coast.'

'How nice.'

'I had to persuade them. Mum's had a bad chest all winter, and I thought she needed some clean air. They're in a little bed and breakfast. John drove them down on Saturday and will collect them at the weekend.'

'John's a nice man, isn't he?'

'He is – he's very loyal. You'd have to be to live with my parents all these years.' Tilly raised her eyebrows.

'That sounded rather heartfelt,' said Violet.

'Oh, I shouldn't complain. But it's not as if we couldn't afford our own house – John has a reasonable salary. The trouble is I promised to look after them all those years ago, and I can't bring myself to abandon them now. I worry it would break my mother's heart, and she's had enough of that in her life.' She paused, blushing. 'Sorry, I don't know what brought that on. Shall we have some tea in the kitchen?'

She led the way down the narrow hall to the kitchen at the back. A little dresser stood along one wall; painted pale blue, it was arranged with oddments of china. Tilly put the kettle onto the gas stove, while Violet looked out of the window. A neat lawn was edged with colourful flower beds, and at the far end espaliered fruit trees provided a backdrop for a vegetable plot.

'The garden looks nice.'

'Yes, that's John's work – he loves gardening. He's got an

allotment too, so we have fresh veg. He's ever so good with his hands.'

The two sat at the kitchen table, a pot of tea between them. 'I've got no biscuits, I'm afraid,' said Tilly. 'If Mum were here, there would be cake.'

'It doesn't matter. I came to see you, not to eat biscuits.'

'So, what can I do for you, Violet?'

'I wanted to speak to you about Charles – or, should I say, Bruv.'

Tilly looked across the table at Violet with her piercing blue eyes. 'How did you know about that? Only the family knows I call him Bruv.'

'Madeleine told me.'

Tilly frowned. 'Madeleine?'

'Yes, Charles's first wife.'

'Is she... have you... met, then?'

'Yes. It turns out we live opposite them – Madeleine and their daughter, Elizabeth.'

'Good God. How extraordinary.'

'Yes, isn't it? A real coincidence. Charles and Elizabeth met in the street quite by accident about nine months ago. Since then we've got friendly. In fact, they came to supper last night, except Charles couldn't join us – he was ill in bed.'

'Nothing bad, I hope?'

'No, just a cold. Anyway, over supper I asked Madeleine how she met Charles, and she told me that he had fought in Belgium – and please correct me if this is wrong – under an assumed name. Did you know about that?'

Tilly flushed, and poured them both another cup of tea. 'Yes, I did,' she said quietly.

'Do you know why?'

Tilly shook her head. 'Not really.'

'What do you mean?' Violet frowned.

'The fact is, I don't know why he did it. He was always a

romantic with grand ideas. He wanted a different life from the one he was born into. Perhaps it was that.'

'That's exactly what Madeleine said. But do people really go into war thinking romantic thoughts like that?'

'Oh yes. The boys round here all had romantic notions before the last war. Their heads were full of heroism and how marvellous it was all going to be. How wrong they were. Thank God my John had the sense to join the police force – he didn't have to go to war, you see.'

'Your brother chose such an odd name – Padraig Devereux. Does it have any family significance?'

'No.'

'So where did he get the idea?'

'I really don't know, Violet. You must ask him.' There was an edge of irritation in Tilly's voice.

The two sat in silence for a moment. Violet was determined to get some answers. 'There was another thing I didn't understand. Apparently, he was visited in hospital by a man who Madeleine thought might have been in the military, or the police. Do you know anything about that?'

Tilly shook her head.

'I only wondered,' Violet went on, 'because it was shortly after that he got a government job – or so Madeleine said. It just seemed rather strange to me. I mean... how he got the job in the first place. After all, he had no clerical experience, or serious academic qualifications.'

'Well, I don't think the job was anything very grand, was it?' said Tilly. 'Board of Trade or something. Maybe John helped – I really can't remember now. We were all just so grateful he'd survived. Mum could hardly believe it – it took her weeks to get over the shock.'

'What shock?'

Tilly flushed again. 'Of seeing him, of course.'

'Why was it a shock? I mean, I presume they'd have been

writing to one another throughout the war. I'd have thought it would be simply relief?'

'You don't understand,' said Tilly, standing up and taking the empty cups to the sink and rinsing them under the tap. 'I'm really sorry, Violet,' she said, turning round, 'but I must get on. I'm writing a piece for *Woman's Weekly*, and they want it by tomorrow.'

'Oh, of course. I understand.' Violet stood up and began to pull on her gloves. 'Well, it's been lovely to see you again, Tilly. Please give your parents my love. And you must all come over in the summer perhaps and see the baby.'

'That would be nice, thank you. I'll see you out.'

Sitting on the bus, travelling south through Camden Town, Violet ran over their conversation. It seemed that her sister-in-law was concealing something, but what? Why was there such secrecy about Charles and his past?

Back in Holland Park, she collected baby Freddie and wheeled him home. There was no sign of Charles, but she found a note on the kitchen table.

Vi darling –

After you'd gone, I felt a bit better and decided to attend my meeting after all. If you don't mind, it's easier if I go straight back to Oxford tonight.

See you in a few weeks and kiss the baby for me.

Yours,

Charles

Violet slumped down onto a kitchen chair and put her head

in her hands, as she attempted to analyse her feelings. There was frustration, of course, and annoyance – at the way Charles could just leave without even saying goodbye. All the way back on the bus, she had been rehearsing how to raise the issue of his false name. Now she wouldn't get the chance. Once again, her husband had run away, and she was left with nothing but unanswered questions.

PART TWO

15 YEARS LATER

27

November 1959

Violet

Violet sat in the front pew of the Our Lady of Victories Church, Kensington, with her sixteen-year-old son Freddie on one side, and Elizabeth on the other. Before her, in front of the altar, lay her husband's coffin.

Six of Charles's friends from the club had stood guard over the body through the night. 'A vigil is a mark of respect,' Simon had explained, when she asked him about it.

'But you'll all be exhausted,' she said. 'Surely it would be simpler if the undertakers brought the coffin here on the morning of the service.'

'No, Violet. It's a club tradition – to honour the passing of a cherished member.'

In spite of years of ill-health, Charles's death came as a shock to his family and friends. He had retired from his job a few years earlier, and at sixty-four was enjoying a more relaxed way of life.

Each autumn he would go south, like a migrating bird, to a boarding house in St Leonards near Hastings, only returning to Holland Park in the spring when London's winter smogs had cleared. While on the south coast, he spent his days writing or walking by the sea.

'It's a perfect existence,' he had told Violet before his last departure to the coast. 'I can breathe clean air down there, I'm fed by my landlady, my bed is made for me, and I'm free to work whenever I like.'

'So, much like being at home, then,' said Violet, with just a hint of sarcasm.

Her tone was not lost on Charles. 'My dear, you don't really mind me being away, do you?'

'No, Charles, I really don't mind, I promise.'

'Are you lonely without me?'

'Sometimes, a little. It's harder during term time, when Freddie's away at boarding school. Otherwise, I'm so busy with my own life, I don't have time to be lonely. Being head of the maths department at the school is very hard work. And there's my music and other hobbies. I do wonder about you though, living like a bachelor. Don't you miss family life?'

Charles studied her face carefully. 'My dear girl, you know I've never been very good at family life. You really should never have married me. I'm an inveterate loner. When I'm away, my writing keeps me company. My characters are my companions, and they are far less trouble than real people. And it's not as if I'm gone for long, is it? Each spring, I return to Holland Park – to you, Freddie, the church and the club.' He smiled and gave her hand a reassuring pat.

Secretly Violet often wondered if it would have been more sensible to get divorced. The marriage was all but over in many ways. And yet something kept them together – a shared responsibility for their son perhaps, or simply a shared past.

For many years, she had been braced for him to abandon her completely, so this part-time marriage was a sort of blessing. She had long ago accepted that it was in his nature to run away from things – to leave when the going got tough. It was not cowardice, exactly, rather an inability to truly commit. A lifetime spent running away instead of standing his ground and dealing with whatever faced him.

Throughout their marriage there had been small clues that hinted at a secret life. The cypher book, the disappearances for 'work', his intimate knowledge of the more obscure byways of government – all that had surprised her. And yet she had never dared to question his work. Neither had she had ever challenged him about his strange alias – she had come close once or twice, but always backed away at the last minute. It was a character flaw of hers, perhaps, not to challenge, not to demand the truth. It was easier simply to get on with her own life and let him get on with his.

But now this maddening, fascinating, mercurial, handsome man she had called her husband for twenty years had gone from her life for ever. And much to her surprise, in the days before the funeral, she found herself grieving – as much for the time they had been apart as for the time spent together. She wept too for the missed opportunities – for the children they would never have, for the houses they would never own, and for the secrets that had separated them throughout their life together. But ultimately she wept because, in spite of everything, she had really loved him.

A few days before the funeral, Violet had arranged to meet Elizabeth in a coffee shop on Kensington Church Street to discuss the funeral arrangements.

She found a corner table, and ordered them both a coffee while she waited. Elizabeth arrived a few minutes later, looking tearful.

'Oh Vi, there you are.' She leaned down and kissed her on the cheek. 'I'm so, so sorry about Dad. Poor you, and poor Freddie – he's too young to lose his father.'

'Yes, it will be a shock for the poor boy.'

'Did the school tell him?'

'Yes. His housemaster rang me last night to say it was done.'

'How did Freddie take it?'

'He was upset, obviously, but being away at school he won't feel it properly, if you know what I mean. It will hit him when he gets home, I suspect.'

'When do you expect him?'

'Tomorrow. He's getting the train.'

'And how about you? Are you managing? You must miss Dad terribly.'

'Yes, of course I'll miss him. But we had... moved apart, you know. Your father spent so much time on the south coast, we ended up living separate lives in many ways.'

'Where's the service being held?'

'The principal Catholic church in Kensington. It's just reopened after being bombed back in the Blitz. I know Farm Street was Charles's favourite church, but I thought this would be more sensible – closer to home and so on.'

'Will he be buried in Kensington too?' Elizabeth asked, stirring her frothy coffee.

'No, he left very clear instructions about that in his will. He wants to be buried back in Enfield – the Lavender Hill Cemetery. He chose the plot himself. I went up there to have a look the other day. It's surrounded by countryside and is very green and quiet.'

'Goodness, that's a surprise,' said Elizabeth.

'What is?'

'I'd have thought Enfield would be the last place on earth my father would want to spend eternity. It always seemed to me that his whole life was a rejection of his past.'

Violet smiled. 'That is true. But Enfield is where he was born, and it's natural to want to return "home", as it were. The thing is, Elizabeth, so much of what your father said and did was odd. Ours not to reason why, and all that. I just hope he finds peace at last in his childhood home.'

'That sounded heartfelt,' said Elizabeth, reaching across the table to take Violet's hand. 'Do you think peace eluded him in his lifetime?'

'To some extent, yes I do,' said Violet. 'He was happy enough when he was writing, or living by the sea, but for the most part I would say he was troubled. Yes... troubled is the word I'd use.'

'By what?'

'Events in his past, I suppose. As you've already pointed out, he was always running away from things. Part of that, I suspect, was shame at his lack of formal education, his working-class background. Beyond that, he carried a lot of guilt at leaving you and your mother, at spending so much time away from me and his son, perhaps. But I think the real guilt goes back much further.'

'To when?'

'I don't really know, but it has something to do with the first war... before he met me, or even your mother. He so rarely discussed that part of his life. Lots of soldiers from that time struggled with what had happened. It was such a brutal war. I tried to get him to talk about it once – a couple of years ago – but he got so angry, I decided it wasn't worth it. But I'll find out one day, I'm sure of that.'

. . .

The following day Violet had met Freddie at Liverpool Street station. Now well over six foot, he was slender and very handsome. She ran up to him and hugged him tightly.

'You must be starving. I thought we'd have some cake,' she said brightly. 'There's a splendid new café on Notting Hill Gate.'

'That would be nice,' said Freddie.

'Let's take a taxi.'

'A taxi, Mum... Isn't that a bit expensive? We normally take the tube.'

'I know, but I can't face the tube today.'

The taxi dropped them outside the café. Newly opened, it was run by an Italian, who greeted Violet warmly and introduced himself as Gino. He guided them to a table near the window. Behind the bar was a new Italian espresso machine, which rumbled and gurgled as it frothed and steamed.

Violet ordered coffee for herself, and a hot chocolate for Freddie. 'And the boy would like cake. What do you have?'

Gino began to list an extensive range of cakes and pastries.

'Just a piece of chocolate cake, please,' said Violet, cutting him off halfway through his well-rehearsed recitation.

Freddie sipped his hot chocolate, but fiddled with his food and left most of it uneaten.

'Don't you like it?' asked Violet.

'It's very nice. It's just quite rich.'

'I'm sorry.' She reached across the table, and took his hand. 'You look very pale, darling. Are you all right?'

'I'm fine. Just tired.'

They sat together in awkward silence for a few minutes. Then Violet paid the bill, and they walked back to Clarendon Road. Standing in the hall, Violet unlocked Charles's room. 'This will be your room now,' she said. Freddie laid his suitcase on the bed by the wall. To her surprise, she saw him lean over and smell the bedlinen.

'What are you doing?' she asked.

'I wanted to see if I could still smell him. He always had such a distinctive scent... pipe tobacco, cigarette smoke, hair oil.'

Violet walked over and hugged her son. 'Oh darling. I'm so sorry. We'll miss him, won't we?'

'Of course,' Freddie replied.

'I'll leave you to unpack. I'll clear his wardrobe soon, I promise. Then you'll have more room for your things.'

Freddie came downstairs a few minutes later. Violet was just taking a casserole out of the oven. Their black cat sat on the table, staring out at the garden. The boy had found the cat as a stray kitten five years earlier at his prep school, and had smuggled it home in a cardboard box. Violet had allowed him to keep it and, thinking it was male, they had christened it Midnight. But since then Midnight had produced four sets of kittens and had been re-christened Milly.

Freddie picked the cat up and buried his face in her thick fur. She purred loudly as Freddie's tears fell onto her glossy black coat.

'Put her down now, darling. It's time to eat.'

Over lunch at the kitchen table, Violet apologised. 'I'm sorry you had to hear about Dad like that – at school, I mean.'

'It's OK.'

'Who told you?'

'Father Garvey. He called me to his study. I thought I must have done something wrong and was braced for a caning.'

'Oh darling. I'm so sorry.'

'Anyway, he was very nice. After he told me that Dad had died, he offered me a cigarette.' Freddie giggled quietly.

'He didn't!' Violet exclaimed. She roared with laughter, breaking the tension.

'He did. He said: "I expect you would like a cigarette."'

'Did you have one?'

'Of course.'

'I didn't know you smoked.'

'Everyone smokes, Mum – the boys, the masters, the staff – everyone. You get six of the best for it if you're caught, but everyone does it all the same.'

His mother tutted. 'More casserole?'

'Yes please. I'm rather hungry. Does that seem wrong?'

'No, of course not.' She reached over and squeezed his hand. 'Poor boy.'

'How did Dad die?' he asked, spooning casserole into his mouth. 'I mean, Father Garvey told me the basics, but what actually happened?'

'Do you really want to know?'

'Yes, I do. I must know.'

'All right. Well, your father was away as usual on the south coast – you know how he loved St Leonards. Oddly, this time he left his typewriter at home before he went, so I knew he wasn't feeling on top of the world. He'd had a bad chest for weeks, and our doctor said it would do him good – the sea air and so on. But while he was there he took a turn for the worse. His landlady called the doctor, who put him into hospital. I went down to see him that weekend, and the doctors were very encouraging. They said they were treating the chest infection, and he was in the best place. They implied there was nothing to worry about. But while I was there, your father kept talking to me about his regrets, how he wished things had been done differently. He asked me to call on Tilly and tell her what was happening. He wanted to see her, he said. That was when he mentioned that he'd chosen a plot for his burial. I told him not to overdramatise things. I said he was being theatrical as always. I regret that now. Anyway, he asked me to go and look at the grave site. I did get a bit worried then, and suggested I should stay. I could have booked into a hotel, but he said I couldn't leave my school in the lurch, and he would be fine.

'So I came home that Saturday night. On the Sunday I went

to the cemetery. It was a lovely plot, I have to admit. I called in on Tilly afterwards. She was very worried about him, obviously, and said she'd go and see him that week. She went down on Monday, I think, and stayed for a night or two.'

'Why didn't you let me know he was ill, Mum?' Freddie's face was taut with anxiety.

'I didn't want to worry you, I suppose. And I thought he would get better. It was foolish of me. Would you have preferred to know?'

'Perhaps. It would have been less of a shock, you know?' Tears spilled down his cheeks again.

Violet reached across the table and squeezed his hand. 'I'm sorry. Forgive me?'

'Yes, of course.'

She handed him a handkerchief. 'Shall I carry on?'

'Yes please.'

'Well, after that, things went rather downhill. Late on Wednesday night, I got a call from the hospital saying he'd developed pneumonia. I got the first train down from Charing Cross on Thursday morning. I arrived at the hospital just after nine, but he'd already gone.' Violet's eyes filled with tears.

Freddie reached across the table and handed her back her handkerchief. 'I'm so sorry, Mum. That's horrid.'

A tear trickled down her face, and she wiped it away with the back of her hand. 'I was upset to miss it – not to be there with him. I felt I'd failed him in some way.'

'I'm sure you didn't. I mean, you went down earlier, and he told you to go home. You did exactly what he asked.'

'Yes, I know. I just wish they'd rung me earlier in the day. I suppose they thought I had a car and could have driven down that night. Perhaps I should have explained...'

'Maybe they should have asked,' replied Freddie. 'Not everyone has a car.'

She nodded. 'There's no pudding, I'm afraid.'

'Don't worry, Mum.'

They spent the rest of the afternoon listening to music on Violet's gramophone. Later, they played a game of whist. 'You really ought to learn bridge,' said Violet. 'Your father was a great bridge player.'

'I know. And I will one day,' said Freddie. 'But this will do – keeps us distracted.'

Violet smiled. 'Whist it is, then.'

On Sunday, she insisted Freddie accompany her to church. 'I want you to see where the service will be held.'

'The funeral's at Farm Street, surely,' said Freddie. 'I've been there with Dad several times.'

'No, we're not doing it there,' replied Violet.

'Why not? That was Dad's favourite church.'

'Kensington's closer... for his club friends, that's all.'

That night, Violet knocked on Freddie's door. 'Are you asleep?'

'No, come in.'

It seemed odd, seeing her son lying there, where her husband had lain before. 'Can't you sleep?' she asked.

'Not really. It feels odd. This room was Dad's – everything in it belongs to him.'

'We can clear it out, make it yours.'

'It's all right. I don't mind. I can feel him here – in the silk pictures he brought back from China, in the clothes hanging in the wardrobe. His desk over there... I can picture him, typing away, a glass of beer on his desk and a cigarette smoking in the ashtray beside him.'

'Yes, he loved that desk. He bought it with his first publisher's advance, apparently.'

'It's locked, you know,' said Freddie. 'I was trying to open the drawers. Where did he keep the key?'

'Do you know, I have no idea. I was married to him all these years and I've never opened that desk. He was rather funny about it. Never told me where the key was.'

'How odd. What was he hiding?' asked Freddie.

'I've no idea. Probably nothing of any importance.'

'But what about money and stuff? There might be something important in there, like bank statements, or other things you may need.'

'Well, we can worry about that later. You try and sleep now, love. Big day tomorrow.' She kissed his forehead and walked over to the door. 'Light on, or light off?'

'On please.'

'You're still frightened of the dark then?'

'Yes. Night, Mum.'

'Night, darling.'

28

Elizabeth

As the mourners gathered at the graveside, a strong north-east wind blew through the cemetery, whipping the fallen leaves into swirling spirals that hovered over the gravestones like mini-tornadoes. Although the cemetery was sandwiched between city and countryside, Elizabeth could only hear the sounds of nature – the rustling of the leaves, the cawing of crows overhead. It was the epitome of England's green and pleasant land, she thought.

Shivering, she slipped her arm through that of her husband, Danny. They had first met on that dark day when Captain Valentine had tried to rape her. Afterwards, sharing an office, they had grown close. Danny was one of the few people she felt able to confide in – he had a journalist's knack for getting people to open up. He encouraged her to speak freely about her lost love David, but also to talk about her father, and the sadness she felt that they had been separated for her entire childhood. She had said to him, 'I was lucky to have such an impressive mother – we adored each other, and she did everything for me.

But when I finally met my father I realised how much I'd missed that male presence – the firm hand, and the sense of protection only a man can provide.'

After the war, she and Danny had gone their separate ways and slipped back into their old lives – he to Fleet Street, and a job on the news desk at the *Daily Express*, while Elizabeth threw herself into her mother's business. But they stayed in touch. And slowly, over time, friendship turned to love. She often said to her mother that Danny had brought her back to life.

'You OK?' he whispered now, putting his arm round her.

'Yes, I'm fine. But I'm worried about Freddie. Violet says he's very upset, but today he's putting on such a brave face.'

'Trying to be strong for his mother, I suspect,' said Danny.

The pair watched as Violet, her face protected from prying eyes by a fine silk veil hanging from a black pillbox hat, threw a handful of earth into the grave. Freddie, whippet-thin and much taller than his mother, put a protective arm round her shoulder, before he too threw a handful of soil onto the oak coffin.

Standing alongside them were Violet's siblings, various neighbours and friends, and Tilly and her husband John. Tilly was the only mourner who wept openly. As far as the assembled mourners were concerned, Elizabeth was just a friend of the family. She had promised to keep her real relationship to her father a secret, and she had never reneged on that promise. But Tilly knew who she was; they had met occasionally over the previous decade and Elizabeth had enjoyed listening to Tilly's memories of Charles, hearing about their childhood together and his ambitions, even then, to 'be someone'.

Notable by their absence were Charles's and Violet's parents – all long dead – and, most importantly to Elizabeth, Madeleine, who had died just the year before from a catastrophic stroke.

The rites and rituals complete, the mourners began to trickle away from the grave. A fleet of cars were lined up at the entrance to the cemetery ready to take them back to Holland Park.

Elizabeth and Danny followed Violet and Freddie, and the four led the walk to the cars.

A fair-haired man in a dark blue overcoat approached Violet.

'Excuse me,' he said. 'I wanted to say how sorry I was.' He had an Irish accent, Elizabeth noted, and was rather good-looking, with twinkling blue eyes. Aged about sixty, he wore an impressive set of army medals pinned to his chest.

'Thank you,' said Violet. 'I don't think we've met.'

'My name is Michael Reilly. I knew your husband in the Great War.'

'Oh, how interesting. I do hope you'll come back with us for a drink. I'd so like to talk to you.'

'I'd be delighted.'

'It's being held at his club – perhaps you know it? The Knights of St Columba in Holland Park.'

Reilly coloured slightly, looking embarrassed. 'Oh, I'm sorry,' he stammered. 'I just remembered, I can't come this afternoon... I have a meeting in central London.'

'Oh, that's a pity,' said Violet. 'Perhaps we could meet another time.'

'If you'd really like to.'

'I would. Perhaps the day after tomorrow? My son, Freddie, will be back at school by then.'

'So, is this Charles's son?' Reilly looked across at the boy. 'It's good to meet you, Freddie. You bear an uncanny resemblance to your father as a young man.'

He shook hands with the boy, who blushed. 'How do you do, sir.'

Violet rummaged in her handbag. 'Here's my address,

Mr Reilly,' she said, proffering her card. 'The day after tomorrow, then – about seven would suit me. All right?'

The drive back to Holland Park took well over an hour, and it was after one o'clock when they finally arrived at the club. Simon, who'd gone on ahead, led Violet upstairs.

'We've taken the same room we used for Freddie's christening.'

'Thank you,' said Violet. 'That was very thoughtful.'

She stood at the doorway with her son, greeting the guests. It reminded her of a receiving line at a wedding, but with rather less to be cheerful about. Nevertheless, she smiled politely and shook hands, and accepted commiserations.

Freddie seemed in curiously high spirits, and, once everyone had arrived, he began to circulate among the guests, drink in hand.

'He doesn't seem very upset,' said Elizabeth sotto voce to Violet. 'Do you think he's all right?'

'I think he's doing his best to be grown up. Plus, I suspect he's relieved to have a few days off school.'

'Or maybe he's hiding his true feelings?' suggested Elizabeth.

'Perhaps. You must realise he has been away at boarding school since he was five, so didn't know his father very well. Charles was away a lot, and I was working, so we had no choice. I suppose he's learnt to become independent. Which is a good thing, isn't it?'

'Yes, I suppose so. As long as he's able to acknowledge his grief.'

'Yes, of course.'

'What I mean is, don't assume that his outward appearance is representative of what he's really feeling. He's probably masking his emotions.'

Violet, who well knew how to mask emotions, nodded. 'I'm sure that's very good advice. Well, I must circulate.'

While Violet chatted to her guests, Elizabeth approached Freddie. 'Hello there. How are you?'

'Hello, Aunty Elizabeth. Not bad thanks.'

'I'm sorry that we're meeting on such a sad day. Perhaps we could spend a bit of time together – and I'd love you to get to know my children. We don't see enough of you.'

'No... well, I'm away so much... school and all that.' He sounded just like his father, Elizabeth thought. It was exactly the sort of response he would have given.

'You're always welcome to spend time with us in the holidays, you know, if Mum's busy with work.'

'Mum's always busy, but I'm used to it.'

Danny joined them both. 'Hello there, Freddie. You've grown about a foot since I last saw you,' he said affectionately. 'You bearing up?'

'I'm all right, sir, thank you.'

Elizabeth interjected. 'I was suggesting Freddie might like to come over sometime and see us.'

'Of course, any time.'

'I'm going back to school the day after tomorrow, worse luck.'

'Come tomorrow then,' said Elizabeth. 'The children will be home from school by four. Come for tea. Bring your mother, if you like.'

'Thank you. I'll ask her. Well, I'd better circulate, I suppose. Isn't that what one is supposed to do?'

Elizabeth smiled, and watched Freddie joining the other guests.

'He still doesn't know, then?' Danny asked his wife.

'Know what?'

'That you're his sister.'

'No!' she hissed, before adding in a low whisper, 'Don't say anything! I promised Dad I'd never tell.'

'But surely even a teenage boy could spot the likeness between you.'

'I agree he looks very like Dad, but I'm more like my mother – everyone says so.'

'There's a lot of your father in you too.'

'As far as Freddie's concerned, I'm just Aunty Elizabeth, a neighbour who lives across the road. Mother never revealed her real part in Dad's life to him, and neither have I.'

'It's all mad... this secrecy,' said Danny, grabbing a glass of sherry from a tray as it passed by. 'It will only come back to bite you – you can be sure of that.'

'My father liked secrets,' said Elizabeth. 'It's what made him tick.'

'That's an odd thing to say. Did he have other secrets, then?'

'Oh, lots, I suspect. But you can put your investigative reporter hat away, darling. There's no story for you here. This is my family we're talking about.'

'Of course. But if you ever do want to find out what he was all about, I'm your man.'

Watching Freddie chat to the mourners that afternoon, Elizabeth thought about her husband's advice. Of course, he was right that secrets within a family were never a good idea. She wondered how long it would be before her real relationship to Freddie could be revealed.

29

Violet

The morning after the funeral, Violet knocked on Freddie's door. 'Are you awake, darling?'

'Yes, Mum. Come in.'

'Hello,' she said. 'I've brought you a cup of tea.'

'Thanks.' He pulled himself up in bed, arranging the pillows against the oak bedhead.

Violet perched on the end of the bed. 'Well done for yesterday. It was quite an ordeal.'

'Well done to you too,' he replied. 'You were amazing.'

Violet smiled. 'Drink your tea while it's hot. What would you like to do today?'

'Aunty Elizabeth invited us both over later, for tea.'

'Oh, that was kind.'

'I might do some work this morning.'

'Must you?'

'I've got exams at the end of the term.'

'All right. Well, I'll leave you. There's bread and eggs if you want breakfast. I might practise the piano if it doesn't disturb you?'

'No, I like you playing.'

Violet got up to leave.

'Mum,' Freddie said quietly. 'I spoke to Aunt Tilly yesterday.'

'Oh yes. What did she want?' Violet's tone was mildly hostile.

'You don't like her, do you?'

'Does it matter? She's never been very friendly to me. I think she resented my relationship with your father. They were always very close. Anyway, did she say anything interesting?'

'Sort of. She said this odd thing before we left.'

'What?'

'That Dad was very proud of me.'

'Well, that's not odd. Dad was proud of you – immensely so.'

'No that wasn't it. She also said, "There are things about your father that you should know, which I will tell you one day".'

'Oh, how ridiculous. She's just being melodramatic. The pair of them were dreamers – I don't know where they got it from. Their parents were very sensible, practical people.'

'What did she mean, Mum? What things?'

'I don't know, but I wouldn't worry about it. She's a very odd woman. Now get on with your schoolwork, and then we can both have a nice afternoon at Elizabeth's.'

At four o'clock, Freddie and Violet went across the road to number 43. As they walked up the path, they could hear Elizabeth's two children squabbling in the sitting room.

'It's my puzzle,' said one.

'No, it's not,' screamed the other. 'Dad gave it to *me*.'

As Violet rang the bell, they heard Elizabeth shouting, 'Will you two stop it right now!'

A few seconds later, she opened the door. 'Hello there. I'm so sorry about that. Children... honestly. Come in.'

Elizabeth led them downstairs to the kitchen, where a coffee cake sat in the middle of the table. 'Do sit down,' she said.

'You made a cake,' said Violet. 'How nice.'

'Would you like a slice?' she asked them. 'I just finished icing it.'

'Oh, yes please,' said Freddie, settling at the table.

She cut a slice and placed it in front of him. 'Tuck in. You look half-starved.'

'Dad used to say I was too thin... "all skin and bone", he'd say.' Freddie tried to smile, but his eyes welled up with tears.

'That sounds like your father,' said Elizabeth, patting his shoulder. 'Eat up. And then go into the garden. The children are dying to show you their bikes.'

Freddie let himself out through the French windows into the wintry garden to join Elizabeth's children, who were now cycling around the edge of the lawn, gouging great rings out of the turf.

'Will Freddie be all right?' asked Elizabeth, pouring herself and Violet a cup of tea. 'It's rather boring for him playing with two youngsters.'

'Oh yes. He's better here than at home. He seems a bit lost there, to be honest. The problem is we never really gave him a proper home – with his own room and so on. I feel rather bad about it now.'

'Oh Violet, don't be so hard on yourself. You did what you could.'

'We should have moved to a proper house years ago. I tried once, you know.'

'What – to move? You never said anything.'

'No... well, it was complicated.'

'I'm intrigued. Go on.'

'You won't tell Freddie?'

'No, not if you don't want me to.'

'The thing is, when Freddie was about four or five, I got pregnant again.'

'Oh, Vi, I had no idea. I didn't think...'

'That Charles and I ever slept together?'

Elizabeth blushed. 'I suppose I did mean that.'

'Well, in some ways you're right – we hardly ever did. But we had a jolly evening one summer and one thing led to another. Anyway, Charles disappeared afterwards for a few weeks. While he was away, I realised I was pregnant. I didn't tell him... I was waiting, you know, till it was safe.'

'I understand.'

'A few more weeks went by, and I pretty soon realised we couldn't stay in Clarendon Road. There was not enough room for one child, let alone two. I was a maths teacher by then, with a good salary, so I thought we should move. I found a lovely house in Wimbledon with a large garden. There was a good school nearby for Freddie. But Charles would have none of it. He was furious. He said having another baby was irresponsible, and moving was impossible. He basically refused to budge. Then, a week or two later, I lost the baby, and after that I didn't have the energy to fight.'

'Oh, Vi... I'm so sorry. I had no idea.'

Violet wiped a tear from her cheek, and smiled bravely. 'It's all right. I suppose it was not to be. It was all a long time ago now. Water under the bridge – isn't that what your father used to say?'

Their conversation was interrupted suddenly by a loud wailing from the garden. 'Oh, no, I've got a flat,' yelled Sandra. 'It's not fair. James will win now.'

Elizabeth pushed open the French doors. 'Do try to calm down, Sandra.'

'Don't worry,' Freddie called out, 'I might be able to mend it. Have you got a kit, Sandra?'

'Yes, in my saddlebag,' replied Sandra breathlessly. 'Oh Freddie, you are marvellous.'

Once the tyre was fixed, she wrapped her arms round his waist, hugging him tightly. 'Oh, Freddie, you are lovely. I wish you were my brother.'

'Do leave the boy alone,' shouted Elizabeth. 'He's fixed your bike, now get back on it.'

Sandra suddenly stuck her tongue out at her brother, who punched her in the stomach. Doubling up, Sandra began to scream, at which point Elizabeth marched out into the garden. 'Don't hit your sister like that again, and Sandra, please stop making such a racket. If you two can't play nicely, you'd better come inside.'

The children and Freddie trudged inside, their bikes abandoned on the lawn.

Violet was already standing up. 'Actually, I think we'd better be going. Freddie has to pack for school tomorrow.'

'Oh, that's a shame,' said Elizabeth. 'You will come again, won't you, Freddie?'

'Yes, of course.'

Upstairs in the hall, they put on their coats.

'Thank you very much for having me, Aunty Elizabeth,' said Freddie.

'You're very welcome, Freddie. Please come back in the holidays.'

'Oh yes, pleeease do,' said Sandra, hugging him again. 'Oh, and Freddie, come into the sitting room a minute. I want to show you my puzzle.'

'It's my puzzle!' shouted James.

'No, it's not,' said Sandra, pushing him away with one hand and pulling Freddie with the other.

She led him to the coffee table in front of the fire, where a jigsaw puzzle lay half finished. Freddie glanced up at the mantelpiece. To his surprise, there was a photograph of a man who looked remarkably like his father in army uniform. 'Is that my dad?' he asked Elizabeth.

'Oh... yes,' she said, flushing. 'Your mother gave it to me years ago. It's nice, isn't it?' Then, turning to Sandra, she said, 'Freddie really has to go now, and you have the Brownies tonight. You can show him the puzzle next time. Now get upstairs and change.'

Sandra ran into the hall and up the stairs, calling out, 'Bye Freddie,' while Elizabeth guided the boy out of the room and shut the sitting room door behind her.

'Well, goodbye then,' said Violet. 'And thank you again.'

As the front door closed behind them, Freddie could hear Sandra wailing from the hall, 'Mum, it's not Brownies tonight. Brownies is tomorrow.'

That night, Violet came to visit to her son in his room.

'Are you all right?' she asked, sitting on the edge of his bed.

'Yes, I'm fine.'

'I'm sorry you're going back to school tomorrow. I'll miss you.'

'I'll miss you too.'

Freddie pulled himself up in bed, and took his mother's hand. 'I was thinking about what Aunt Tilly said at the funeral – about there being things I should know about Dad.'

'Oh, Freddie. Pay no attention to her.'

'No, Mum. The thing is... that photograph of Dad on the mantelpiece at Elizabeth's house. Is that what Aunt Tilly was talking about?'

Violet felt her heart racing. Should this be the moment she revealed the truth about Elizabeth being Charles's daughter? It felt too soon. The ground had not been properly prepared, and she needed to discuss it with Elizabeth first. 'Of course not,' she said firmly. 'Tilly has never been to Elizabeth's house. Now, stop worrying and lie down.'

She stood up, and stroked her son's forehead. At the door, she turned. 'Sleep well, darling.'

30

Violet

Michael Reilly stood on the doorstep of Violet's house and rang the bell. She opened the door wearing a dark navy dress that emphasised how pale and thin she had become.

'Hello again, Michael. I'm so glad you could come.'

'Good evening, Violet. It's a pleasure.'

Violet led him downstairs to the sitting room. The fire was lit, and the coals were glowing cheerfully.

'What a lovely room,' said Michael, looking around.

'Thank you. It's small but cosy. Please sit down... drink?'

'Yes please.'

'I have sherry, whisky or gin.'

'Gin please – with tonic if you have it?'

'I do. I'll have the same.'

When they both were settled, Michael cleared his throat. 'It was a lovely ceremony, Violet. I'm sure Charles would have liked it.'

'Thank you. I gave it a lot of thought – the music especially.'

'I can see you're musical. I couldn't help noticing the beautiful piano.'

'It is my private passion, yes.'

'I don't recall Paddy – I mean Charles – liking music much.'

'He appreciated it, certainly, but he didn't play.'

'And how are you?' he asked.

'Oh, I'm OK,' she said briskly. 'It's an adjustment, of course, but the truth is we spent a lot of time apart. I'm quite used to living alone.'

'My own mother was widowed when my brother and I were just children,' said Reilly. 'She coped well without my father, and if I'm honest I didn't really miss him. It's an awful thing to say, but I think I was too young.'

'Our son is much the same. At sixteen, he's older than you were, but he's been away at boarding school since he was five, so he didn't see his father that much. They played cards together sometimes in the holidays, and Charles took him to his club occasionally. But the truth is, they weren't that close.'

Reilly nodded. 'Perhaps he wasn't an easy man to get close to.'

Violet studied him. 'You may be right. I don't know why, though – he had a perfectly nice family who all adored him. But something made him withdraw from the people who loved him.'

She blushed suddenly. 'I'm sorry, I don't know why I feel the need to tell you all this – you're a complete stranger, after all.'

'Maybe it's because I'm a stranger that you feel able to talk about it. And please don't apologise. I'm a plain speaker myself. If I'm honest, I too was mystified by your husband's behaviour sometimes.'

'Tell me how you met. Was it in the trenches?'

'No,' replied Michael. 'Our friendship began before that...'

Violet listened, wide-eyed.

'I met him on the first day he came to Dublin. He looked

like a tramp. Said he'd been travelling for weeks. He implied he'd come from the south, had got as far as Liverpool, and then taken the ferry to Dublin. I liked him. He had nowhere to stay, so I took him home.'

'A complete stranger?' asked Violet.

'Yes... it seems odd, I suppose. But there was something about him. He didn't call himself Charles, of course. He introduced himself as Padraig Devereux, an orphan.

'My mother took to him straight away. He was very good-looking as a young man, and was the same age as me – seventeen. Mammy treated him like her own son. My elder brother was already fighting in France, and I think she missed him. Paddy filled the gap.'

'How long did he stay with you?'

'A few months. My mother was furious when he left.'

'Why, what happened?'

'He just disappeared one morning. We woke up and found a note saying he'd joined up.'

Violet smiled. 'Charles was an expert in running away from things. Perhaps that's where it started. But Michael, I'm a little confused. There are so many things that don't make sense. Firstly, my husband was not an orphan. He had a mother and a father and a sister, called Tilly. Secondly, he wasn't seventeen in 1915. I've seen his birth certificate. He was born in 1896, so in 1915 he would have been nineteen. Why did he lie?'

'I don't know... but it seemed he lied about a lot of things.'

'And what was he doing in Dublin in the first place? It makes no sense. He always told me he joined up as soon as he could in 1914, but that obviously isn't true, is it? What was he doing for all those months?'

Reilly chuckled. 'He was a conundrum, I'll give you that. Looking back, he told so many lies. He said his mother was from County Wicklow, and his father's ancestors were French and that they were both dead. But that was all just nonsense, wasn't it?'

Violet shook her head. 'His real father was a stoker named George, and his mother Kathleen was a housewife – and definitely not Irish. He became a novelist later, you know – perhaps he was practising.' She smiled, and sipped her drink.

'So he never told you about Dublin – or any of it?'

'Good heavens, no. Charles never told me anything. I don't even know what he really did for a living. He told me he worked for the Board of Trade, but I'm not really sure that was true either.'

'Why do you say that?'

'Can you keep a secret?'

Michael nodded.

'Some years ago I found an odd notebook in Charles's suitcase. It was filled with all sorts of random letters and numbers. Wait there. I'll fetch it.'

Violet hurried to the kitchen and returned a few minutes later with a folded piece of paper, which she handed to Michael. 'I made a copy of some of it all those years ago, which I've had folded up in a biscuit tin ever since. See what you make of it.'

Reilly studied the piece of paper. 'I'm not sure but it looks very like code to me.'

'That's what I thought. Now, at the time, I began to imagine all sorts of crazy things. But on reflection, it's possible he was just playing around with ideas for a novel. He did write detective stories. It might be as simple as that.'

'What crazy things did you imagine?' asked Michael.

'Well, I know it sounds ridiculous, but it crossed my mind he might be some sort of spy. But of course, I have no evidence of that. I suppose it doesn't really matter now, does it?'

'Did you ask him about the notebook?'

She shook her head. 'No. I'd have been far too frightened of upsetting him. I asked him once exactly what he did. He always said that he was just a paper-pusher. But on this occasion, I decided to see if I could get him to be more explicit. I asked him what paper-pushers did. Well, he got so angry, I thought he might have a heart attack. His health was not good, you know. After that, I never tried again. I had a feeling that he would never tell me the truth anyway, so what was the point?'

'I understand.' Michael nodded. 'At the funeral, I noticed a rather pretty woman who looked very like someone I knew a long time ago.'

Violet smiled. 'I think you must mean Elizabeth – dark hair, and brown eyes?'

'That's her.'

Violet had a sudden rush of guilt. She had been debating since her husband's death whether she should reveal to Freddie that he had a sibling – albeit one who was old enough to be his mother. Now she pushed the thought aside. 'I'm not sure I should talk about her. It's a secret.' She bit her lip.

'I'm going back to Dublin tomorrow. I'll probably never come back here. Your secrets are safe with me.'

Violet studied her visitor. 'All right, if you promise I can trust you.'

Michael nodded.

'That woman is Charles's daughter from his first marriage. He married a nurse he met in the field hospital in Ypres.'

'Ah, so he married Maddy, did he?'

'You knew her?'

'Oh, yes. We were all a little in love with Maddy. I came to visit Paddy a few times in the first couple of weeks after he'd been shot, and I remember thinking it would almost be worth being gassed and blown up to be looked after by her.'

Violet's smile concealed an uncharacteristic emotion – envy. She couldn't imagine anyone saying anything so flattering about herself.

'Sadly, the marriage didn't last,' she went on. 'Charles was sent abroad for work, and they split up when the child was just a baby. Needless to say, our son doesn't know he has a half-sister, so I'd be grateful if you kept this to yourself.'

'Of course, I won't say anything,' said Michael. 'But wouldn't it be better to tell him? These things have a habit of coming out.'

'You may be right – and perhaps I will, one day, but not yet. He's got enough to deal with. Another drink?'

'Thank you, yes.'

She refilled their glasses. 'Going back to when you first met him... I still don't understand why he turned up in Dublin calling himself Padraig Devereux. And to join up under an assumed name – surely that was a risk?'

'I agree. I was hoping you might have an explanation. Have you thought of asking the War Office? There might be records.'

Violet shook her head.

'Maybe you should.'

'Maybe I will. But in all honesty, Michael, I wonder if there's any point. It was all so long ago, and no one really cares except me.'

31

December 1959

Violet

Michael Reilly's advice to tell Freddie the truth about his half-sister preyed on Violet's mind. As Christmas approached, and with the prospect of her son coming home for the holidays, she decided to discuss it with Elizabeth.

'Could we meet for coffee?

'Yes of course, Violet. How about somewhere on the Gate? I can usually get away from the salon at lunchtime.'

'How about the new place – Gino's. Tomorrow?'

The café was bustling when Violet arrived. Elizabeth was already sitting at a corner table, pen in hand and a notebook in front of her.

'Hello, dear,' said Violet, sitting down opposite her, 'doing the accounts?'

'Yes. I never seem to have time when I'm at the salon. I

spend most of my time pacifying the staff. Danny says I should get a manager, but the profits would disappear to nothing if I did that.'

Elizabeth beckoned to the waiter, ordered coffee and closed her notebook. 'Now, what do you want to talk about?'

'Who says I want to talk about anything in particular?' asked Violet defensively. 'I might just have fancied a chat...'

'Violet, I know you well enough to know that you never just "fancy a chat". You've got something on your mind. What is it?'

Violet cleared her throat. 'You're right, of course. I want to discuss you and Freddie.'

'I'm not sure I understand.'

'Your relationship. I wonder if it's time for him to know the truth.'

'Ah, I see. What's brought this on?' asked Elizabeth, stirring her coffee.

'Oh, just something somebody said. A man called Michael Reilly – he was at the funeral.'

'Was he the rather good-looking Irishman?'

'That's right. He didn't come to the wake, but he came to see me afterwards. He'd known your father in the war.'

'The first war?'

'Yes.'

'How fascinating.'

'He knew your mother too. In fact, he noticed you at the funeral and said you reminded him of her.'

'How wonderful,' said Elizabeth. 'I wish I'd had a chance to speak to him. I'd love to find out more about my mother's wartime experiences. She was always so self-effacing about it.'

'By all accounts, she was a great beauty,' said Violet. 'All the soldiers were in love with her.'

Elizabeth smiled. 'Maybe I could meet up with him?'

'I'm afraid he's back in Dublin now.'

'That's a shame. Anyway, what did he say that made you think again about Freddie knowing I'm his sister?'

Violet recounted what Michael had told her about Charles's time in Dublin, his false name and the discrepancy about his age. 'It seems your father's entire life was built on lies,' she said gloomily.

'Good God,' said Elizabeth, 'I don't know what to think.'

'It's a shock, isn't it? I mean, I knew your father was a secretive man, but never imagined he was capable of such deception. Anyway, it just got me thinking about you and Freddie. Charles's life was based on so many lies, perhaps it would be better if Freddie at least knew the truth about having a sister. Imagine if he found out later in life – he'd feel so betrayed. On the other hand, knowing the truth might spoil his memory of his father. Children are capable of the most extraordinary flights of fancy. He might start imagining all sorts of things that aren't true.'

'It is difficult, I agree. For what it's worth, Danny has been telling me for years we should explain that I'm his half-sister. I'm sure Freddie knows something anyway. He noticed that photograph of Dad on the mantelpiece last time he came to see us, and I could tell he was confused. I'm sure he didn't believe my explanation – that you'd given it to me. I mean... why would you? It makes no sense.'

'So you think we should be honest then? That he should be told.'

Elizabeth nodded. 'Well, he should be told about me, yes. I'm not sure about the rest of it. The false name, the missing year, living in Dublin – that might upset him. It's all rather a lot to take in – and we don't really know why Dad did it, do we? The fact that he was married before, had a child, and that the marriage broke up is far more straightforward.'

'I think you're right. One secret at a time.'

'Would you prefer to do it alone, or would you like me to be with you?'

'Alone, I think. Then perhaps we could come and see you afterwards. He's very fond of you – in fact he told me he wished you were his real aunt, and not just a friend. So perhaps finding out you're his sister will be a blessing.'

Elizabeth reached across the table and squeezed Violet's hand. 'Let's hope so.'

A few days before Freddie was due to come home for Christmas, he wrote to his mother to say he'd been invited to spend the first week of the holiday with a school friend at their family home in Suffolk.

> *If you're agreeable, Jolyon's mother asks if I could stay until the 22nd. I told J it would be fine – as you're always so busy and would probably appreciate a bit more time to yourself.*

Violet wrote back to say she was happy about the arrangement, and hoped he'd have a good time.

In fact, she was seriously disappointed. Ever since her conversation with Elizabeth, she had been impatient to tell Freddie his father's secret.

As Christmas approached, Violet went down to the local greengrocer and ordered a Christmas tree. 'Can you deliver it on the twenty-second? My son will be home that day, and he likes to decorate it with me.'

She walked back from the shops filled with excitement and anticipation. Since the death of her husband, Freddie had taken on a more significant role in her emotional life, and she couldn't wait to see him again. This would be their first Christmas alone together, and she was determined to make it special.

Freddie telephoned the evening before he was due home.

'I'm getting the eleven twenty into Liverpool Street. I should be home by mid-afternoon.'

'I could meet you,' Violet suggested eagerly.

'No, don't bother. I'll just get the tube. See you at home.'

She knew he was trying to save her the trouble, but his casual remark hurt. 'All right, if you're sure,' she said quietly.

After Freddie had hung up the phone, she found herself sobbing.

Freddie let himself into the flat to find their Christmas tree propped up in the hall. 'Hi Mum, I'm home,' he called out.

Violet ran upstairs excitedly. 'Hello, darling. How lovely to see you. How was the journey? How was your friend – Jolyon, isn't it?'

'The journey was the same as normal. And Jol was OK. His folks are quite nice. But he has a very annoying little sister. She wouldn't leave us alone.'

He pushed open his bedroom door and flung his bag onto the bed.

'You must be tired,' Violet said. 'Come down when you're ready. We'll have some tea in the sitting room.'

Violet had lit a fire, which was glowing merrily when Freddie came downstairs. He collapsed onto the sofa, his long legs sprawling across the carpet. 'It's actually nice to be home.'

'Well, don't sound so surprised,' said Violet. 'If I didn't know you better, I'd be quite hurt. Do you want tea? I've bought crumpets as a treat.' She poured two cups of tea and loaded a crumpet onto a toasting fork.

'Yes please. I didn't mean it that way. It's just... it was nice of Jol to invite me. I suppose he thought I might need cheering up. But it was quite hard work making conversation each evening with his parents. There were times when I just wanted to lie down with a good book.'

'Well, you're home now. And it's good for you to be sociable with other families. What does his father do?'

'He's something in the City – a banker, I think. He lives in London during the week.'

'Is the house nice?'

'I suppose so. Big, with a huge garden. Quite chilly though.'

Violet smiled. 'Not cosy then.'

'Not at all. Shall I toast that?' Freddie knelt by the fire, holding the crumpet to the coals.

She laid a cup of tea on the floor by his side. 'Drink it while it's hot, darling.'

'OK.'

They sat for a while watching the flickering flames, as the crumpet browned at the edges. Finally, Violet nervously broke the silence.

'Freddie... I've got something to tell you.'

He turned round, his face etched with concern. 'You're not ill, are you?'

'No! Not at all. Oh darling, it's nothing like that. No, in fact it's something nice – well, I think it's nice.'

His shoulders dropped as he relaxed. He buttered the crumpet, smeared it with jam and crammed it into his mouth. Butter dribbled down his chin.

'Manners, darling! Not all at once. I hope you didn't eat like that at Jolyon's house. His mother will never invite you back.'

Freddie waited until he'd swallowed his mouthful and wiped his chin clean with the back of his hand. 'Mother dearest, I was the perfect guest – Jol's mother said so. "Oh, do come back, Freddie. It's been wonderful having you."' His impersonation of an upper-middle-class, middle-aged woman was perfect, and Violet laughed out loud.

'Freddie, you are naughty. That's very good.'

'I've been practising. I've been cast as Cecily in *The Importance of Being Earnest*.'

'You! But you don't act.'

'I do now. It's quite fun.'

'And playing a woman!'

'Well, someone has to. I'm at a boys-only school. Besides, I'm quite good at it. Father Peter said so.' Freddie slipped into Father Peter's deep sonorous voice: 'Boy... you have a remarkable talent for playing a young woman. If I didn't know better, I'd say you had a fistful of sisters at home.' He laughed, and buttered another crumpet. 'So what's this news then?'

Violet cleared her throat and sipped her tea. 'It's about Aunty Elizabeth.'

'Oh yes, what about her? Oh, God, I don't have to go and babysit that awful Sandra, do I?'

'No, it's not that. Although Sandra seems quite nice to me.'

'Oh, Freddieeee, please can I give you a hug?' he squealed in a high-pitched voice.

'You're a very bad boy,' she said, smiling. 'The poor girl's got a crush on you, that's all. You're very good-looking, Freddie. She can't be the first girl to adore you from afar.'

Freddie blushed.

'No,' Violet went on, 'it's about Elizabeth and who she really is.'

Freddie looked up at his mother. 'What do you mean, who she really is? She's Aunty Elizabeth.'

'Well, in actual fact, she's... your sister – your half-sister, to be precise.'

'What? Are you telling me you had another child? How's that possible... she's almost the same age as you, isn't she? I may not know a lot about biology, but I do know a girl has to be a certain age before she can have a baby.'

'Not me, you silly boy – your father.'

Freddie sat for a moment absorbing this information, his

mouth open in astonishment. 'Dad had another child before me?'

Violet nodded.

'And you've only just found out?'

'Not exactly,' said Violet.

'How long have you known?'

'Quite a while.'

'Why haven't you told me before?'

'I know it must seem odd to you, but your father didn't want me to. He was quite insistent.'

'But why? It would have been nice to have a sister – or a half-sister, or whatever she is. I would have been less lonely.'

Violet heard the pain behind his remark. 'Oh darling, have you been lonely?'

'Yes,' he said, tears welling up in his eyes. 'All my life.'

He threw the toasting fork down and ran from the room. She heard him calling for the cat, his feet thundering upstairs, and the sound of his bedroom door closing with a slam, followed by the unmistakeable sound of weeping.

Violet sighed. She had hoped the news would bring her son joy. But instead she had spoiled his homecoming. Not for the first time, she felt despair that she had never been able to provide the sort of comforting home her son really needed. She just hoped he would feel differently in the morning. At least one secret had finally been told.

32

Elizabeth

The day before Christmas Eve, Elizabeth woke to the sound of her children squabbling in the drawing room below her bedroom. Sighing, she got up, put on her dressing gown and came downstairs.

Throwing open the sitting room door, she found the children squaring up to each other in front of the mantelpiece.

'You're the meanest boy I ever met!' screamed Sandra.

'Well, you're the wettest girl in the world,' shouted her brother.

'Sandra, James! Will you stop shouting,' said Elizabeth. 'The whole street must be able to hear you. Apart from anything else, I've got a hideous headache. Quite honestly, if you can't get along, I'm not sure Father Christmas will be inclined to make a stop at number forty-three this year.'

'Oh Mummy – don't say that,' said Sandra dramatically. 'It's not my fault. *He* finished my puzzle.' She pointed theatrically at her brother, who simply shrugged.

'James, is that true? Did you finish the puzzle?'

'What if I did? There were only a few pieces left and it was so obvious where they went. A monkey could have done it.'

'I hate you!' screamed Sandra.

'Not as much as I hate you,' James hurled back.

'Stop it this minute, both of you. Go to your rooms and don't come out until you've calmed down.'

Elizabeth watched the backs of her children as they reluctantly stomped upstairs, then breathed deeply and headed down to the basement kitchen. The smell of coffee drifted towards her. Danny was pouring beans into his new coffee grinder.

'I'm not sure we'll make it as far as Christmas Day,' said Elizabeth, sitting at the table. 'Either Sandra or James will have killed each other, or I may have committed infanticide. Please give me coffee now.'

Danny smiled. 'Patience. It won't be ready for a few minutes. In the meantime, have a piece of toast.' He placed a slice, thickly buttered, in front of her and tipped the ground coffee into an Italian stovetop coffee pot.

'Thanks. Didn't you hear them shouting?' asked Elizabeth.

'I did.'

'Then why didn't you stop them?'

'They've got to sort these things out for themselves.'

Elizabeth sighed. 'That's the sort of "hands-off" parenting I've come to expect from you.' She smiled, and crunched down on her toast.

'You're welcome.' The coffee pot on the stove began to rumble. 'I mean it. If we constantly intervene they'll never learn to negotiate.'

'It didn't sound like negotiation to me. It was more like World War Three!'

'They're just excited because it's Christmas.'

'And bored. Can you take them somewhere today? I've got a full day at the salon. Every woman in Notting Hill Gate is getting her hair done before Christmas. How about the Science Museum?'

'No can do, I'm afraid. I'm on a big story. Got to be finished by tomorrow night.'

'Oh marvellous. A scoop for Christmas,' said Elizabeth sarcastically. 'What is it?'

Danny put his fingers to his mouth. 'My lips are sealed, but it involves senior figures in government, and is deeply shocking.' He laughed, poured out two cups of espresso and handed one to Elizabeth.

'You enjoy torturing people, don't you?'

'Not at all. But if people in the public eye set themselves up as virtuous, moral leaders, I expect them to behave accordingly. If they don't – if they, in fact, have half a dozen love children, and a mistress in every port – it's my job to expose them. It's really very simple.'

Elizabeth sighed. 'I suppose I understand. It just seems so tawdry... I mean, none of us live perfect lives, do we?'

'No, but we don't try and tell others how to behave. That's the difference.'

'So you'll be busy all day.'

'Yup. Won't be home much before nine.'

'Oh dear. I was hoping to invite Freddie over later for supper. Violet gave him the news yesterday.'

'What news?'

'About us being siblings.'

'Oh well, I'm glad that's out at last.'

'I'm not sure it was such a good idea. He left the room in tears, apparently, and has been holed up in his room ever since. Violet's frantic.'

'It was a shock, I'm sure. He'll get over it.'

'I hope you're right. Do you think it's too soon for supper?'

'No, it's a good idea, if only to normalise things. And he'll soon get used to it.' Danny leaned over and kissed his wife. 'I mean, who wouldn't want you as a big sister?'

Elizabeth smiled. 'All right, I'll invite him over for supper.'

'Good. And I'll try to join you for pudding. Now I really must go.'

'Will you be working all over Christmas?'

'Once this story's filed, I'll be off till after New Year.'

'Oh, that's good. I wonder if you could do something for me over the holiday?'

'Take the kids to a museum, you mean?'

'That would be lovely, obviously – but I meant some research.'

'I'm intrigued... go on.'

'Violet met a man called Michael Reilly at the funeral, who knew my father in the First World War. He revealed some rather bizarre information. My father apparently enlisted under an assumed name.'

'That's odd.'

'Isn't it? Apparently, he joined up in Dublin under the name of Padraig Devereux, saying he was seventeen. But the fact was he was nineteen by then. And what was he doing in Dublin in the first place? Violet is completely baffled by it all. I said you might be able to find something out by using one of your contacts.'

Danny raised his eyes heavenward. 'I'm a journalist, darling, not a spy or a government minister.'

'Oh come on! You know heaps of people.'

'Well, I do still have a couple of contacts at the War Office. I suppose it wouldn't do any harm to ask. Although be careful what you wish for. You might discover something you'd rather not know.'

'I've thought of that, but I just feel I have to try, in order to understand him, you know?'

'All right, he's your father. But don't tell the boy.'

'No. Violet and I agree about that. One shock at a time.'

'Quite. Now I really must go.'

When Danny had gone, Elizabeth went up into the hall and rang Violet. 'Morning, Vi... I wondered if you and Freddie would like to come over later for supper?'

'That's kind, but I'm not sure. He's still very withdrawn.'

'Has he emerged from his room yet?'

'Just. But only because the cat needed feeding. They're both eating breakfast now.'

'Tell me if this is a silly idea, but I wondered, might he take the kids somewhere this afternoon – to one of the museums, perhaps? They'd love it, and it might be good for him. I've got to take them to work with me, but they'll be climbing the walls by lunchtime. It would be such a help if he could come and collect them.'

'I can ask him, but I won't make any promises.'

'Try to persuade him. But whatever happens, come for supper tonight. We'll get the little ones settled with a card game or something, and then we three can have a long chat. OK?'

Freddie reluctantly agreed to accompany Sandra and James to the Science Museum.

'But the moment they start squabbling,' he told his mother, 'I'm dumping them both there, and coming home alone.'

'I'm sure they'll be on their best behaviour. And when you get back, I thought we could decorate our tree.'

'All right.'

'Don't forget we're having supper with Elizabeth later. She's very keen to see you.'

Freddie nodded. 'My big sister.' He smiled quietly to himself. 'That sounds rather nice actually.'

Violet kissed him on the cheek. 'I'm so glad you feel that

way. Please wear your warm coat and scarf – it's jolly cold outside.'

The Science Museum was full of Christmas visitors as Freddie steered the two children inside. 'Wait here while I get tickets,' he instructed, 'and don't squabble.'

'We won't,' said Sandra, gazing at him longingly.

He returned a few minutes later. 'Where shall we start?'

'The Children's Gallery,' shouted Sandra.

'No, I want to see the cars,' demanded James.

'I'm sure we can do both. I suggest we start at the bottom and work our way up.'

The cars were part of a larger display of machinery on the ground floor. While James and Freddie admired the first jet-propelled car, built in 1950, Sandra imagined herself in the first Rolls-Royce, built in 1905.

When they finally reached the Children's Gallery, they joined long lines of children keen to try out the most popular exhibits – the revolutionary self-opening doors, and, more excitingly still, the tape-recording machine, which allowed them to hear their own voice played back to them.

'I sound funny,' said Sandra after her turn. 'My voice doesn't really sound like that, does it Freddie?'

'It does,' said Freddie. 'But I think you've got a nice voice.'

'Have I?' Sandra cooed. 'I think you have a beautiful voice.'

Her brother put his fingers into his mouth and pretended to be sick.

'Come on, you two,' said Freddie, 'we'd better hurry up. We don't want to get home too late. Mum and I still have our tree to decorate.'

'Can we help?' asked Sandra. 'I'm awfully good at decorating.'

. . .

Violet was delighted to see Freddie returning in relatively high spirits, with the two children in tow.

'Would you all like tea?' she asked as they trooped into the hall.

'Oh, yes please,' replied Sandra. 'Can I help you make it?'

'What a polite little girl you are – and yes you can. If you come down to the kitchen with me, perhaps Freddie and James can bring the tree down to the sitting room. Freddie, put it in the pot in the corner of the room.'

As Violet played carols on the piano, the three children ate digestive biscuits and drank mugs of tea while they decorated the tree. Violet watched as they worked, admiring her son's ability to intercede between the two warring siblings, and suddenly felt sad that she and his father had never had more children. Perhaps James and Sandra might become some kind of alternative family one day.

Later that evening, the four of them trooped across the road for supper. Elizabeth opened the door. 'Hello! You all look very cheerful. Freddie, I think you must have brought the wrong children back from the museum.' She smiled and kissed his cheek.

Freddie laughed. 'They were very well behaved, actually.'

'Well, that was a miracle. Shall we all go into the sitting room? I've got the fire lit.'

The Christmas tree stood in the bay window; it reached almost to the ceiling – some eight feet or more.

'It looks very impressive,' said Violet, admiring it. 'Ours is a little smaller.'

'We helped Freddie decorate it,' said Sandra.

'They did a very good job too,' said Violet.

'Oh good. I'm glad they could be useful. Drink?' asked Elizabeth.

'Sherry please.'

'Is Freddie allowed?'

'Oh yes, of course he's allowed. He's in the sixth form now – practically an adult.'

'I'll have a sherry too, please... Elizabeth.' He looked at her and winked.

'Why didn't you say, "Aunty Elizabeth"?' asked Sandra.

'Because she's not really my aunty,' said Freddie.

'Yes,' interrupted Elizabeth. 'There's something I need to tell you about that.'

As Elizabeth delicately explained that her father and Freddie's were one and the same, the children listened intently. 'So you and Freddie are brother and sister,' said James, matter-of-factly.

'Half-brother and half-sister,' his mother corrected.

'So is Freddie my brother too?' said Sandra excitedly. 'Oh, I do hope he is.'

'No,' said Violet, 'he's your half-uncle... I think.'

'How exciting,' Sandra gushed.

'Why haven't you told us before?' asked James.

'Because we wanted Freddie to know first,' replied his mother. 'Now, who's hungry?'

'Me!' chorused the two children, trooping off to the kitchen.

When they'd gone, Elizabeth took Violet and Freddie by the arm. 'I think that went well, don't you?'

Violet nodded. 'Yes, as well as can be expected.'

After supper, Elizabeth told the two younger children to go up to bed.

'I don't want to go,' wailed Sandra. 'I want to stay here with Freddie.'

'If you don't go upstairs this minute, Father Christmas won't be coming tomorrow night,' snapped Elizabeth. 'He never visits children who are tired and grumpy.'

Sandra stood up, pouting.

'And remember, you'll see Freddie the day after tomorrow,' said Elizabeth more gently, 'he and Violet are coming for Christmas lunch.'

'Are we?' said Violet quietly.

'Yes, Vi... if you don't have other plans. We'd like it very much.'

'Freddie, what do you think?' asked Violet.

'That would be nice, thank you.'

Pacified, Sandra and James disappeared upstairs.

'Shall we go through to the sitting room?' suggested Elizabeth. 'I'm sure you must have lots of questions, Freddie.'

'It's nice here,' said Freddie, as they settled down in front of the fire.

Elizabeth smiled. 'Thank you. It's all my mother's taste really. I've hardly done anything to the house since she died.'

'Do you miss her?'

'Yes, every day. But I have Danny and the children – and now you and Violet. I hope you're OK with the news about your father?'

'Yes, although it was a shock at first. Why did he leave you and your mother?'

'He didn't really leave us. He was sent abroad for work.'

'Is that when he went to China?'

'That's right. I understand why he felt he had to go – it was a great opportunity. Unfortunately, the marriage just didn't survive. It was no one's fault.'

'There's a boy at school – his parents have just got divorced. It's a huge scandal, being a Catholic school.'

'It happens,' said Violet gently. 'You mustn't think badly of your father.'

'I don't,' said Freddie. 'Not about that anyway.'

Violet and Elizabeth caught one another's eye.

'The thing you have to remember, Freddie,' said Elizabeth, 'is that me being your sister wasn't my secret to tell. It was our father's. So your mother and I had to respect his wishes. I'm glad you know, now. And I'm happy to have a little brother.'

'Aunty Tilly told me at his funeral that Dad had secrets, and that she'd tell me what they were one day. Is this the secret she was talking about?'

'I suppose it must have been,' said Violet hurriedly. 'I can't think what other secrets he could have had.'

Freddie visibly relaxed. 'That's good to know.'

'Well,' said Violet. 'I think we ought to go now. It's been a long day, and I'm sure you have heaps to do.'

'All right,' said Elizabeth, kissing them both. 'We'll see you both on Christmas Day. Come about one o'clock.'

As Elizabeth stood at the door watching her little brother walk away, his arm protectively round his mother's shoulder, she felt a pang of sisterly love. He was such a handsome, but vulnerable, boy. He looked very like his father, but he had his mother's gentle nature and sensitivity. With their relationship now out in the open, she was looking forward to their first Christmas together as brother and sister.

33

JANUARY 1960

Elizabeth

The Christmas holidays were finally over; the children were all back at school, and, as January was normally a quiet month at the hairdressing salon, Elizabeth had taken a day off work. Danny was also at home, working in his attic study.

'I thought you could do with a break,' she said, bringing him coffee.

'That's kind. I've been working since seven.'

'I know. I was there when you got up, remember. How's it going?'

'Oh, all right. I'm finalising a couple of big stories. Easier to think here than in the newsroom. Too many distractions.'

'Too many trips to the pub, more like.'

'Ha! You know me so well. Actually I'm glad you popped up, because I've just put the phone down to an old mate at the War Office.'

'Oh yes...' Elizabeth sat down in an armchair in the corner of the room.

'He's been doing a bit of digging for me about your father.'

'And...?'

'It's all a bit odd.'

'Tell me.'

'He managed to unearth a file on a man named Charles Frederick Carmichael, otherwise known as Padraig Devereux.'

'How exciting! Can we see the file?'

'No.'

'Oh, why not?'

'It's effectively under seal.'

'What does that mean?'

Danny picked up his reporter's notebook and read out loud: 'Under section 3(4) of the 1958 Public Records Act, and I quote, "files can be withheld, if, in the opinion of the person who is responsible for them, they are required for administrative purposes or ought to be retained for any other special reason".'

'What does that mean?'

'It's government-speak for the fact that there's something in the file they don't want anyone to see. Files from the First World War are subject to a fifty-year rule – in other words they can't be released for fifty years, which, in the case of your father, would take us to roughly 1970.'

'This is bizarre. Why does he have a pseudonym, and why does he have a secret file?'

'I don't know, but the usual reason is that the individual was involved in some sort of undercover role.'

'Spying, you mean?'

'Yes if you like, spying.'

'But Dad wasn't a spy – he worked for the Board of Trade.'

'So he said.'

'What do you mean?'

'Darling, I hardly knew the man, but if he were just an ordinary bloke there would be a boring civil service file about him. And there's nothing. It's like a void.'

'I see. How very odd. Should I tell Violet?'

'Yes. I don't see why not. She has a right to know.'

Elizabeth arranged to meet Violet that evening.

Violet led her down to the sitting room and they sat opposite one another, each with a glass of sherry.

'I've got a bit of news for you,' said Elizabeth. 'Well, news is perhaps not the word – more a lack of news.'

'I don't understand,' said Violet.

'I hope you don't mind, but I asked Danny to have a dig around about Dad, using a contact of his at the War Office. You remember Danny worked there during the war.'

'Yes, I recall that. What did he find out?'

'That's the thing – not much. There is a file on Dad, but it's sealed.'

'Sealed?'

'Yes, no one can see it. Danny says – and forgive me if this sounds mad – it's the kind of thing they do if it's a matter of national security.'

'Oh...'

'You don't seem surprised.'

'No, perhaps that's because I'm not.'

'What do you know?'

'Wait there.'

Violet went to the kitchen and returned with the folded piece of paper she had kept for so many years in the biscuit tin. 'Read that.'

'It's just gobbledegook,' said Elizabeth. 'What does it mean?'

'I think it's code – a cypher, if you like. I found it written in a notebook in your father's suitcase during the war. I made a copy on that piece of paper, and have kept it ever since.'

'Did you ask him what he meant?'

'Oh no, of course not! He'd have been furious if he knew I'd been rummaging around in his things. For years, I've thought he might have been playing around with ideas for his novels – what would a cypher look like, that sort of thing. Now, I'm wondering, was it real? Was he actually a spy?'

Elizabeth felt the hairs on her neck stand on end. 'My God... Dad, a spy?'

Violet shrugged. 'It's an explanation, isn't it?'

'Do you think he was capable of it?'

'I don't know. In some ways I do. He was the most secretive man I've ever met.'

'Could I have another sherry?' asked Elizabeth.

'Yes, help yourself. I'll have one too.'

They sat for a while, nursing their drinks, staring into the fire.

'It makes one question one's whole relationship with someone, doesn't it, when you realise they're not who they seem,' said Elizabeth.

'I know what you mean. But we have no actual proof, so we should perhaps be a little circumspect. We can't condemn the poor man without evidence.'

'No, I suppose not.'

'I think everything hinges on solving these two mysteries. What was he doing in Dublin? And why did he change his name? Those are the things I want answers to.'

'Do you think his sister knows anything?' asked Elizabeth.

'Tilly? I'm sure she knows something. I asked her years ago, but she clammed up.'

'Might it be worth asking her again?'

'I suppose it's worth a try,' said Violet.

. . .

Tilly and John had finally acquired a telephone, and Violet arranged for her and Elizabeth to visit them the following Saturday afternoon. As they approached the house, Violet took Elizabeth's arm. 'I'm a bit nervous.'

'Don't be. What's the worst that can happen? She sends us away with a flea in our ear?'

Tilly was sitting at the kitchen table, a typed manuscript laid out in front of her covered with bright red pencil comments.

'Hello, you two,' she said brightly. 'Do sit down. I was just editing my latest short story. John has made a cake – isn't he clever?' She gestured towards a lemon cake that sat in the middle of the table, surrounded by four plates, cups and saucers.

'It looks delicious,' said Elizabeth. 'And how exciting to be working on a new story. You and my father must have inherited a powerful creative gene!'

'I suppose so. Would you like tea?'

They made polite conversation for a while, about the state of the roads, how Freddie was getting on at school, and the problems with running a hairdressing salon, until finally Violet could contain herself no longer. 'Tilly, Elizabeth and I would like to ask you a couple of questions about Charles.'

'Oh yes.'

'I know I asked you once before, and at that time you were not keen to break his confidence. But he's gone now, and I think we have a right to know.'

'Know what?'

'There are so many things, but chief among them is why Charles fought in the war under an assumed name. Since you and I had that chat all those years ago, I've met a man who knew him at the time. Apparently, he met Charles in Dublin in 1915, but Charles introduced himself as Padraig Devereux. Did you know about that?'

Tilly glanced across at her husband. Elizabeth noticed John discreetly shrugging his shoulders, as if to say – why not?

'I knew about the name, yes,' said Tilly. 'But I don't know why he did it, so don't ask me.'

'But Tilly, surely he must have told you. You and he were always so close.'

'He didn't tell, and I didn't ask. It wasn't my place.'

'John,' interjected Elizabeth, 'can you talk some sense into her? Violet needs to know the truth, and so do I.'

'Tilly gave her word,' replied John. 'You can't ask her to break it.'

'Charles is dead. Surely you can tell us something,' said Violet desperately.

'I think you should leave now,' said Tilly, standing up.

'Oh, Tilly, please don't be like that.'

'I'm sorry, Violet, I really am, but my loyalty to my brother comes above everything else. If he'd wanted you to know, he'd have told you himself.'

'That woman is so stubborn,' said Elizabeth on the way back to Holland Park. 'She obviously knows something. It's so frustrating.'

Violet nodded. 'All I can think is that the reason he took that name and concealed his past is because something really terrible happened. Perhaps he killed someone, or took part in some revolutionary activity. I don't know, but it's obviously something he took great pains to cover up.'

'I think you're right, Violet. And I wonder if we'll ever get to the bottom of it.'

34

FEBRUARY 1960

Violet

The sleet that had been falling since dawn had now turned to snow, and was beginning to settle across the lawn. Violet pulled herself up in bed and stared out at the garden. It looked really quite romantic, blanketed in white; even the much-maligned ash tree in the corner took on an air of mystery, its branches covered in snow.

It was half-term and Freddie was spending the holiday with his friend Jolyon in Suffolk. Although Violet would miss him, she was determined to keep busy. She had a pile of marking to get through, and had also promised her son that his bedroom would be cleared out by the Easter holidays. It was time to create a room Freddie could call his own.

After breakfast, Violet went upstairs, and unlocked Charles's door. Three months after the funeral, her husband's clothes still filled the wardrobe, and a half-finished manuscript lay untouched on the desk. To any casual observer it looked as if Charles was still alive. But the room felt cold, and there was a damp musty smell. She opened the curtains and watched the snow falling onto the pavement. Inside, the wintry light illuminated the room. Every surface was covered in dust, and there was a general air of neglect and melancholy.

She opened the wardrobe and began to take out Charles's old suits and jackets, laying them on the bed, sorting them into piles as she went. Good-quality clothes would go to the charity shop in Kensington Church Street. Shabbier items – albeit quite wearable – would be donated to the local Church of England Society. At the back of the wardrobe, she discovered Charles's dress suit. It had been made for him in China back in the 1930s. It was very good quality, double-breasted, with a black satin collar. Incredibly, there was no moth damage. 'That will do for Freddie when he's older,' she said to herself, hanging it up on the door to take to the dry-cleaners.

Finally the wardrobe was empty, but the bed was now piled high with clothes. Violet had never learned to drive, and now she rather wished she had. It would take several trips to the charity shops to clear the mess.

Charles's own novels – almost forty of them – filled the only bookcase in the room. She left them where they were, hoping that Freddie might read them one day. Their writing style might be a little old-fashioned, but they were a huge body of work, and something of his father's to be proud of.

Finally, Violet decided to tackle Charles's beloved maple desk. Throughout their marriage Charles had made it clear that it was to be left alone at all times. Soon after their wedding, she had made the mistake of tidying his papers. He had come home that evening and fumed. 'How dare you?' he had shouted. 'It's my property, my desk. You must never, ever go near it again.'

'But I was only dusting,' she protested.

'I don't care. Leave it alone. If it needs dusting, I'll do it.'

. . .

Her hands now trembled as she gathered up all the papers he had left lying on the desk and placed them in a folder. The typewriter keys were grimy, and the glass top of the desk was smeared with tea stains and cigarette ash. She removed the ashtray and fetched warm water, a cloth and some polish.

First, she cleaned the typewriter keys, wiping each one with the damp rag. To clean the desk surface, she heaved up the typewriter with both hands and placed it on the pile of clothes on the bed. As she was replacing it afterwards, the typewriter slipped from her grasp and landed heavily on the desk surface. There was a tinkling sound of metal hitting glass. Looking under the typewriter, she saw a tiny key on the desk surface, and above, still stuck to the machine, a length of sticky tape, now yellowing with age. Was this Charles's secret hiding place for the missing desk key?

Holding her breath, she inserted the key into the central drawer, and found that it fitted. She pulled it open to reveal nothing of interest – Sellotape, pens, paperclips and drawing pins. There was a cupboard on the left-hand side. Again, its contents were unremarkable – stacks of fresh typing paper, carbons to make copies, and envelopes.

Then she turned her attention to the drawers on the right-hand side. The top two drawers contained several buff-coloured folders. Upon inspection, they turned out to hold letters from his publisher and ideas for future novels. She laid them on the desk to examine later.

When she unlocked the bottom drawer, her heart missed a beat. It was filled with diaries. She removed them one by one, and laid them on the floor in date order. In all there were fifteen, the first dated 1914, the last 1929 – the year Charles returned from China, and his writing career began.

She sat for while on the bed, staring at the haul. Should she read them, she wondered. Her husband had obviously wanted to keep them private, otherwise why lock the desk and hide the key? She picked one up and handled it – it was nice-quality leather, although slightly mouldy around the edges.

She returned it to the floor with the others, nervous about reading it. Might she discover things she would rather not have known – private thoughts of her husband's that would be better left unseen? Mentions of other women – lovers perhaps, or even children. He had already tried to conceal one family. Could there be others?

By now it was lunchtime, and the snow was settling thickly on the pavements. Feeling hungry, Violet went into the kitchen and boiled the kettle. While the tea stewed in the pot, she made herself a sandwich. Back in the bedroom, she sipped her tea, plucking up the courage to open a diary.

Finally, she could contain her curiosity no longer. She picked up the earliest diary, marked 1914, hoping to find out what Charles was doing in that 'missing year', when he went to Dublin and changed his name. Her fingers trembled as she opened the first page, dated 14 September. The handwriting was clearly that of her husband – neat, with a hint of copperplate. Not quite the adult hand she had known so well – more the studied, immaculate handwriting of an intelligent young man.

Mr McMasters gave me this diary today and asked me to keep a record of my time in the army. He knows I want to be a writer and suggests this will be good training for me. I hope he's right. I feel a bit of a fraud – I mean, what is there to say? But here goes...

Yesterday, I joined the Middlesex Regiment with Jimmy and Tom. We're off to training camp next week in Essex. Mum is furious; she thinks I'm throwing my life away. I can't seem to get her to understand how important it is. I feel I must do my duty and fight for my country. Nothing is more important.

Violet was confused. Charles had always told her he joined up in Ireland. The diary made no sense.

She leafed through the subsequent 1914 entries, reading about the training camp he had attended, and the lack of weapons and uniforms. Gradually, Charles's style became less like a diary and more like a novel. It seemed he had taken his teacher's advice to heart and was practising his craft.

5 December

I arrived this morning at regimental headquarters – the Ingliss Barracks, Mill Hill, North London. It's a grand, imposing building, like a country house. At the front gate I gave my name. I have to admit I felt very nervous. My orders were to report to Major Marchant.

His office was on the ground floor. I stood outside in the corridor, and knocked. He called me inside – his voice was strong and a bit frightening, like the headmaster at school. Gingerly, I opened the door and introduced myself. I fumbled my words a bit – nerves, I suppose.

'Well, don't lurk in the doorway, Private.'

I stepped inside, and he looked me up and down for a bit: 'So, you're my new batman, are you?'

Violet sat up with a start. 'I didn't know he was a batman,' she said to herself. 'He never mentioned that.' She continued to read, fascinated...

Once inside, I dropped my pack on the parquet floor and saluted.

The major was about forty, I should think. Good-looking

with neat features, and a moustache. His tone was firm but not unkind. His accent though – very upper-class.

He told a corporal to show me to my quarters up on the first floor. My room had a single bed, a chest of drawers, and in the corner was a wash-hand basin. It was much bigger than my room at home, and compared to the tent I'd been living in for the last three months it seemed like luxury.

A connecting door led to the major's room. It was far larger than mine, with a pair of armchairs in the bay window, and a small table to one side with drinks and a pair of decanters. I was surprised that we had adjoining rooms. I thought I would be in a dorm with the other soldiers.

'No good you being miles away from him, is there?' the corporal said. 'You've obviously never been a batman before.'

I admitted then that I hadn't the faintest idea what the job involved. So the corporal told me my duties: press the major's uniform, polish his medals, buttons, shoes and boots, launder his shirts and underwear, and do his ironing. On top of that, I have to bring him tea in the morning, make sure his decanters are filled up with wine, port and whisky, and clean his guns.

I don't mind admitting, I couldn't believe it. When I volunteered for the post of batman, I hadn't realised it would be such a lot of work. 'I joined up to fight the Germans,' I told the corporal, 'not do some bloke's ironing.'

Well, he laughed out loud then. 'Don't worry, lad. Once we get over the Channel you'll see some action, and this will seem like luxury.'

Before he left, he told me that the major is second-in-command in the regiment, so I'd better mind my p's and q's. 'He's important, all right? So watch your step, lad,' were his parting words.

12 December

It's been a week now, and I've hardly seen the major. He works long hours and I'm glad to say he's not too demanding, which is a relief, because there's a lot to learn.

Being a batman is not as easy as people think. All my duties – like washing and ironing and such – have to be done in my own time. I fit them in alongside my training as an infantryman. So I'm up with the lark to prepare the major's uniform and black his boots. Mum would be proud of me – I remember her blacking Dad's boots before work.

It's exhausting. At night I collapse into bed and hardly have time to write my diary before I'm asleep.

Violet laughed out loud at this. She couldn't imagine her husband blacking someone's boots and ironing their shirts. He always appeared totally helpless domestically. Looking back over their twenty years of life together, she felt as if she didn't know him at all.

24 *December*

The major seems nice enough, and I must be doing something right because he's not complained yet. I had to polish his golf clubs the other day. When I brought them to him, he asked if I'd ever played. When I said I hadn't, he said I should.

'You've got the figure for it – tall, with long arms – you'd have a good swing.'

I honestly hadn't the faintest idea what he was talking about.

We had a carol service in the chapel this evening. It was lit by candles and was really beautiful. I don't mind admitting I had a tear in my eye, as I thought of Tilly and Mum and Dad. This will be my first Christmas away from them. I got a letter this morning from Mum, and she says there's a Christmas parcel in the post. I just hope it gets here soon.

Most nights I hear the major playing music on the gramophone he has in his room. Tonight it was an aria from La Traviata *by Verdi. I recognised it – because Mr McMasters once took a few of us to hear a performance of it at the local theatre.*

Violet smiled at this. Although her husband never played an instrument himself, he had always loved music. When she and Charles had first met, she had sensed many similarities between them, and this diary confirmed it. Like her, he had been born in a working-class family with no artistic pretensions. And yet, like her, he had an intuitive interest in the arts – clearly nurtured by his favourite teacher.

In some ways the diaries were bringing her closer to the man she had shared her life with. She drank her tea, and picked up the next diary, for 1915.

1 January

Today was a red-letter day – I received my Christmas parcel from Mum. As soon as I snipped the string on the parcel I knew what it was. The scent of fruit, sugar and nutmeg filled my room. The major came in to get something and asked what that delicious smell was. I explained it was a fruit cake from my mother.

'Perhaps we'll toast the new year later with a cup of tea and piece of cake,' he said.

Tucked into the parcel was a pair of socks, which I really needed, and a separate package from Tilly. I had mentioned in a letter that I needed a new diary, and blow me down, she had bought me one. It was so kind of her. I'm really lucky to have her as a sister. There was a note too. 'Dear Bruv, don't forget to keep your diary. We all look forward to reading about your exploits!'

The more she read, the more Violet liked this young man. He was open and honest, kind and thoughtful. What had happened to him, she wondered, to make him so remote, so difficult to love?

2 January

Last evening, I shared some of Mum's cake with the major. He was very nice about it and asked me to thank her. Then, to my surprise, he told me to pour him a glass of sherry from his decanter and offered me one too.

It didn't seem right to be enjoying a drink with an officer, but I wasn't going to turn it down. We were getting on so well, I decided to ask him about the aria he had played a few days before. I said I thought it was from La Traviata *by Verdi.*

The major was surprised I recognised it. I explained about Mr McMasters.

He asked me then about my favourite subjects at school. I told him I loved English Literature, and that if the war hadn't come along I was going to apply to university.

The major raised his eyebrows. 'What an extraordinary young man you are. No one told me I was to have such an erudite young batman.'

I felt a bit embarrassed – perhaps I had been showing off. I made my excuses, and told him I had to iron his shirt for the morning.

I think I'm very lucky to work for this man. Although an officer, he seems really friendly and interested in me. Not what I'd expected at all.

3 January

Earlier this evening, I was about to start writing in my diary when the major came into my room. I didn't want him to know about the diary, so I hid it under my pillow. He asked if I wanted to listen to some more music.

I followed him into his room, and he told me to sit on an armchair – there are a pair of them in the window. I said I was happy to stand, but he insisted.

I thought he'd sit in the other chair, but instead he lay down on the bed. Next to him were a pile of records. He flicked through them, reading the titles out loud. Eventually he suggested Aida.

'I heard it played once in Verona,' he said. Apparently, the opera house there is in the open air, and the seats are made of stone and are very uncomfortable. He laughed about it as he told me. Anyway, he put the record on the gramophone and then lay back down, with his head resting on his hands. 'What was that you were writing, just now?' he asked.

I told him about the diary and how my teacher had suggested I should fill it in each day to practise my writing. I said, 'He thinks I have talent as a writer, sir.'

Marchant rolled over onto his side, resting his head on one hand, and stared at me 'Do you?' he asked.

'That's not for me to say,' I said. I could feel myself blushing, and felt such a fool.

'Why not let me be the judge? Go and bring your diary to me.'

I know he's an officer and I'm supposed to do as I'm told, but I refused. I said, 'I don't mean to be rude, sir, but a diary is private.'

'Fair enough,' replied Marchant, rolling over onto his back. 'But I can't pretend I'm not a little disappointed. Let's listen to the music.'

We listened to an aria. When it was over, he got up and removed the record, slipped it back into its paper sleeve, and said we'd listen to the rest tomorrow.

He's a nice man, but sometimes he doesn't behave like an

officer should – at least I don't think so. He treats me like a friend, almost. But of course, he's not my friend. He's a major, and I'm just a private.

4 January

After parade, I met up with Jimmy and Tom. We discussed the rumours that the regiment will be shipped out to Belgium within the next few weeks. We all agreed we were a bit nervous, but excited. 'Time to get over there and show them what we're made of.'

Then Jimmy asked me how I was getting on with the major.

I said I thought he was a bit too friendly. They thought I was making a fuss. But it doesn't feel right – that's all I know. It's just not right.

Violet read the entry with a sinking feeling. Charles obviously had a sixth sense about this relationship. Several days went by without any entry at all. But on 10 January Charles started writing again; this time the handwriting was erratic and uneven, as if the lad was hysterical.

I hardly know where to start. I'm in a such a state. Oh God, what have I done? Perhaps if I write it down, it will make it more bearable. As if, somehow, it all happened to someone else – a character in a novel perhaps, but not to me.

Rumours had been swirling for days about us shipping out. The major said it would be two more weeks at least. He asked me to pack up his golf clubs, although how he expected to use them out there in Belgium I have no idea.

Then a couple of days ago, he attended a regimental dinner. I'd polished the buttons on his red tunic and saw him off down the corridor. He had already had a few sherries before he went, and stumbled slightly. I spent a quiet enough evening, sorting through his laundry, but decided to get an early night.

I was fast asleep when I woke to find the major crouching down by my bed, whispering in my ear. 'Are you asleep?'

I sat up, and the major turned on the bedside light. 'Would you like to listen to some music?' He stank of drink.

'It's a bit late, sir,' I said.

'There will be no time for music when we're in Belgium, lad... come next door.'

It was odd him calling me 'lad' like that. But I didn't like to say no, so I got up and pulled my army tunic on over my pyjamas, and went to his room. Marchant was by the gramophone, placing the needle onto the disc. He took his jacket off, threw it on the chair and poured himself a large brandy. He was already quite drunk, swaying round the room. He lay down on the bed, his head resting on his hands. 'Come and sit next to me.' His tone had changed, and he pretty much ordered me to do it.

I sat as far away from him as I could.

'How are you feeling about our adventure together, Private?' he asked.

I was confused and really uncomfortable – being so close. I can't remember what I said. I mumbled something about being a bit nervous.

Then he said this odd thing: 'We're off to Belgium in a week or two, and we'll be standing shoulder to shoulder like Spartan warriors.'

Well, I didn't understand. I'd never heard of the Spartans. He must have seen my blank look, because he began to explain. Apparently, the Spartans took the view that men fought better together if they had formed a relationship.

Then he began to stroke my hair. 'You are a lovely boy,' he said. 'You remind me of someone I knew at school. Your voice, of course, needs work, your manners too, but these things can be changed.'

I felt my heart racing, my hands sweating. I stood up abruptly. 'I'm sorry, sir,' I told him, 'But I really must leave now.' Then I saluted. Looking back, it was an odd thing to do but I felt I had to get things back onto an even keel.

I got as far as the door linking our two rooms, and suddenly he was behind me. He grabbed me, put his hands on my crotch, and pushed me then against the door, pulling down my pyjamas. The pain when he... I can't even write down what he did. I just can't.

Afterwards, he lay back down on the bed as if nothing had happened. He asked me to bring him some tea in the morning.

I was crying, but I couldn't let him see. 'Very good, sir,' was all I could say.

I went back to my room. I was shaking and weeping, and had to scrub myself clean. I couldn't believe what had happened. Finally, when my skin was red raw, I lay down, but couldn't sleep. I kept trying to tell myself it had been a bad dream, but of course it wasn't. It was real and he would do it again. That's what he meant about the Spartans. He would use me like that from that day on. That would be our 'special bond'.

That's when I realised I had to get away. Even though it was still dark, I got up and dressed. I looked around for what to take with me. My diary, a pencil and pen, my letters from home, and the old clothes that I'd joined up in – trousers, a jacket, a pair of shoes, a shirt. There was still some of Mum's cake left, so I wrapped it up, put it all in a knapsack, and crept out down the corridor and out of the building. I couldn't risk going through the main gate – the guard on duty would have seen me. But I knew there was a side entrance in the wall. Thank God, the gate was unlocked. Once out of the grounds I just ran and ran. I didn't know where I was going. I wanted to go home to see my mum and tell Tilly what had happened. But I couldn't risk that. I must have run for miles because eventually I found myself on the banks of the River Lee.

The sun was just coming up. I sat down on the bank, trying to decide what to do. I couldn't go back, I knew that. I had deserted, and the penalty for that was execution. And I couldn't tell anyone what had happened; they would never believe me. That's when it came to me... that I could pretend to kill myself. I could leave a note, saying I was committing suicide. That way I wouldn't have deserted, I would be dead.

I felt really bad about Mum and Tilly and Dad. I knew they'd be devastated. But better that than having to hear that your son had been shot by a firing squad.

I changed into my ordinary clothes, folded my uniform and placed it on the river bank, with a suicide note inside the tunic pocket. Then I ran... I just had to get away – as far away as I could.

Violet laid the diary down next to her, tears running down her cheeks. 'Oh, the poor boy,' she murmured. 'Poor, poor little Charlie.'

Suddenly, all the pain, all the secrets, all the running away from responsibility made sense. Charles had spent his life running away from an awful experience that he could never forget.

35

Elizabeth

Elizabeth was just putting on her coat, ready to head out to the salon, when the doorbell went. She found Violet on the doorstep in floods of tears.

'Oh, my dear, what's the matter?'

'I've had rather a shock,' muttered Violet. 'But I'll come back later. I can see you were just going out.'

'No, it's all right. I was only going to work – they'll survive without me. Come in... we'll go down to the kitchen.'

While Violet sat at the kitchen table, Elizabeth brewed a pot of coffee. 'Now, dry your eyes Vi, and tell me what's happened.'

'I was clearing Charles's room and found these,' replied Violet wiping her eyes. She fished into her handbag and pulled out two leather volumes, which she lay on the table between them.

'They look like diaries,' said Elizabeth placing a cup of coffee in front of her. 'Did you read something that upset you?'

'I did rather,' said Violet. 'There are fifteen diaries in all, from 1914 to 1929. I haven't had a chance to go through the others yet, but I presume there will be things about you and your mother. I'll show you them later of course, but I wanted you to read these two first. It explains such a lot about your father.' She pushed the diaries across the table towards Elizabeth. 'I've marked the relevant entries. But I warn you they are rather shocking.'

As Elizabeth read of her father's assault, tears streamed down her face. 'Poor Dad, I can't believe it.'

'I know. I felt the same. Oh, Elizabeth, why could he never tell me about it? I'd have understood.'

'Shame, I suppose. People never talk about these things – I should know.'

'What do you mean?'

Elizabeth took a gulp of her coffee. 'Many years ago something similar happened to me. The man I was working for at the time nearly raped me. If it hadn't been for Danny coming into the office at the vital moment, it would definitely have happened. It was so close.'

'Oh my dear, how awful,' said Violet. 'I had no idea.'

'I never told anyone, not even my mother. The only person who knew, apart from Danny of course, was Dad.'

'You told your father?'

'Yes. We met by chance that evening in the pub, and I only had to hint at what had happened. He knew immediately. Now I know why. He'd been through it himself, and recognised a fellow sufferer. The thing is, Violet, I know from experience that you never get over such a thing. You can push it away, spend months, even years not thinking about it. Then suddenly, out of nowhere, a smell or a sound can bring it rushing back. I've been lucky, because Danny knows what happened. He's there for me in the middle of the night if I have a nightmare about it. I don't know what I'd have done without him.'

'And poor Charles had no one,' said Violet sadly. 'At least no one he trusted. Do you think your mother knew what had happened to him?'

'I don't know. If she did, she never let on. Somehow I doubt he'd have told her.'

'Why?'

'She could be quite unsympathetic.'

'Is that why you didn't tell her about your experience?'

'Possibly. And I suppose I didn't want to upset her. Back in wartime, there was already so much suffering. People being bombed and death everywhere. So it seemed rather unimportant.'

'But it wasn't unimportant,' protested Violet. 'Oh, you poor girl. Thank God for Danny. Is that how you met?'

'Yes.' Elizabeth smiled. 'Not the most romantic introduction, but the fact that he knew... that he understood, somehow cemented our relationship. I never even told my fiancé, David. Do you remember him? I came home that night, after this awful experience, and there he was asking me to marry him. I couldn't spoil the moment with such a ghastly revelation.'

'Was Charles kind about it?'

'Oh, very. And he was furious with the man. He told me he "had contacts" and there might be something he could do. I'm convinced now that he helped to get the letch moved. I certainly never saw the man again.'

'How would he have done that? I mean, he never struck me as that influential.'

'I don't know, but he must have done something behind the scenes. Now, enough about me,' said Elizabeth, quickly changing the subject. 'What I've read in this diary is just tragic – not just for him but for his parents. How must they have felt? Their only son apparently committing suicide. And Tilly! She would have been devastated too. Such a burden for her knowing about it all this time, and not being able to share the hurt with anybody.'

'You're right,' said Violet. 'And I agree, his poor parents. They were always rather shy and retiring. Nervous almost. Looking back, I wasn't very kind to them. I found them hard to get close to. And as for Tilly, we've never really got on. I always thought she resented me somehow. I got the impression that she saw Charles as her property. In his will, he left the dividends from his shares to Tilly, not me or Freddie. At the time, I felt quite cross about it. I mean, I had a son to look after, and she has a husband of her own.'

'Oh Violet. Was it a lot of money?'

'No, not a lot, but it's the principle of the thing. Anyway, Tilly is a closed book. I've been to see her twice now to ask about Charles, and each time she clams up.'

'Maybe we should go and see her again, and confront her with the evidence. I could drive you there if you like.'

'Would you? I think that's a very good idea. And this time, I won't let her fob me off or take no for an answer. She's going to tell me everything she knows. It's time to get the whole story at last.'

36

Violet

The drive from Holland Park to Enfield took over an hour. The snowy roads were slippery and there were times when Elizabeth nearly lost control of her Morris Minor Traveller.

'Oh dear,' said Violet, gripping the edge of her seat. 'Perhaps we should have taken the bus after all.'

'No, it's all right,' said Elizabeth. 'This car is tough as old boots. We'll make it, don't worry.'

Tilly's husband John came to the door. 'Violet, Elizabeth – what a surprise!'

'Yes, I'm sorry,' said Elizabeth. 'We should have rung ahead. Is Tilly in?'

'Yes, but she's working. You'd better come inside.'

The pair stood on the mat in the polished tiled hall, stamping the snow off their boots. Tilly emerged from her office. 'Hello, this is rather unexpected.'

'Yes, I'm sorry to barge in like this,' Violet began, 'but Elizabeth and I wanted to have a word.'

'All right, come in.'

Tilly led them into the front room. Not for the first time, Violet noticed the similarities between her sister-in-law's office and her brother's, with a desk in the window, and the same typewriter – a heavy black Imperial.

'Do sit down,' said Tilly, indicating two armchairs set against the wall. She sat facing them. 'So, what can I do for you?'

Violet reached into her handbag and removed one of Charles's diaries. 'We wanted to discuss this.'

'What is it?'

'Charles's diary for 1915. I was clearing his room yesterday and found it – along with fourteen others. He stopped writing a diary in 1929 when he came back from China. As I understand it that's when he went on sabbatical and started writing novels. Perhaps the impulse to keep a diary ebbed away at that point. Anyway, there is something written in this one that I wanted to show you. I think it explains a lot.' Violet held the diary out.

Tilly took it, holding the leather-bound book in her hands like a precious relic, her fingers trembling slightly. 'I'm not sure I should. I mean, it's private – a diary – not meant for others.'

'I know what you mean, and I understand,' said Violet. 'I felt the same at first, but there's something in there that answers so many questions, and I think it's vital we all read it.'

Tilly bit her lip. 'I don't need to read it. I already know what it says.'

'What do you mean? Did he show it to you?'

'No, but I know what happened.'

'So, you know about the...' Violet paused, still struggling to say the word, '...the assault.'

'I know what that terrible man did to him, yes. I didn't know at the time, you understand, but Charlie told me afterwards when he was in hospital after the war... when we found him... still alive.' Tears trickled down onto her cheeks.

Violet stood up and went to kneel by her side, wrapping her in her arms. 'Oh, Tilly. Oh, my dear, I'm sorry. I didn't mean to upset you. It's just such a shock. I felt I had to see you. I hope you understand.'

Some minutes passed before Tilly was able to speak. 'You have no idea, Vi, what it was like. The pain, the agonising pain. I thought it would kill my mother.'

'When you found out about what happened to him, you mean?'

'No, we didn't know about that then – that came out much later. No, what I meant was when we thought he'd committed suicide. I thought my mother would die. I really did.'

'I keep thinking how I would feel if one of mine did the same,' interjected Elizabeth. 'It would be unbearable. Your poor mother.'

'She was your grandmother, remember,' said Tilly.

'Yes, of course. I'm sorry I never knew her.'

Violet sat back down on her chair. 'Tell us everything, Tilly – please, I beg you.'

Tilly laid the diary tenderly on the desk, and wiped her eyes.

'It all started with a telegram.' She opened her desk drawer and pulled out a large brown envelope buried at the bottom. On it, the word 'Bruv' was written in her neat handwriting. She opened the envelope, removed a delicate piece of paper and handed it to Violet. 'You'd better read that. It's the telegram we received from the War Office in 1915.'

'God, how awful,' said Violet, scanning it quickly. 'How absolutely awful to receive such a thing.' She handed it to Elizabeth.

'Then, a few days later, we received this.' Tilly handed

them a letter. 'Read it out loud, Violet. You have such a lovely voice.'

Dear Mum, Dad and Tilly,

I know you'll never understand, and maybe you'll never be able to forgive me for what I'm about to do, but believe me when I say, I can't take it any more. Army life is not what I had imagined. Something terrible has happened and the situation is intolerable. I can't say anything to anyone about it, and no one would believe me anyway. Desertion is unthinkable, so I must do the only honourable thing and end my life.

Please believe that I love you all, and try not to think too badly of me.

Your loving son and brother

PS: Mum, if you believe in the afterlife, have faith that we will be reunited one day. I promise.

Violet looked first at Elizabeth, who was weeping, and then at Tilly. 'So, what did you think, when you received this?'

'It seemed to confirm the telegram. You see, I couldn't believe he'd killed himself at first. I knew my Bruv, and he would never have done such a thing. He had a love of life that burned brighter than anyone I knew. I kept saying, after the telegram arrived, "It can't be true. They've made a mistake." But then the letter came. It was enough for my parents. They accepted it then, but I never did.'

'The PS is interesting,' said Elizabeth, wiping her eyes. 'Do you think he was trying to tell you something – that he wasn't really dead?'

'Possibly,' said Tilly. 'Then after the war I got another telegram. Here...'

She handed it to Violet, who read it out loud.

Tilly. I'm alive and at St Barts Hosp. Love Bruv.

Violet glanced at Elizabeth. 'Your mother told us Charles asked her to send a telegram from the hospital, do you remember?'

Elizabeth nodded. 'You must have been amazed when you got this.'

'I was. I didn't tell my parents at first – didn't want to raise their hopes. I mean, it might have been a hoax. But he signed it "Bruv", so I was pretty sure it was from him.

I went to the hospital and there he was. He looked so pale and thin. Oh Violet, I was so happy. I thought I would crush him, I hugged him so much.'

Tilly turned to Elizabeth. 'That's when I met your mother – she was his nurse. Anyway, I went home and brought Mum and Dad to the hospital the next day. My dad, well, he couldn't believe it – he looked like he had seen a ghost. And Mum collapsed on the floor screaming. I thought she might have a heart attack.'

'You must have been so happy,' said Elizabeth.

'Happy doesn't describe it. Ecstatic, more like. And in shock. It was months before we could take it all in.'

Elizabeth nodded. 'I can imagine.'

Tilly looked across at Violet. 'So now you know.'

Violet was sitting quietly, staring at the two telegrams and the suicide note in her hands. 'I just wish he'd told me. I just wish I'd known. I'd have been so different with him. More understanding perhaps. Why couldn't he tell me?'

'I don't know, Vi. He was proud, I suppose. Didn't want you to think badly of him.'

'But that's ridiculous. I wouldn't have thought badly of him.

It would have made me love him more.' She broke down, sobbing.

Elizabeth took her in her arms. 'Oh Violet. I'm so sorry.'

'Well, at least I know now – we all know,' said Violet finally. 'Should I tell Freddie – what do you think, Tilly?'

'One day maybe, when he's older and can cope with it. It might help him understand.'

'Understand what?' asked Violet.

'Why Bruv was so distant from everyone.'

'You felt that?'

'We all felt it. He could never trust anyone. That experience changed him, Violet... changed all of us. That and...' Tilly hesitated.

'What?'

'No, I shouldn't say.'

'It's too late for secrets now,' said Violet. 'What else was he concealing?'

Tilly paused, and took a deep breath. 'You must never tell anyone this – no one, not even Freddie. Do you promise?'

'Of course,' said Violet.

'When we found him in hospital, he was scared he'd be prosecuted for desertion.'

'Surely not,' said Violet. 'He fought so gallantly – nearly died for his country.'

'I know, but the rules were very strict. I was married to John by then. He was policeman, and he had a word with his chief constable. They decided not to prosecute. But there was a price to pay. Nothing comes free in this world, does it?'

'What price, what do you mean?'

'He had to work for them.'

'For who?'

'The secret service.'

'Undercover, you mean?' interjected Elizabeth. 'A spy. Is that what you're saying?'

'I shouldn't say any more,' said Tilly hurriedly. 'We were sworn to secrecy. But that's why he went to China. He never told me the details, and when he came back he never spoke of his work.'

'Do you think he wrote about it... in the diaries?" asked Elizabeth.

'Of course not,' said Tilly impatiently. 'He wasn't allowed to speak of it to anyone. He certainly never told me anything, and to be honest, I didn't want to know. What you have to understand is that he just wanted to do his best. All he ever really wanted was to be a good writer. And he tried so hard. He was so clever, so talented. He wrote all those books, and poems – and all on top of a demanding government job. Remember him like that, Violet, not as the difficult man he could be at times. I knew him better than anyone, I think. He could be selfish sometimes, and secretive, of course. But what else could he be after what he'd gone through? Remember that and try to think well of him.'

As Violet and Elizabeth drove away from Tilly's house, Violet asked, 'Can we visit his grave? It's not far, is it?'

'Yes of course. That's a good idea.'

They stopped at a florist near the cemetery, and Violet bought a small bunch of snowdrops. When they arrived at the cemetery's ornate gates, Elizabeth suggested they drive to the graveside. 'I seem to remember the grave was a long way from the entrance,' she said.

A single-lane road led through the graveyard, and Elizabeth had to drive slowly in the icy conditions to avoid sliding off the path. Finally, they abandoned the car, and trudged through the snow until they found Charles's grave, beneath an ancient yew towering above their heads.

Violet bent down and removed the dead flowers that had

lain there since his funeral. 'I really should have come back before now. It's a mess. I feel ashamed.'

'Don't be silly,' said Elizabeth. 'You've had a lot on your plate.'

Violet placed the snowdrops in the small urn on top of the grave. 'There, that looks better.'

Elizabeth took her arm. 'It looks really lovely.' She moved a little closer to study the headstone. 'That poem is rather good, isn't it? Who wrote that?'

'Your father,' said Violet, with tears in her eyes. 'He left instructions in his will to include it on the headstone. I didn't really understand it at the time. I just did as he asked, and thought no more about it. But I can see now what he was trying to say, from beyond the grave.'

You bear your dead away;
No plumes about him sway;
No proud barge waits to ferry him
To cypressed isle of Heroes blest.

What secrets shall I hold from prying eyes?
What merit now have barriers or ties?
The winds of Dawn deride us;
And chill we creep towards our End.

Standing on the grassy slope of the cemetery, the two women stood silently beside the grave thinking of the man they had both loved. The snow began to fall once again, and rooks cawed in the trees above.

'I can see why Charles wanted to be buried here,' said Violet. 'To be left in peace – no more lies, no more mystery, no more secrets – just an eternity of tranquillity.'

A LETTER FROM DEBBIE

Thank you for choosing to read *The Telegram*. I hope you enjoyed it, and, if you would like to keep up to date with all my latest releases, just sign up at the following link. Your email address will never be shared, and you can unsubscribe at any time.

www.bookouture.com/debbie-rix

Secrets are a perennial theme for so many wonderful stories. They are the driver for the action in many ways. As a novelist, you have to consider whether the reader will know the secret from the outset and watch the characters 'catching up', or whether you leave them in suspense until the end. My novel, *The Secret Letter*, based on the lives of my own parents during World War II, drew on this idea. The discovery of the secret letter is the pivotal moment in the novel that forces the central character to change her life.

The eponymous telegram of this latest novel is the starting point for the story. But the reader doesn't quite understand the significance of it until the final pages. Only then does its full impact become apparent.

If you read my historical note, you will understand the background to this novel, and how important it has been to me and my family. The telegram was real, as was so much of the detail in the novel.

I hope the story of Charles, Violet and Elizabeth touches

you – and perhaps resonates with family stories of your own. If you have enjoyed it, I'd be so grateful if you could leave a review. Reviews are really the only way new readers can discover my books.

Finally, if you would like to get in touch, please do so via social media or my website.

Thank you.

Debbie Rix

www.debbierix.com

HISTORICAL NOTE

Writing this novel has been unlike any other. In the past, I have created fictional characters who interact with real people – famous figures in history such as Goebbels, Hitler and Himmler. Although the characters I invented experienced events which are historically accurate, they themselves are not real.

However, *The Telegram* is about a real man who also happens to be my father-in-law: Frederick Anthony Edwards, born in 1896.

He is the direct inspiration for the novel's main character, Charles Carmichael. Sadly, I never met my father-in-law. He died in 1961 when his son Tony Edwards (my husband) was in his mid-teens. But Tony has occasionally talked about him, as did my late mother-in-law; so, over the years, I have absorbed quite a few scraps of information about him.

What emerges is a man of many parts. A talented and highly productive writer who wrote over thirty novels (under three pseudonyms), while being ostensibly employed as a Clerical Grade administrator in the Ministry of Food – a fairly lowly position for someone of his keen intelligence and sensibilities. He had been given that post after returning from China, where he spent the 1920s working in the British Legation in Peking (now Beijing) – doing what, he never said. I began to research the sort of job he might have had in China at that time, and discovered that men were sometimes sent abroad by the British Government in lowly jobs (as clerks, for example), but who were actually spies. Given my father-in-law's reticence to discuss his time in China, and after discussion with my husband, it seemed possible that his father might have been a spy. This became more likely when my husband told me that his father had been 'friends' with William Joyce (Lord Haw-Haw) – which puzzled him, as his father seemed totally apolitical. Joyce's statement in the novel that, before leaving England for Germany in 1939, he had told my father-in-law that "he always loved England" is an exact quote from life.

Also 100% true is that, just like Freddie in the novel, Tony was unaware he had a half-sister (a daughter from his father's first marriage to the nurse who cared for him in hospital) until after his father's death. Equally true to life is the fact that his half-sister lived in a house opposite their basement flat in Clarendon Road, Holland Park – a coincidence that seems too far-fetched to be true. But it was.

Those facts alone might have been enough to hang a novel on. But what made my father-in-law's story totally compelling was a remarkable family secret, only divulged to my husband by his father's sister 'Tanny' on her deathbed in 1984. She told him that in 1915, Fred had faked his own suicide as a young army private, and then fled to Ireland, where he joined up in an Irish Regiment under the name of Henry Charman. Although using euphemistic language befitting a respectable old lady, she made it clear that he had been raped by the Major for whom he had been the batman, and that a faked suicide was his only way out of a hazardous predicament with no obvious solution. Just as in my novel, Fred re-joined up under an assumed name, went to the trenches in Belgium and was nearly killed in no-man's-land.

Tanny also revealed how, lying wounded in a London hospital after returning from the front line, Fred 'came back to life' by sending her a telegram signed by her pet name for him, thus ensuring she knew it was genuinely from her brother. My husband and I are pretty sure the pet name would have been "Bruv" (as in my novel), because that's how he signed her personal copies of his books – still preserved in our bookshelves at home. Another wholly accurate element in my novel is the fact that Tanny's husband was a policeman, who reported Fred's reappearance to his commanding officer without repercussions – or so Tanny claimed. But I wasn't convinced. I have therefore invented the scene where Fred is subsequently visited – and recruited – by the Intelligence Service.

However, espionage apart, Charles Carmichael's fictional life in my novel closely follows what is known about his real-life counterpart, Frederick Edwards.

As I say, I never met him. He was by all accounts utterly charming and a great raconteur; his young adult photos also show him as exceptionally good-looking and dashing. But his whole life would have been burdened with the memory of a closely guarded secret – an extraordinary event which must have been deeply painful both to him and his immediate family in Enfield. Perhaps that explains why he chose to be buried there – symbolically interring the past among his family roots.

During my research for the book, I visited the tranquil semi-rural cemetery near Enfield where he was laid to rest in 1961. The simple plaque set in the earth above his coffin has disappeared, but I have re-imagined his gravestone in my novel, taking its inscription from the words in an epic poem he penned in 1953.

In writing this novel, I have felt increasingly close to the father-in-law I never knew; I sincerely hope he approves of my book and is smiling at me kindly from Above.

ACKNOWLEDGEMENTS

As always, I am indebted to my publisher Bookouture, and in particular to my editor Natasha Harding, for her support for this book. I had wanted to write this story for some time, and she understood how important it was to me.

But I am most grateful to my husband Tony Edwards, who has helped me by revisiting his childhood memories of his father. He is also the author of a stage play 'Charman', about his father's extraordinary experiences in the Great War, and it was generous of him to allow me to take this story and develop it into my novel.

PUBLISHING TEAM

Turning a manuscript into a book requires the efforts of many people. The publishing team at Bookouture would like to acknowledge everyone who contributed to this publication.

Audio
Alba Proko
Melissa Tran
Sinead O'Connor

Commercial
Lauren Morrissette
Hannah Richmond
Imogen Allport

Cover design
Eileen Carey

Data and analysis
Mark Alder
Mohamed Bussuri

Editorial
Natasha Harding
Lizzie Brien

Copyeditor
Jacqui Lewis

Proofreader
Tom Feltham

Marketing
Alex Crow
Melanie Price
Occy Carr
Cíara Rosney
Martyna Młynarska

Operations and distribution
Marina Valles
Stephanie Straub
Joe Morris

Production
Hannah Snetsinger
Mandy Kullar
Jen Shannon
Ria Clare

Publicity
Kim Nash
Noelle Holten
Jess Readett
Sarah Hardy

Rights and contracts
Peta Nightingale
Richard King
Saidah Graham

Printed in Great Britain
by Amazon